Praise for *Fire Mountain*

"A masterful blend of high-octane suspense and heart-pounding mystery. Mentink delivers an explosive thriller where danger lurks on every page. Clear your schedule—you won't be able to put this one down."

Lynette Eason, bestselling author of the FBI: Strange Crimes Unit series

"Dana Mentink is at the top of her game in this heart-pounding thrill ride. Danger explodes onto the page as Kit and Cullen fight to survive a volcanic eruption while relentless killers pursue them. An action-packed, gripping suspense, Fire Mountain will keep readers riveted until the end!"

Elizabeth Goddard, award-winning author of *Perilous Tides*

"An unlikely trio struggles to escape a volcano on the verge of erupting in the pulse-pounding latest from Mentink. This starts with a bang and never lets up."

Publishers Weekly

"What a read! This is the first book I have read by Dana Mentink, and it certainly won't be the last. The plot is well written and exciting."

Midwest Book Review

Books by Dana Mentink

Elements of Danger

Fire Mountain

Raging Waters

ELEMENTS OF DANGER #2

RAGING WATERS

DANA MENTINK

a division of Baker Publishing Group
Grand Rapids, Michigan

Published by Revell
a division of Baker Publishing Group
Grand Rapids, Michigan
RevellBooks.com

Printed in the United States of America

Library of Congress Cataloging-in-Publication Data
Names: Mentink, Dana author
Title: Raging waters / Dana Mentink.
Description: Grand Rapids, Michigan : Revell, a division of Baker Publishing Group, 2026. | Series: Elements of danger ; 2
Identifiers: LCCN 2025025478 | ISBN 9780800746537 paperback | ISBN 9780800747947 | ISBN 9781493452774 ebook
Subjects: LCGFT: Christian fiction | Romance fiction | Thrillers (Fiction) | Novels | Fiction
Classification: LCC PS3613.E496 R34 2026
LC record available at https://lccn.loc.gov/2025025478

Cover design by Ervin Serrano

Baker Publishing Group publications use paper produced from sustainable forestry practices and postconsumer waste whenever possible.

26 27 28 29 30 31 32 7 6 5 4 3 2 1

To Mom and Dad, thank you for teaching us the meaning of the word *family*.

ONE

AS HE DODGED A SKULL-SPLITTING KICK to his temple, Gideon Landry wondered again if this side hustle was going to pan out. His legs ached from fighting the current, and the cold water sapped his strength like a leech on an open wound.

Isn't being an Air Force SERE instructor enough for you, Gid? No, he had to go and set himself up to teach civilian classes during his precious leave time.

In a backwater nowhere of northern Washington.

During torrential rains. With most of his class bailing out at the last minute.

Why hadn't he just canceled the whole thing like a sane person?

Because his service days were numbered, and that was the exit strategy he'd come up with for a variety of reasons. Why should he let a weather calamity put the kibosh on his early preparations? Man against nature. He always thought he'd win. Probably why his brothers never wanted to go camping with him.

Another splash of bone-chilling river water renewed his resolve.

Suck it up, buttercup.

Gideon continued to tread water, ignoring the pain pulsing in his shoulder as he tried to formulate a rescue plan for the drowning young doe. The animal had flipped from stomach to back, its frantic hooves batting the spray, eyes rolling in terror.

On the muddy bank, the only student who'd actually followed through and shown up for his survival skills class looked, in a word, terrified. Rain coursed from Roger's yellow hat as he watched Gideon struggling with the deer, who'd been trapped in a tangle of branches in the bloated river.

The water on the rugged eastern flank of the Cascades was freezing at the end of February. Of course. Puffs of snow stacked the peaks ringing the town. He and his brothers had camped beside this very river when they were kids, and he'd relished these acres in all their summer glory. This was definitely *not* summer.

But leave was leave, and even a handful of students would be enough to provide glowing testimonials for the website he was planning.

The torrent beat against Gideon as he circled and splashed his way to a better angle to free the drowning deer, whose panicked bleating was growing fainter as it succumbed. Behind Roger, the bushes parted and Gideon's heart sank as a full-grown male deer stepped out.

He yelled to Roger over the roar as he pulled out his knife and sawed through the intertwined branches.

"Huh?" Roger yelled back from his place atop the bank, his cell phone capturing the action.

Unbelievable.

"The buck, behind you!" Gideon shouted at a volume he rarely attained. Yelling generally indicated a complete inability to deal with a situation, which was exactly where things were headed. He stifled the litany of bad words scrolling through his mind and continued to hack away.

The buck, agitated about his mate's situation, was about to mow down the clueless Roger. Gideon's one and only client was close to having his clock cleaned by a two-hundred-pound deer. That'd look swell on the Yelp reviews. A testimonial would definitely be out of the question. He should give up on the doe.

Go save your client.

But the doe's terrified eyes locked on his, the water millimeters from inundating her quivering nostrils. She had no hope except for him. Her death was certain.

He shouted again to Roger without taking his attention off the knife. He continued to work the blade across the entangling branches, focused so he didn't cut off his fingers with the weapon he kept sharp enough to split atoms.

He didn't think Roger had heeded his command, but he couldn't spare a look. Since the class had only just begun when he spotted the entangled animal, they hadn't yet covered the "be mindful of your surroundings" topic, and clearly Roger had zero prior knowledge on the subject. The man was probably still trying to video the moment for his social media instead of looking for a way to help. *This is real life*, he wanted to shout. *Fix it, don't film it.*

With a snap, the last branch finally gave way. He sheathed

the knife, grabbed the deer around the neck, ignoring the hooves that battered his stomach, and hauled her to the shore against the pummeling current.

In the shallows, braced in the mud, he shoved at her flanks until she got her wobbly legs situated. It took one last heave from Gideon to propel the exhausted creature far enough onto terra firma for her to find traction. The buck was there immediately, nosing the female away from the water and Gideon before they disappeared into the woods. Mission accomplished. Doe saved.

With all his remaining energy, he hauled himself through the mud and up the bank. His weak shoulder complained every inch of the way. As usual, he ignored it. He expected to see Roger in a crumpled heap when he finally pulled his way clear. No Roger.

He shook the water out of his eyes.

Still no Roger, but someone else was there.

Gideon stood upright, water running down his freezing limbs as he tried to shake away the hallucination. He must be hypothermic, seeing things. But even that made no sense, none at all. Why would he hallucinate the woman he had no desire ever to clap eyes on again? He swiped the moisture from his face, but she was still there.

And Roger wasn't.

Mackenzie Bardine arched a delicate brow at him. "Where's the rest of your class?"

That soft, feathery tone concealed the talons underneath. His stomach knotted into a fist as he barely caught the towel she tossed him.

His mouth finally started to pitch in and help out his

brain. “What are you doing here, Zee?” The nickname bestowed on her by her brother, Aaron. His best friend.

Her lips firmed into a line. “You can call me Mackenzie. I’m not a teen anymore.”

No, she wasn’t. She wasn’t even the same woman he’d last seen two years before at the funeral, or the one who’d tried to strong-arm him into her cause. She was tall and more slender than he recalled, her wet rain gear plastered around her athletic physique. Drops beaded on her chestnut ponytail, much longer than the previous short bob, as she regarded him with those gray eyes from under the brim of a boonie cap.

“What are you doing here?” he repeated through chattering teeth because he couldn’t think of anything different to ask. He looked for her car and saw only his own rain-slicked Jeep Wrangler.

“I was in the area. Thought I’d join your class. You take walk-ins, right?”

He didn’t get out a response before she rushed on. “By the way, I suggested your guy, Roger, move to a safer position to save him from being flattened by the buck. Oh, and I told him there’s concern about the Cotton Flower Dam. Some signs of pending failure. Whole town’s talking about it. He decided to get on the road home. Said to tell you adios and he’d had a wonderful time. I assured him I’d pass on the message.”

Anger ballooned in his belly. “You did what?”

She smiled. “He paid up front, I’m sure, right? So no biggie?”

Roger had prepaid, in fact, but that wasn’t the point.

"Wrong time of year for a wilderness survival class, isn't it?" she said. "Wouldn't August be better for the city folk?"

"Turns out people need to survive, no matter what the season," he managed between clenched teeth. "What do you want?"

"Just what I said. I saw online that you were teaching your class again. Thought I'd take a refresher course, but . . ." She shrugged. "No fun with only one student and a storm, and what with the risk of the dam failure and all . . ."

He finally broke through the stupor and stalked to his vehicle, turning his back on her and stripping off his shirt as he went. He felt her watching him as he yanked on a dry one from the back seat and added a jacket before he spun to face her again. "You're lying, obviously."

She stared at him, unperturbed. No explanation. No apology. Typical.

"Why are you really here?" The rain increased to a relentless sheet of misery. She pursed her lips, as if she were considering a reply. He realized he was teetering on a dangerous precipice. *Do not get involved with her.* "Never mind. I don't want to know."

And he didn't want anything to do with Mackenzie Bardine or her plans. Not after he'd declined her request for help with her vigilante social media campaign and received a dose of her wrath to add to his own measure of guilt. Whatever her newest crusade was, it was no concern of his.

"Can I have a ride back to town?" Her casual tone annoyed him further.

"How did you get out here without a vehicle?"

"Staying at the hotel in Oakleaf. I ran here."

"It's five miles."

She shrugged.

Of course. Five miles would be easy for Mackenzie, who'd been a marathon nut in her college days. He wanted to leave her there and drive away from the feelings she awakened in him. The pain. But the pewter eyes cooly observing him were the exact shade of her older brother's. Aaron could run five miles too, joking the whole way, and handle every problem with a wink and a shrug . . . until the last one that took his life.

And nestled deep, way down in Gideon's soul, was the knowledge that he might have saved his friend. Might have, but didn't. Mackenzie thought so too.

He heaved a sigh. "Fine."

He'd use the drive to ferret out her real purpose, buried under the lies. Or maybe he wouldn't. Stony silence was an acceptable option too, and whatever she was up to didn't concern him, after all. Not anymore.

Get her to town and out of your life.

They got in. He cranked the ignition and jerked them onto the road, windshield wipers working double time.

The radio report confirmed Mackenzie's information, though she'd dialed up the timeline of the impending disaster for the hapless Roger. Authorities were concerned about a failure of the Cotton Flower Dam, which had needed repairs for decades. Gideon had known all that. Engineers were monitoring the situation, but residents had been told to stay alert, as evacuation orders could be issued in the upcoming week. He'd totally have been able to complete an eight-hour survival class and get Roger safely on the road before midnight. Had she been trying to scare Roger away out of spite? But why show up at his class? Now? There had to be plenty of other people she could harass besides him.

Her expression was impassive. "Still on active duty? Teaching in your spare time at the old stomping grounds?"

Their family friend owned this hunk of soggy land and gave permission to Gideon to use it for free. "Yes."

"Why? Most guys would be feet up in a recliner or on a boat fishing on their leave time."

None of your business. But the manners drilled into him by his parents kept him from articulating the thought. Instead he turned the tables. "Finish the police academy?"

She shook her head. "No. Quit that for good."

He hadn't heard. She'd been working on her academy requirements when Aaron was murdered. He'd assumed she would eventually go on to complete the program and earn her badge. So she wasn't law enforcement. That explained plenty. "That's how you get away with saying that stuff on your podcast."

Her tone hardened. "I don't 'get away' with anything."

"Podcasting theories, no matter how unproven."

"I tell the truth and dig into cold cases."

"Like your brother's."

She looked out the window into the pounding rain. "Yes. Like his. I've covered four so far," she added in a defensive tone. "And thanks to the podcast, three have been solved."

But no one had been arrested for the assassination-style murder of Aaron Bardine during a drug deal gone bad two years prior. Gideon remembered how she'd come at him when he'd gone to pay his respects at the house after the funeral. The image of her face, swollen from crying and seething with rage, was burned into his brain.

"Aaron was your best friend. Did you know something was wrong?"

He had, and heard the question she couldn't voice. *Why didn't you make him tell you?* And he caught on to her self-recrimination as well. *Why didn't I do so either?* He blinked away the memory. The rain continued to smash against the Jeep's windshield as he drove.

It was hard to look at her and not see Aaron.

A wet, windblown branch caught in the wipers. He saw her glance in the side-view mirror at the white truck he'd noticed when they turned into the town of Oakleaf. Only five hundred residents lived in this wooded hollow settled in a valley rich with stunning views. Several of the shop owners were busily boarding up their windows. The ones who'd already invested in storm shutters had rolled them into place. None of those measures would help if the dam failed, which they well knew.

Survival meant hoping for the best while planning for the worst. No place for pessimists.

Her fingers gripped the door handle as they rolled toward the main drag. He pulled to the side to allow the white truck to pass. The driver wasted no time speeding by, a bearded guy behind the wheel soaking in Mackenzie's profile as he went. Not out of the ordinary. Mackenzie was not a cover girl type, but there was something about her that made people, particularly men, pay attention. Gideon had been paying attention forever, or so it felt.

Her gaze stayed forward-facing, but he saw her making note of the plates as the truck vanished down the street.

"What's going on, Zee?"

"Not much. Just a little vacation here in lovely rural Washington. Figured it was time to get out of Seattle. How about with you?"

"Knock off the coy routine." He jutted his chin. "Who was that in the truck?"

"I don't know."

"Sure it doesn't have something to do with your online crusade?"

She didn't look at him, but her jaw tightened. "I use my platform for good. You don't approve of that?"

"Depends on your motivation." Still, she gave him no eye contact.

"And what do you think that would be, in my case?"

He shrugged. "I'm sure the advertisers on your podcast are thrilled with your follower count. Close to twenty thousand, right?" He cringed inwardly at his slip.

"Flattered that you looked me up. If you'd helped me, like I asked . . ."

He heaved out a breath. "Let's not fire up this whole argument again."

Mackenzie was silent, fingers drumming on her knee.

"Look, Zee. Like I told you then, I—"

"I know. You couldn't go on camera because of your job. And you wouldn't review the timeline of that night, your impressions, anything related to the case because you'd gone over it all with the police. You had other priorities."

"You should too," he snapped. "This is a police matter.

You have to move on with your life, like I told you when you asked me."

"And what if I can't do that?" A ripple of emotion crossed her face, a shimmer of anguish—there, then gone—hidden under quiet anger.

He didn't know the answer, wasn't sure he'd done much better than she had in accepting Aaron's death.

She'd thrown herself into the podcast, and he'd watched her grow more brash about her theories as she told her viewers that the kingpin responsible for a huge portion of the drug trafficking in the Pacific Northwest, a man she referred to as "Bullseye," would be brought to justice. She didn't shirk from stating that she believed Bullseye—someone who fed on desperation and peddled pharmaceutical relief—was responsible for Aaron's death as much as if he'd pulled the trigger himself. As far as she was concerned, Aaron was an innocent victim in the whole mess.

Gideon wasn't as convinced, which was another reason he'd declined to help her investigation. Better for her to grieve the brother she'd known.

The FBI and DEA also had Bullseye on their radar, and Gideon imagined they didn't enjoy her taking the case to the social media world.

A vein still jumped in her jaw.

Only another mile until he delivered his passenger. Might as well try not to inflame things further. He took a breath. "So you're here because of your podcast."

"I have a contact in this area."

This area. His suspicions were correct. "That's why you're in town?"

A sly grin overtook her anger. "What? You don't believe I'm here because I wanted to take your class?"

"Not in any way, shape, or form."

She chuckled. "You always were a suspicious one, Gideon, that's why you have a permanent furrow between your manly eyebrows."

And you always knew how to disarm my defenses. Annoying, the way she commanded his attention. He could still picture her in that green dress, her eyes dancing in a way that would disappear forever in a matter of hours when her brother was murdered.

He recalled a similar gaze—her brother's—on that sultry August night in California when Gideon had discovered Aaron wrecked in a ditch on the base where they'd both been sent for SERE training. He'd reeked of whiskey.

"*Oh man, Gid. Glad it's you. Not gonna rat me out, are you?*"

And Gideon had made a choice that night, one with deep roots reaching all the way back to their high school trauma.

"I'm sorry, Aaron. I can't do it again." And he'd called it in. Aaron was remanded into the equivalent of Air Force jail until his discharge.

Publicly, Aaron laughed about it to anyone who had the bad taste to bring it up, as if the whole episode was a youthful prank, though Aaron had landed back in civilian life stripped of his pension and military benefits.

Mackenzie's gorgeous silvery eyes, so like her brother's, were hard now, stripped of their luster.

He shifted on the seat, kicked up the windshield wipers to full against the blasting rain. "When's your meet?"

"Depends," she said with a vague shrug.

They drove by the police station, a squat relic with ugly cement trim and putty-colored paint. Mackenzie scanned the building.

"My contact was arrested yesterday. She's here being processed."

Arrested. Interesting. So the cops would have forty-eight hours to charge the detainee or cut her loose. Was that why Mackenzie was here, in case the woman was released? Waste of time otherwise. No one would be let in unless they were a lawyer. His vague unease began to swell. "How do you know that?"

She hesitated. "Sources."

"What sources?"

"None of your business."

So much for civility. "Bummer for your podcast. Must have been a blow to have your contact arrested before you could record her." He didn't keep the sarcasm from his voice, nor did she react to it. Strange. Their rapport since Aaron's death had been at the matches and gasoline type of reactivity level. Now he was getting nothing. "Think they'll charge her?"

"Yep."

Mackenzie had her nose in everything. So why would she wait around? *Not your concern, Gid.* He had to offload Mackenzie before the match touched the fuel. At least he could do that much. "Where do you want me to drop you off?"

"Coffee shop, please. There."

He eased into the nearly empty lot of The Daily Grind. Only two vehicles and a squad car were parked on the slick asphalt. The rain slackened for a few moments, but the gunmetal clouds proclaimed it was only temporary. A monster storm was coming, and soon. The dam was about to be sorely tested, along with anyone who stayed.

He idled, waiting for her to get out. When she didn't, he fiddled with the heater and waited some more.

She turned to him. "How long are you on leave?"

"Another week."

"Seeing your folks?"

"Yes."

"Your mom doing okay?"

The fact was, his mom and dad were struggling to maintain their family farm.

His oldest brother Duncan was up to his earlobes with sole custody of three kids, and his other brother, the newlywed Cullen, couldn't do everything, even though he loudly proclaimed that he could. His cousin Johnny helped out when he wasn't deployed with the Navy. It was Gideon's turn to step up, and he wasn't going to let anything divert him. "They're fine."

She nodded, rubbing a spot of mud from the knee of her leggings.

Was she making small talk? His nerves prickled with an undercurrent of danger, though he couldn't for the life of him decipher why. It felt like the moment before a storm touched down in a completely different place than expected. He scraped a palm over his chin. "Look. Why don't you just tell me what's really going on with you and why you're sitting in my car? And don't give me that excuse about taking my class. You know I don't play games."

"Oh, but I love games." The mischievous grin enticed him in spite of himself.

Get rid of her. "I don't want any part of whatever you're . . ."

But Mackenzie's attention was diverted as someone exited the shop, a stocky older man holding a to-go cup as he wrestled with his hood. She watched the man.

"Who's that?"

She didn't answer, just continued to watch and fiddle around with something in the footwell before she got out, walked around to his side, and gestured for him to roll down his window.

"Thanks, Gideon. For the ride, I mean. I know we aren't exactly buddies, and I appreciate it." Before he knew what happened, she leaned in and kissed him, touching his cheek with one fingertip.

Her lips were warm and soft. He hadn't been this surprised since his brother called to say he was trapped by an erupting volcano. There was no way he could get his brain to command his mouth to offer one single word in the wake of that kiss and the sparks it sent cascading through his nervous system.

A smile tugged the corner of her mouth. They were playing a game, but he didn't know the rules.

"And I really am sorry I scared your student away," she said.

She actually did sound regretful. Maybe he'd misjudged her.

"I stowed a bag in the back of your Jeep while you were swimming with the deer. Would you mind hauling it out for me?" She touched her neck. "Pulled a muscle."

He got out and opened the rear door. Abruptly, she moved behind him. He was unprepared when she looped a foot around his ankles and toppled him stomach first to the ground.

The air whooshed out of him. Shock didn't begin to describe it. "What are you doing?"

"Give me your wallet," she shouted.

His what? "Zee, this isn't funny."

Her knees pressed into his shoulders, grinding his chin into the wet pavement. He made a move to turn over, but she leaned harder on his back.

"Sorry, Gid. Nothing personal." Then she started barking out commands again, as if she was a bad actor in a television drama.

He didn't move. This was some kind of a bizarre dream. Had to be. "Are you joking?"

"Like I said, I'm sorry."

Anger began to bubble in his gut as his thoughts came back online. He figured she was trying to create some zany footage for her podcast, but her phone wasn't in her hand. There was no one else around to catch it on video.

"Mackenzie, I'm about to toss you off of me like an old backpack, so you'd better have a good explanation—"

"No, Gid," she said, sad and sweet, and then her voice rose to a sharp command. "Give me your wallet."

He saw from his uncomfortable position that her antics had attracted attention. The rotund man who'd just exited the coffee shop jerked a look at them, spun around, and bolted inside.

"Zee," he said through gritted teeth. "I don't know what

you think you're doing, but now we're gonna have cops involved. Get off me. We'll tell them it was a joke."

She didn't move.

"Quit messing around."

"We'll be done here soon." She pulled the wallet from his back pocket.

"Mackenzie, so help me . . ." He started to roll over, but the coffee shop door flew open, and a uniformed cop with a damp coffee splotch on his shirt barreled out, gun drawn.

"Police!" the cop roared. "On your knees, hands up."

The cop hustled over, ordered her onto her belly, and cuffed her hands behind her back. A second officer appeared to check her for weapons. Gideon climbed to his feet, all the while trying to understand what had just happened.

With her cheek pressed to the asphalt, Mackenzie gave him one lingering smile.

....

Hours later, Mackenzie sat in her stiff coveralls in a holding cell, waiting. The bare cement space, gray upon gray, was cool, and she wished she'd been allowed to keep her jacket. At least they gave her soft slip-on shoes, but they didn't do much to warm her toes.

The jail was charged with energy, a hum of urgent chatter and feverish movement in the corridor that made her think the officers were dealing with increasing flood-related issues. That'd be ironic, if the dam really was going to fail immediately, like she'd casually hinted to Gideon's student. The beginnings of a smile curved her lips when she flashed on the memory of Gideon's face, made even more vibrant by his outrage.

Why did he have to be so handsome? And why had the man actually believed her about her reason for needing a ride to the coffee shop? He was smart, savvy, clever, and yet he'd acquiesced. Guilt over how he'd refused to help her go after Bullseye, maybe? She swallowed a sudden lump in her throat. Ends justified the means, in this case. The impending trouble with the dam might even work in her favor by adding to the distraction level in the jail. All sufficient thoughts to push away her unease at duping Gideon.

Arms folded around herself, she waited. Through the narrow rectangular cell window, a slice of the wall clock was visible. Eleven a.m. No wonder her stomach was growling. She'd skipped the free breakfast bagel and reconstituted eggs at the hotel in order to be sure she didn't miss Gideon before he led his student into the wilderness or outright canceled his class due to the rain. The run from the hotel was easy, fairly flat if somewhat muddy, and she'd made good time—but now she regretted that she hadn't hammered down at least half a bagel beforehand.

Her stomach rumbled again, and she tried to find a more comfortable position. Hopefully a meal of some kind would be offered. And she'd wait until it was provided and eat it without complaint, whatever it was. She'd been a hairbreadth away from putting on a badge herself, and she knew serving in law enforcement was an impossible job. No need to make it any more difficult for them by asking for food or anything else. Hunger could wait anyway. There was only one thing on her agenda. Her informant.

Pleased as she was that her podcast had thus far contributed to the solving of three cold cases she'd highlighted, the last few months had focused mostly on Aaron's murder. Recent episodes outlined Aaron's last moments. She publically theorized from the very first session that her brother had died meeting a dealer who worked for an operation run by a shadowy boss nicknamed Bullseye. She'd overheard Aaron say that name while on his cell phone.

Lorraine, the woman she had arranged to talk to in Oakleaf, would provide details about that very clandestine network, but she was scared. Confirmation, that was all Mackenzie needed. Some mortar to cement the facts.

Lorraine's untimely arrest had thrown a wrench into the plan, but not an insurmountable one. Gideon's presence in the area was a happy accident that made Mackenzie's altered scenario easier to execute. He was her ticket in, and she'd punched it.

The new plan was still the longest of long shots, a reckless attempt, but it had been now or never. Lorraine's fear was palpable in their brief messages. She believed she was being watched, targeted even, at her place of work, a shipping company owned by Bullseye. She'd disappear the first moment she was able to, so the meeting had to happen now. With an arrest pending, Mackenzie wasn't sure if Lorraine was trustworthy or not. Mackenzie had no other choice.

There wasn't a guarantee she could even locate and talk to Lorraine, but she figured she'd have a slim chance since it was a small-time jail with a communal eating area, according to her research. Slim chances were better than none. It wouldn't take long. A five-minute exchange. That was all she needed. Worst case, with the help of her jail accomplice, a filing clerk she'd paid handsomely, perhaps she could slip a written message with the first of her two vital questions. *Is Bullseye headquartered here in town?*

The answer had to be yes. She believed it down to the cell level. She'd meticulously tracked every tiny tremor of activity through various social media avenues and on web channels where people spoke in code looking to score drugs or dealers arranged sales. If there was a dark cyber alley, she'd crawled down or slithered through it. As much as she could, she protected herself, never showing her face or broadcasting her location, using a virtual private network to conceal her IP address, stripping metadata from images.

She had scores of fake identities she used to monitor the stinking channels of her cyber web for all the cold cases she'd investigated. Some tidbits she'd gleaned from local police reports, all public information she'd scoured, analyzed, mapped, cultivated, obsessed over, like Gollum with his ring.

Or maybe she was more like a giant spider, waiting for the slightest vibration on the elaborate web she'd spun. It wasn't pretty, inhabiting the same places as the lawbreakers she was trying to expose. Sometimes she felt as if no endless shower of hot water would scald the taint from her skin after a particularly long research mission in those lightless corners.

She wriggled on the hard seat.

You're doing what's necessary for Aaron and all the other people whom you've helped.

Each tiny quiver of information pointed her to this

region, this town, and hours of research and inquiries had led her to her source. Lorraine would confirm if she was correct or not. In a best-case scenario, she would also answer Mackenzie's crucial second question. *What is Bullseye's real name?*

Or maybe Lorraine would give her something else to narrow the field, point her to someone who could help. But one way or another, Bullseye would be exposed.

Mackenzie had gained a following on her podcast, *Boots on the Ground*, thanks to the modern fascination with true crime and the cases she'd been able to help solve. Every time she launched a new case, tips flooded in, but the majority never panned out. She garnered her share of haters too—mostly men who objected to her message, her words, her presentation, her clothes, her age, and her very existence. The same type of hatred she'd seen in the eyes of the bearded guy driving the white truck. Just an unfriendly local? Or one of Bullseye's people who had somehow tracked her? She'd abstained from posting updates since she hit town, but Bullseye might be every bit as adept at tracking as she was. She'd made no secret of the fact that Aaron Bardine was her brother.

And Bullseye was a filthy drug lord who was going to pay for his death.

Her body still tingled from the strip search. Hot shame licked her cheeks. Though she'd been treated respectfully, there was no way to avoid feeling humiliated and exposed while standing naked in front of a rubber-gloved stranger. It pained her to be deceiving the police. Part of her identity would always be law enforcement, even though she hadn't finished the academy. Down the road she'd have to come clean with the cops and FBI about what she learned and how she'd collected the information, but that wasn't important now.

Aaron often said, *"Use your powers for good, Zee."*

And she intended to.

An image of her parents swam through her mind, how they'd react when they heard what she'd done, their daughter, arrested for robbery. Her parents did not have the will to fight. Instead they comforted themselves with a future reckoning. *"No one escapes God's justice,"* her father said. *"He wins in the end."*

But God put her here on this planet to act, and act she would.

Her mission was not a quest for attention, as Gideon believed.

His expression when she'd taken his wallet was not something she'd ever forget. Shock, anger, and the worst emotion, disappointment, cascaded over his face. He had no idea what she was doing, and she wasn't sure why it mattered anyway. Gideon wouldn't want to even try to understand someone who reminded him of how he'd failed. She experienced agony whenever she recalled how she had done the same.

Her mom and dad would understand someday that it was the only way, the best chance she had to get enough information to help her prove that Bullseye was responsible for employing the dealer who'd murdered Aaron. He had a network of people who sold for him, transporting the drugs on small planes from Canada into the US. She knew it, from a thousand different bytes of information, but she couldn't prove it.

Not yet, anyway.

"Hungry?"

She snapped out of her reverie to find a cop talking through a slot in the cell door.

"Oh. Yes, actually."

"There's a light snack in the dining hall. I'll need to shackle your ankles."

Mortifying, but her chance had come. She stood.

"Okay."

He started to unlock the door. "We're working on your arraignment details, but the—"

Another cop hustled up before the door swung open. "We gotta evac the prisoners to county," he said to the first cop. "Two trips. I'll drive the women out first, Dan will follow to back me up. We'll get the males out next."

Evacuation? Mackenzie's chest tightened. *No, no, no.* Once they reached the larger county jail, she might never have her chance to talk to Lorraine.

"Wait," she started, but the officers weren't listening. It was clear the unit was in "handle it" mode. In a matter of moments, she was handcuffed and escorted to a covered garage and loaded into a small van, where her cuffs were fastened to the welded O-rings on the side of the vehicle. There were no windows save for the front, where she could get a partial look.

She strained to see as two other women were ushered in, one with a frizz of gray hair and the other younger with braids tight to her head and . . . Mackenzie stared . . . a broken front tooth, the only physical descriptor she had for her informant.

"Lorraine?" Mackenzie said to the woman across from her, as loudly as she dared.

The woman's freckled brow creased. She nodded, chewing her lip. "Yes."

Mackenzie's heart soared. *Thank you, God*. "I've been hoping to talk to you."

Her eyes flew wide, the little freckles on her brow dancing. "You're Mackenzie?"

"Yes."

Lorraine gaped. "What are you doing here?"

"Trying to find you."

"I thought for sure it was all off when I got arrested."

Mackenzie waited impatiently while the officer rechecked their seating arrangement and restraints. He let himself through a cage and locked it behind him before he strapped in and turned on the engine. Through the caging, she watched him ease the van into the storm. The deluge was instant, the front wipers barely able to keep up.

"What'd they get you for?" Lorraine asked.

"Robbery. After I heard you were in here, I figured it was the best way I might be able to see you."

Lorraine's complexion paled. "You got yourself arrested to talk to me?" She grimaced. "Wasted effort. It's all out of control now."

Mackenzie tried to break into the woman's tirade, but Lorraine continued, chewing on her dry lower lip. "He's not done punishing me. I know it. He's got people everywhere. If I talk to you, it'll get even worse. He'll end me."

"No one will know."

"He will. He already does." She yanked on her cuffs.

"That's why I'm in here, don't you see?" Tears collected on her lashes.

"Tell me what happened."

"I was arrested at my job. I work in the front office for a delivery company downtown that Bullseye owns. Somebody reported me for stealing, and they found the money in my company locker. It was so humiliating. But I didn't do it." Her voice raised in pitch. "Don't you get it? They found out I was communicating with you. Jail is the price now, but if I talk to you, it'll get worse." Her voice broke on the last word. "How am I ever going to get another job now with an arrest on my record?"

Mackenzie's stomach churned. Lorraine was suffering because Mackenzie had reached out to her. Why hadn't she anticipated such a thing? She'd been arrogant enough to think she was hidden from Bullseye.

"I'm sorry. I never meant to cause you trouble." She so badly wanted to take the woman's hand.

Lorraine sniffed. "I should have known better. I thought I could help you and maybe you could shut him down and he wouldn't find out. What was I thinking?"

"It's not over. The only way through this is to send him to prison, and we can still do that." She leaned forward, wrists cinched tight against the restraints. "His headquarters is here? In this area?" Lorraine nodded and Mackenzie's excitement flamed. Question one answered. "Do you know his name?"

Lorraine went still, and the hunted look in her eyes told Mackenzie the answer was yes. The moment had come. "I need to know."

"I can't tell you. He'll have me killed for sure."

"I promise I will never reveal to anyone that we spoke." She had to talk loudly enough to be heard over the rain.

"They might be following us right now." Lorraine looked around, jutting her chin at the other prisoner. "What about her?"

But the woman with the silver hair stared out the front.

"She's not listening. Please tell me what you know. This will be our only chance, Lorraine. You know that." Her throat clogged. "He can't go on ending people's lives. Help me shut him down. Please."

Lorraine cocked her head. "Aren't you afraid of what he'll do to you?"

"My brother's dead." She felt such a rush of white-hot anger, it took her a moment to finish. "He's not taking anything else."

Lorraine was silent for a beat before she swallowed hard. She was going to talk. Her bravery was breathtaking, and Mackenzie would see to it that she used every mote of information to its full advantage.

"You need to do something for me," Lorraine said.

"I will if I can."

"My mom is hoping to move to Jamaica next month to live with her sister. You need to help her, make sure she gets there. She'll be safe then."

"I'll try."

"No," Lorraine snapped, tone steely. "You'll do better than try. Even if you have to put her on the plane yourself, you're going to make it happen. Promise, or I don't tell you a thing." Her fingers were twisted together, jaw tight.

Mackenzie looked at her. "Lorraine, I promise I will make sure your mother gets to Jamaica."

"How do I know you'll do it?"

What could she say to vouch for her integrity? "My brother's gone. That's why I'm here. That's why I got myself arrested. There is nothing else in this world I want more than to bury Bullseye in a prison cell and shut down his drug dealing permanently."

Lorraine went still, thinking.

Mackenzie's whole mission hung on Lorraine's decision. What if she was right about Bullseye's reach? That even now the drug lord might know exactly where they were. How would he choose to deal with his two betrayers?

She held her breath and waited as the police van rolled on through the pummeling rain.

TWO

THE OFFICER HAD TAKEN Gideon's statement about the "robbery." He'd tried to explain that it must be some kind of prank, but even as she was led away, Mackenzie was loudly proclaiming she'd needed money to pay some bills and Gideon was a handy mark since she knew where to find him and he'd trust her.

Like a sap.

Two cups of bad police station coffee later, he'd finished giving his statement. "I don't want to press charges."

The weary cop in charge had looked at him, fingers still poised to hunt and peck on his keyboard. "You don't mind some lady mugging you?"

Oh, he minded all right, but that was between him and Mackenzie. "I'm leaving. I'd like to forget the whole thing. I got my wallet back, so . . ."

"Uh-huh. Well, the DA isn't a fan of crime in our little hamlet, so Ms. Bardine is going to be charged anyway."

"She's not a threat."

The officer simply stared at Gideon, who realized he sounded like he was off his rocker.

"Mr. Landry, if we hadn't been right there, she might have injured you or worse."

Been right there. And that was the fact he couldn't dislodge. She'd chosen to pull her little stunt at the coffee shop, knowing there was a cop inside. She *knew* she'd be arrested quickly, and he had a lousy feeling he understood the timing.

The cop stretched his neck as if he had a kink in it. "Look, sir. It's a bad time to be in Oakleaf. Place is flooding inch by inch, and we may be issuing evac notices anytime now because of the dam. You go on home and let us handle this, okay? The less people in town, the better."

At that point another officer poked his head in. "Sarge, update. Back lot's flooding and the river's gonna crest by nightfall. Fire chief is starting voluntary evacuations of the east side in thirty minutes, which includes us. County's making room at the jail in Clover for us to transport the detainees. We gotta get out now ahead of the evacuees."

Gideon had been hustled from the chair and out of the building. He should have left right then. Hit the gas and not looked back, but instead he'd waited in his Jeep in the coffee shop parking lot next door until the prison van departed in the pouring rain. He'd watched the loading of the prisoners, the first, slender, with her head ducked against the deluge.

How's your plan looking now, Zee?

For some inexplicable reason, after the van rolled slowly away, he was still there in his Jeep, staring out the front windshield, thoughts raging like a tempest. He grabbed the last bag of peanuts from his supply and chewed them thoughtfully as he considered. The truth of Mackenzie's question was like a poison dart. He *had* known something was off when fear began to creep into Aaron's devil-may-care persona, when the communication between them had ceased.

He and Aaron had been inseparable since sixth grade all the way until their senior year of high school when it had all gone catastrophically wrong. In spite of the wreckage, they'd both decided enlisting in the Air Force was the answer after graduation. They'd pieced their relationship back together, the years of friendship cementing the cracks. Mostly.

The discharge for drinking deposited Aaron stateside, but the texts continued between them in spite of it all, even while Gideon completed the training pipeline that carried him all the way to airborne school in Georgia. And Aaron? He'd rallied, started a successful computer software company that afforded him a tidy condo and a nice set of wheels. He'd made the best of it. Hadn't he?

But the reality of it was that Gideon *had* noticed Aaron's trepidation.

"I'm good, Gid," Aaron had said. *"You don't need to keep asking me like you're my parole officer."*

But Gideon knew deep in his gut that all was not well during that final family dinner, where jazz played in the background and Mrs. Bardine's roasted chicken graced the table.

He'd actually decided to follow Aaron that night, but he dallied a moment to answer a question from Aaron's father, and by the time he made his way to the car, Aaron was gone.

Two hours later, a frantic phone call from Mackenzie rocked his world.

"Aaron's dead, he was . . . shot in the head, behind a fast-food drive-through."

It appeared he'd gone to buy drugs and something had spooked the dealer. The police almost apprehended the suspect, but he was killed running in front of a delivery truck as he fled.

"Aaron was your best friend. Did you know something was wrong?"

She'd called Gideon weeks prior and flat out told him Aaron wasn't acting like himself. Gideon had promised to try again to get Aaron to talk. And his soul wondered why he hadn't pushed harder for answers, why he'd let his friend dance around an explanation. And why had he refused to help Mackenzie later when she'd started her quest for the truth? It was the subject of much tortured prayer.

Gideon's thoughts zinged back to the present. Mackenzie's plan to get arrested had worked well. Clearly, she wanted to get to her contact before she was sentenced, probably with the help of her inside source who likely worked at the jail. He marveled at her sheer audacity. Or was it frightening recklessness? Probably both, but she hadn't counted on the fact that the jail would be evacuated. Maybe it would work in her favor. Give her more unsupervised access to her informant. More likely, it would sink her whole plan as she was escorted to the larger facility.

He realized he'd eaten all the peanuts and still hadn't moved from the coffee shop lot. What was he waiting for? He reached for the ignition just as the same white truck from earlier rolled by at a glacial pace, the bearded driver not even trying to hide as he stared at Gideon.

Flat, muddy eyes, a mustache and beard that flowed together in a snowy mass, a cap with a worn brim tipped back on his head. The intimidation factor was unmistakable. The guy's look promised punishment if Gideon crossed him.

Gideon stared back, sending his own message as he calmly folded up the empty peanut bag and settled back in the comfortable seat of his beloved Jeep. It had been far too trying a day to be complacent, even if he was inclined toward passivity, which he certainly wasn't. He blazed a look at Hairy to eliminate the possibility of any misunderstanding.

Whoever you are, whatever you're doing, is immaterial to me. I'm not moving until I'm good and ready.

No flinching on Hairy's part, only the hint of a cruel smile. Message received. They'd come to an understanding. The guy moved on.

Gideon tracked the truck's progress along the street, which was covered with an inch or so of water. Mackenzie. The stranger in the truck. The prison van. The situation was a nebulous pool of unknowns, but three facts floated to the top.

Hairy was a problem.

Mackenzie was up to her neck in trouble.

And something bad was going to happen. Soon.

Not his concern. He was only a means to an end for her, clearly. She'd used him to get what she wanted. She was like that. His ridiculous attraction aside, they weren't friends anymore. Maybe they never had been. Their connection was Aaron, and he was dead and gone.

Gideon's goal remained unchanged. He owed his parents more than he could ever repay, but he intended to try his best.

There was nothing he could do about today's failed wilderness class but redouble his efforts on the next one. Host classes when the farm duties were lighter. Do whatever was needed during the in-between times to support. A clear plan, the kind he liked most.

Rain slapped at his windshield, and that wasn't about to improve either. He'd been tracking the weather for a week now. The storm was growing. Widespread flooding was expected in the next few days, which was why he'd intended to have his class finished and be on his way by now.

Possible dam failure added to the mix too.

No good reason to stay in town, just like the cop had said. *Go on home and let nature take its course.*

He watched the truck vanish around the corner on the road to the bridge, the same direction the prison van had taken fifteen minutes prior at a much slower speed. His drumbeat of anxiety would not be quieted. He thought of the question Aaron used to put to him.

"Why do you clutter up your life with worry?"

Worry was a useless feeling that didn't help anyone. Preparedness, on the other hand, could save lives. And that was what he was trained to do.

A little intelligence gathering wouldn't hurt. He'd detour around the bridge, wait on the other side, relay any useful information to the cops in the unlikely event he collected any. Observe and report only. If his instincts were wrong, no one needed to know.

If they weren't . . . He let the thought die away as he turned on the engine and took off.

* *

Just tell me his real name.

Mackenzie was bursting with impatience, but she kept quiet and still so as not to yank her cuffed wrists. She wanted to convince Lorraine of her motives. Her work wasn't just for Aaron but for the families of all addicts who could not shake their loved ones loose. Agonized mothers who'd left comments on her podcast about their beautiful children who were now cadaverous slaves to their next fix. Parents who were waiting in a perpetual purgatory for the phone call that would inform them their son or daughter had lost the battle. And also for children in schools who were encouraged and groomed for addiction, preyed upon by those who made them believe drugs were the answer.

But most of all it was for her parents, who lost their will and joy and zest for life the moment Aaron was murdered. They carried on in body but not in spirit.

That had died with Aaron.

The rain hammered down upon the van. Mackenzie noted that the cop bypassed the flooded turnoff to the highway in favor of the bridge, a longer route, the hills alongside the road sodden and slick. There were literally no other vehicles on the road, not that she could see anyway, except possibly the police car she'd heard would be following them. The cops were stretching their staff to the brink since two more officers would be required to transfer the men to the county jail and the rest to move cars and equipment before the station was inundated.

In the distance she could barely see the metal beams of the bridge that spanned the river. Far upstream, lost to view, was the Cotton Flower Dam. If it really did fail, two hundred thousand acre-feet of water would empty itself with deadly force into the river, which would promptly submerge the town. Goose bumps prickled her skin as she scanned the heavily forested surroundings through the windshield. Aaron would have loved to ride the trails here. Of course, he'd want to overnight at a luxury inn somewhere. What had happened to make him start using drugs?

Aaron could lie to their parents, to his sister, and probably to his girlfriend, Leah, whom she'd never met, in that charismatic way that fooled everyone.

But not Gideon.

If only Gideon had forced Aaron to come clean that night since he wouldn't confess the truth to her. Deep down she was absolutely certain Gideon could have saved her brother.

But neither of them had stopped the tragedy from unfolding. *You are just as much to blame, Mackenzie.*

She refocused on Lorraine.

Lorraine blew out a breath. "Okay." She hunched her shoulders and strained toward Mackenzie as far as the cuffs would allow. "My boyfriend, Cal, is . . ." Lorraine sighed. "He *was* my boyfriend. Probably won't want anything to do with me now that I've been arrested. He works at the airport in town, and they let him bunk there. He's not a pilot, he does the office work and helps load and unload cargo, but he started to notice strange patterns. Small planes that flew in without proper flight plans or paperwork, and pilots who refused help and unloaded packages themselves when there were few people around."

"Where did the packages go?"

"Cal wasn't sure at first, but after a while, he noticed the same truckers who picked it up all worked for—" She stopped as the van shimmied.

Mackenzie pulled against the restraints. "Who?"

"Sorry," the cop called. "Hit a patch of standing water there when we rolled onto the bridge. Driving this thing is like steering an elephant."

Lorraine clutched the side to steady herself, breathing hard.

"Who did the truckers work for, Lorraine?"

Lorraine started to answer when the cop suddenly grabbed his radio.

Mackenzie didn't hear what he said over the clatter of rain, but his urgency caught their attention.

Mackenzie pulled the restraints to the limit to get a look. She caught a snippet of the cop's conversation.

"Dispatch, transport one."

"Transport one, dispatch."

"A white truck behind me."

Her blood went cold. A white truck . . . like the one that had been popping up in her sights since she hit town. The officer's eyes widened in the rearview mirror. He squeezed the radio.

"I no longer have a visual on transport two. Request . . ."

In a blur she saw the white truck pull adjacent.

Lorraine was right. Punishment was coming.

As the truck drew even, she got a quick look just before it smashed into the side of the prison van. The women ricocheted hard against the metal interior.

Lorraine screamed.

The silver-haired lady flopped forward in the seat like a rag doll. Her eyes were enormous, petrified. “That truck’s going to shove us over the side of the bridge!”

Mackenzie didn’t want to believe it, but her gut told her that was exactly what was going to happen. With a flash of nausea, she also knew this was her fault too. Bullseye found out she was talking to Lorraine and sent his people to eliminate any threats.

The cop, the two terrified women . . . *What have I done to them?*

The sergeant fought valiantly to keep the van on the road, pushing their speed to get ahead of the truck as he shouted an update into his radio.

His words were cut off as the truck slammed them again, causing the van to scrape against a metal bridge support with a scream of metal against metal.

He gripped the wheel, jammed the gas pedal to the floor, and outpaced the truck. Mackenzie’s breath came in spurts. She could see the far side of the bridge ahead. If they made it across, they’d have a chance. Another officer might have time to rendezvous. She called out to Lorraine, but the woman was frozen in shock.

Without warning the truck dropped back and out of her view. Sweat gleamed on the cop’s brow as he pushed them onward. The exit to the bridge was only twenty feet away. He was actually going to get them off.

Her hope popped like a soap bubble as a second vehicle, a black 4x4, rolled onto the far side of the bridge facing them. It wasn’t help. Like a cork bottling up the fluid inside a shaken bottle, they were trapped.

Heart in her throat, she watched as the 4x4 bore down on them from the front. No doubt the white truck was still pursuing as well. She wished she could hold Lorraine's hand, comfort her or the silver-haired woman who had done nothing to deserve what was about to happen. The handcuffs prevented her from doing anything but holding up her palms in the universal "calm down, don't panic" gesture.

Useless, as there was every reason to panic.

Something popped. A tire exploding. Theirs?

The cop continued to holler details into his radio. There was a rifle locked in a holder in the console. To use it, he'd have to slow, to stop. Defend them as best he could until backup arrived. The glass was probably bulletproof, so maybe if they stayed put . . .

A brutal impact slammed her forward, and the restraints jerked her back, cutting into her wrists. Glass fractured around her. She did not feel any bits of it raining down, but she could hear the breakage and the shearing of metal. The wires threaded through the glass kept it in place in spite of the spiderweb of cracks. Small comfort. The glass would hold. But there was nothing that would keep them from drowning if they went over. The railing flashed closer and closer.

"No!" Lorraine cried, halfway between a wail and a sob.

With a screech of metal, the van punched through the rails and flew out into the air.

Her stomach tumbled as if she were on an amusement ride. In her peripheral vision she saw the officer clinging to the steering wheel, his knuckles white as if he could somehow still control the van as it sailed free from earth.

But they were dropping toward the thundering river.

The terror of the situation pressed into her every cell as she recalled that she was chained in place.

What awaited Mackenzie instead of the justice she sought?

A slow drowning in a frigid river.

Bullseye's deadly web had killed her brother.

And now he would murder her and three innocents as well.

....

On the far side of the bridge, Gideon flung the binoculars into the passenger seat and cranked the wheel to escape the shrubs where he'd concealed his Jeep. His hands strangled the wheel.

The white truck had shot past his place of concealment and continued at breakneck speed away from its terrible handiwork. The 4x4 that burst on the scene had paused a moment at the rupture where the police van had gone over and then spun a U-turn and followed the route of its escaping cohort.

Gideon hadn't seen what happened to the police escort supposed to accompany the van, but it hadn't made it onto the bridge. No help coming from that quarter. His heart slammed into his ribs.

New plan. He flat-footed the gas. Thanks to his shortcut, he was parked on a high point up a soggy riding trail where he had a perfect view of the van as it approached the bridge and crossed it. The road funneled down into a pinch point, the prime location to stage an ambush if one was so inclined. He'd anticipated some sort of attack, and the guy in the white truck who'd just slammed into the van had not disappointed.

His instincts had been right.

His teeth clamped tight as he bounced down the trail and onto flat ground before he sped across the bridge.

He called 911 as he drove, shouting the situation over his roaring engine. They heard, and probably were already alerted to the danger by the cop before the van went over, but he didn't have a spare moment to elaborate before he disconnected.

He raced to the breach, yanked the Jeep off to the emergency shoulder, and jammed it into park. He grabbed his pack, zipped the phone in a waterproof case inside, and slid it on, pulling it tight to his body. The roadway was slick as he sprinted to the point where the metal had given way.

Below, the van was floating driver's side up in the rapids, the rear already sinking. The equilibrium would eventually be restored as the water crept in, but the current was sucking them on a wild path as the van took on more water. He scrambled onto the guardrail, perched there staring at the white eddies gobbling the van in inches.

This was going to be messy and potentially lethal.

And he'd thought the day couldn't get any worse.

One breath to pray, the next to inflate his lungs. Then he jumped, arms tucked against his body as he dropped feetfirst into the water.

THREE

THE FORCE OF THE WATER and the intense cold assaulted Gideon like a fist, stripping him of breath as he fought to orient himself in the tumult. When his head broke the surface, he saw fifty feet to his left that while he was underwater, the van had struck the bridge support, which temporarily held it in place. A blessing, but the current would have its way soon. It always did. He struck out, swimming hard against the rush. This was why he chose to train in the ocean when he had the opportunity. Even better when he could practice with his Navy cousin, Johnny, who pushed him like no one else.

A placid swimming pool was nothing like a ferocious expanse of living water.

First a deer rescue, now three women and a cop trapped in a police van. Two dives in one day exceeded his usual conditioning. Though he kept himself in the best physical shape he could manage, he had to labor hard to fight the violence around him and the painful freeze. Something bashed his bad shoulder as he propelled himself, a branch or piece of debris. At least he'd seen no sign of the trucks returning before he dove, but there were other monumental challenges to the rescue.

The glass of the vehicle was reinforced, so he wasn't going to be breaking any windows to extract survivors. The passengers, who happened to be prisoners, were undoubtedly locked in place, save for the officer, who he wasn't even sure had survived the crash.

How was he going to free them all before the vehicle sank?

Return with honor, the SERE motto. At the moment, that meant using everything in his power to bring back as many as he could from the wreck. He tried hard not to fixate on the fact that one of those lives was Aaron's little sister.

Stubborn, mercurial, maddening Mackenzie who shouldn't even be in a police van in the first place.

He clawed his way over until his palm slapped the prison van's dented metal. The frigid water numbed his limbs, and he hardly felt the impact. He figured he had about three minutes tops before the flow overcame the van. He used up thirty precious seconds fighting his way to the driver's side, which was tilted to the sky.

The window was rolled down as the cop struggled to push the door open. He'd survived.

Gideon swam up.

The cop spluttered, eyes wide, one hand disappearing from view as he reflexively reached for his weapon, no doubt wondering if Gideon might be in league with the guys who had just driven him off the road.

Gideon stopped, laboriously treading water, and showed the man his palms. "I'm here to help, sir," he shouted over the roar. "Staff Sergeant Gideon Landry, US Air Force."

After a tense moment, the cop nodded. "Sergeant Martin Rodriquez," he hollered back. They worked together to wrestle the door open, icy water thundering around and in.

"Souls aboard?" Gideon shouted. He wasn't positive how many prisoners were loaded in addition to Mackenzie. There might have been others he wasn't aware of.

The cop hesitated, water splashing his face, still not completely trusting, but Gideon didn't have to say anything further. Rodriquez knew whoever he was transporting would soon be dead.

"Four," he said.

Cop plus three.

Rodriquez was already moving, stripping off his body armor. "I'll unlock. You'll help me get 'em out?"

Gideon nodded. "Yes, sir."

The cop tucked his weapon into his waistband, unbuckled his heavy utility belt, and dropped it. The van was leveling down as the rear filled with water. Gideon levered himself inside.

With shaking hands, Rodriquez unlocked the security door between the driving compartment and the prisoner area. Together they wrestled it open and swam into the interior. The water had already crept within a foot of the ceiling.

At first he only spotted two women, Mackenzie and another with braids. Their heads were barely above the water as it swirled around their necks. Mackenzie's eyes flew wide at the sight of him.

"Help her." She jutted her chin to where he finally noticed the third woman farther to the back, the water just beginning to inundate her nostrils. Silver hair puffed around her head. Her expression was wild with panic. Rodriquez immediately swam to the lady, dove under, and suddenly one of the woman's hands was free. She screamed and thrashed, striking the officer in the face.

Gideon crossed the distance in one second and pinned her in place with a bear hug. "Stay still," he thundered. "And you'll get out alive."

His tone cut through her panic. She stilled enough that in another second the cop had gotten her completely free and propelled her toward the exit.

"Keys," Gideon called to him.

He could read the cop's expression. Allowing a civilian to free the prisoners was against all his training.

"I will get them out," Gideon said, voice hard with resolve.

The cop blinked, gave one sharp nod, and slapped the keys into Gideon's hand. "I'll move her to safety and come back and assist." He continued urging his terrified prisoner to the door. "We'll swim to the bridge support and you're gonna hold on there. Help is coming."

Whoever was en route would not arrive fast enough. Gideon turned back to the two remaining women. The water level had risen and they both had to strain, heads craned toward the precious pocket of air. Mackenzie thrust out her chin again, this time indicating he should release the braided woman.

Still giving orders. He didn't need her direction.

In any case, he did as she suggested because the freckled

lady was clearly starting to panic, breathing fast, inhaling snorts of water that made her cough.

He swam over, dove down, found the wrist cuffs, and unlocked them. She immediately bobbed up into the narrowing pocket of air where he joined her.

"Can you swim?"

She nodded, sucking in huge breaths.

"Okay. Swim the direction you saw the cop go. It'll be hard work, but you can do it. Kick clear of the van when you get out." He didn't want her getting sucked in as the water completely claimed the vehicle.

Her face was dead white, lips bluish. "I can't. I'm scared."

"You can," he snapped, "or you'll die."

She pressed her lips together and started to cry.

She wasn't going to move unless he figured out how to convince her. *Patience, Gideon. She's a civilian, remember?* He said more gently, "What's your name?"

"L-Lorraine." Her voice was barely a whisper, wet lashes spiky around her terrified eyes.

He took her hands. "Listen, Lorraine. This is scary, for sure, but you have someone who needs you, right? Someone who's going to be mourning you forever if you don't get out of here?"

She nodded, and a gleam of determination infused her eyes.

"You can do this. I'll be right behind you in a minute, and I'll help you if you need it. I'm a stranger, I know, but you can trust me. You've got to."

She gave him a tiny nod.

He squeezed her shoulder, assisted with a push that propelled her toward the driver's compartment.

He couldn't spare any more attention on her because the water was now lapping at Mackenzie's upper lip. She was not yet in panic mode, but her nostrils were flared, muscles straining.

He dove, following the feel of her arm to the restraints. It required more seconds than it had for Lorraine because he was almost completely numb and his movements clumsy. Praying he wouldn't lose his grip, he inserted the tiny key and unlocked the cuffs. With one swift kick, she bobbed up to the air pocket. He joined her there just as the van lurched and began to fill in earnest. They had seconds, no more.

"Big breath," he called over the rush.

They inhaled as deeply they could, dove, and kicked their way toward the driver's compartment.

When she began to fall back, he took her arm, tugging her next to him. The force of the water shooting in required their combined strength to fight, and she had been in the water longer. By the time they made it, the driver's area was fully engulfed, so they bobbed to the roof where there were a few precious inches of air. They gulped it in.

He pointed, directing her to shove off the seat to get momentum enough to clear the open window. There wasn't a spare moment to tell her to swim as far from the vehicle as possible, but her cop training should help unless she completely freaked out.

He didn't think she would. Mackenzie had grit, no matter what she lacked in judgment.

Without hesitation, she disappeared into the void. The moment he kicked off in her wake he felt powerful suction as the van sank behind him. He powered hard, fighting cold and fatigue, straining with each stroke until he broke the surface. As he blinked away the blur, he caught sight of the cop and the two prisoners clinging together atop the cement platform of the bridge support pier twenty feet from his position. The women's arms were linked together as they stood, shivering, Rodriquez with them, watching the surface of the water.

Two women.

Where was Mackenzie? He pivoted in a circle without spotting her.

Gideon caught the cop's attention.

Rodriquez gave him an "I don't know" gesture.

He swam in another tight circle, once, twice. Water foamed around him, weighing him down. He stared every which way, trying to calculate where the water might have dragged her. It was not possible that she hadn't made it out.

His memory churned and brought him back to that moment from the past, Mackenzie's voice blazing with anger, disbelief, anguish, all of the above.

"He's dead, Gideon."

He heard again the glass-sharp words when she'd told him her brother had been murdered. The bullet shattered five lives that day. Aaron's and his sister's, their parents', and Gideon's. Maybe Aaron's girlfriend's too.

And if Mackenzie drowned now, how would he tell her parents?

Not her too. It wasn't possible.

"Do you see her?" he shouted to the cop, uncertain if he could even be heard.

The cop's position was higher; he'd have been able

to spot her. Rodriquez looked, almost slipping from the bridge support as he scanned.

Five seconds, ten, fifteen. The cop shook his head.

Unacceptable answer. He'd find her himself.

He struck out a few yards away from the pillar and peered around again.

She'd been tired, injured maybe, unable to reach the first bridge support. The flow would have pulled her closer to the next one. He let the current carry him a few yards downstream, dodging a whirling hunk of wood pallet a millisecond before it would have bashed his skull in.

The next nearest bridge support on the west side was concealed behind plumes of white water. He pushed himself harder and came abreast of it, certain he'd see her.

She wasn't there. His heart dropped.

Pinpricks of black danced in his pupils. He was breathing hard, his strength slowly draining away. He stopped, treading water, shouting above the roar.

"Mackenzie!"

The river answered, but he heard no human reply.

He hollered again, throat tight, fear ripping through his soul. In the far distance, he could still make out the bridge support where the survivors clung.

The cop was gesturing forcefully, the message clear. *She's gone. Get out of the water or you're going to die, you fool.*

The sergeant was right. Adding another victim wasn't going to save her. But she could not be gone, and there was no way he could give up the search. That wasn't in his creed, nor his DNA. Not for anybody and especially not for Aaron's sister.

"Mackenzie!" he shouted.

To his left, he thought he heard something. He yelled again and then he was certain he heard a high-pitched answer. Through the pummeling water he saw a pile of debris. Pulse pounding, he swam hard until he approached a mass of branches that had formed a snag. A flash of orange jumpsuit made his spirit soar.

Thank you, God almighty.

The branches had caught her as she'd tried to reach the other pier. The water seized him in a freezing grip, doing its best to yank him onto another course. He doubled down, tucked his chin, and hauled.

When he finally reached her, she was clinging to a twisted branch, only her head and shoulders above water. He made it close enough, secured himself to a protruding branch next to her, and let the water pin him in place rather than fighting against it.

Her teeth were chattering, lips blue. "Did they make it out? The women and the cop?"

"Affirmative. They're holding in place, waiting for rescue, like you should be."

She didn't answer, just shivered, her fingers like white marble as she held on.

He tamped down his combination of anger and relief and focused on calculating an ending where they didn't both drown. "It's too far and too rough to swim back to their position," he told her. "Can you make it to the next pier if we go together? The water will do most of the work."

She nodded, hair plastered to her face. "Then what?"

Isn't it obvious? "Then we wait for rescue. Gonna hope

the cop's got reinforcements rolling and your would-be assassins are gone."

She cocked her head. "I'll go back to jail."

Anger chewed his gut. "But on the plus side, you won't be dead," he snapped. "Nor will they."

She actually looked contrite. "I didn't mean to put anyone else in danger."

He figured with everything going on, he wasn't required to listen to her lame apology. "We'll edge around this pile and then we kick off in that direction." He pointed. "Hold on to my belt. Ready?"

She looked as though she wanted to say something, but instead she clasped his belt at his lower back when he turned. He was so cold he felt only the barest hint of her touch. His limbs were numbed, hers too, their reflexes slowed. As their core body temperatures dropped and hypothermia set in, decision-making, reaction time, and even their ability to communicate would be impaired.

Move it, Landry.

"We'll get around this pile and then the challenge will be not letting ourselves get swept past the pier."

He grabbed at the branches, broken ends threatening to puncture his palms. Not that he'd likely feel it anyway since they were submerged in an ice bath. She clawed her way too—trying, he supposed, not to add to his exertion by being a dead weight.

When we're out of here, I'm going to tell you exactly how I feel about this situation you've dragged us into, Zee.

The pier seemed impossibly far away when they reached the edge of the tangle. He didn't stop to let that sink in. Movement was the only thing keeping them alive. He did a visual check to make sure she was still hanging on since he could no longer trust his frozen senses and gestured to communicate it was go time.

He swam for all he was worth, Mackenzie doing the same. Every single moment of physical training he'd forced upon his body paid off as he crossed the treacherous distance, though his right shoulder felt like it was going to snap off. She cleaved the water as cleanly as a half-frozen person could. The waves roiled and sucked at them, and once they had to reroute around a sharp spine of rock that protruded in their path. It was so taxing he prayed they'd have enough strength to haul themselves up the slippery cement pedestal.

Focus on the now.

For an eternity it felt as if the river would win, but inch by inch they extracted themselves from the tumult and finally reached the pier.

When they made it, gasping and panting, he found a series of metal pins embedded in the cement that provided footholds. He insisted she climb first.

She shook her head.

"Not in the mood, Zee," he snarled. "Out."

She must have been too cold to argue with her usual bullheaded vigor because she followed his command, leaning on his knee for leverage. When she was clear, she reached a shaking hand to help him. He ignored the gesture and used every last bit of strength to extricate himself.

They crouched on the narrow concrete lip that was no more than eight inches wide, the water pouring off their clothing. When he could force himself to move, he slithered around a couple feet to a spot where he could get a visual on the cop. He waved, almost losing his balance and toppling in. Rodriquez finally spotted him and offered a thumbs-up. The guy probably couldn't believe they were alive. Gideon could hardly comprehend it either.

"Backup coming?" Mackenzie said in his ear.

He jerked. He hadn't realized she'd moved so close to him. "Likely."

He checked his waterproof watch. Twenty-five minutes since he'd entered the water. Backup should have already arrived, even in this bad-weather condition. But it was a scant police presence in a small town with a dam failure looming in addition to the flood—and a whopper of a complication when the two trucks had taken out the prison van. During an emergency, people had to be ready to take care of themselves. He wasn't at all sure how that was going to work since the cop and the other two women were likely as close to hypothermia as he and Mackenzie.

The two stood shivering, limbs quaking. She swayed. It was becoming difficult for her to maintain her balance on the narrow rim, so he looped an arm around her and pulled her to his side. She did not resist, a clear indication she was starting to succumb. He had no dry clothes he could share in their precarious position, no escape from the frigid temps, only the scant comfort of a shoulder to steady her until help arrived. They half leaned, half stood, the minutes ticking by in excruciating slow motion as the cold knifed into them.

If rescue didn't arrive soon, it would be too late.

Over the cacophony of the rushing water, he heard the thin wail of a siren. "Cops, finally."

"One squad car?" She squinted through the spray. "How's that going to help?"

Before he could answer, a red boat with *Rescue* on the side motored into view with lights strobing. Two life-jacketed men stood on deck, another at the controls, scanning the water with binoculars. His worry ebbed away in a rush of euphoria. He muttered another prayer of thanks as he watched the vessel. The twenty-three-foot Zodiac was made for complicated rescues, with plenty of room for all of them and two motors that would provide enough horsepower to easily handle the current. Never had he thought a boat beautiful before, but this one deserved its own magazine cover.

Mackenzie grinned. "Chic. I would have settled for a rowboat."

"Me too."

As they clutched each other, the boat approached the pier where the officer and two passengers clung. They'd put a swimmer in the water, maybe deploy their floating stretcher to convey the passengers to safety if the victims were too weak to manage the transfer.

Rodriquez pointed to their location, and a voice came over the PA from the vessel.

"This is Oakleaf Fire and Rescue. We see you and will render aid soon. Stay put."

As if they had a whole lot of choice in the matter.

He'd opened his mouth to shout a reply when the white truck rolled into view in the marshy grasses along the access road that paralleled the flooding river. His heart thumped and the words died on his lips.

Mackenzie gasped. "They can't be back."

The narrow road next to the bridge was closed by

a gate—he'd checked when he'd taken up his recon position—off-limits since it was submerged in some places already. The truck had found a way through the barriers.

He couldn't see the face of the driver, but he knew it was Hairy, the man with the beard who'd forced the van off the bridge.

But there were cops now, and fire response. Surely they weren't desperate enough to—

He was already turning to draw Mackenzie to the far side of the support when the first rifle shot pinged into the cement pier.

• •

Mackenzie forced her sluggish senses to process. They were under attack. Again. The cops in the squad car returned fire as the rescue boat continued to race toward the stranded trio.

She and Gideon were out of view of the shooter at first, but the angle of the shots indicated the truck was moving, likely searching.

For her? And Lorraine? As she surveyed the violent eddies of the water, she worried Bullseye's orders would be carried out. Their time was ticking down until death came via a bullet or exposure. Somewhere out there, the other vehicle, the black one that had assisted in the initial attack, was closing in as well.

Her thoughts finally tumbled out her mouth, past her chattering teeth. "They were watching from somewhere. They saw us escape the van."

Gideon didn't seem to have heard her. He was half crouched, analyzing. The water made his shorn hair stand up in prickles. His teeth weren't chattering, but his body convulsed with shivers.

The way she saw it, there were only two choices, stay or move, and they had to decide now.

The seconds were ebbing away until they died from the cold.

Until they weakened and fell into the water.

Until the second shooter spotted them clinging to the support, or the first corrected their aim.

"We have to swim for it again." She peered across to the far side of the river. "Current should take us toward that next snag, right? We can crawl our way out."

He did look at her then, furious. "Get real. We don't have the strength."

She tried a smile. "Speak for yourself."

"I'm speaking for both of us. Our best bet is to stay here, keep out of the line of fire, and wait for reinforcements. That's the smart way."

She shook her head.

The muscle in his jaw jumped. "You know how much of my career has been spent learning from stories about people who *didn't* choose the smart way?"

Another volley of shots indicated the officer on the bank had engaged the white truck. They scooted around the pier in time to see the cop who'd driven the van jump feetfirst into the rescue boat where the two women were already sheltering. The boat began a slow turn.

Relief that the women and cop would not die because of her was heady.

A second police car rode up, sirens screaming, and immediately took up position to support the rescue boat.

Their combined fire caused the white truck to back up and execute a wild U-turn.

"Hairy's retreating," Gideon crowed. "Give it to 'em, boys." He leaned away from her another few inches.

Mackenzie thought it over. She had to keep going, and Gideon would only get hurt trying to dissuade her. While his attention was elsewhere, she would stay busy moving toward her goal. If she waited like he'd demanded, she would wind up back in custody somewhere and her chance would pass her by. She no longer had access to Lorraine, but Lorraine's boyfriend, Cal, worked at the airstrip, and there was a chance he hadn't yet evacuated. Maybe he could tell her what she needed to know.

It was her last fragile opportunity, and she had to risk it.

But not Gideon. He was right about waiting for help. It was definitely the best choice for him. He'd get warmed up, back to his vehicle, and escape without suffering any more consequences. She didn't like Gideon—still felt the hurt of his refusal to help with the case against Bullseye—but she didn't want him to die for her. Best to protect him from it all.

She peered into the swirling water, body quaking to remind her she had very little strength left. But all she had to do was make it to the snag and haul herself out. She'd find some dry clothes somewhere, warm up, regroup. Finish what she'd started.

It was an absolutely reckless choice. But it was hers to make.

Gideon was still turned away from her. "Cops are pursuing the white truck. Boat's making a circle. They'll come around to—"

Before he finished, Mackenzie made her move.

FOUR

GIDEON LUNGED FOR MACKENZIE. She had to have fallen, slipped. But his brain observed that her arms were neatly folded to her chest, her toes pointed as she entered the water.

Not slipped. Jumped.

Why? His brain reeled. It was absolutely nonsensical that she'd dive right back in when they just escaped drowning by inches.

Fury choked him. He should've let her carry on with whatever harebrained scheme she'd cooked up.

The moment she pretended to steal his wallet should have been the official end of his involvement.

The squad car on the bank had taken off in pursuit of the shooters, who were no longer in sight. That was something, anyway. He sucked in an enormous breath and yelled at the rescue boat as it tossed side to side like an old porch rocker. He finally got the cop's attention.

Rodriquez pointed to his ear in a "can't hear you" signal.

No kidding. Gideon used his entire body to try to convey

where Mackenzie had gone in. Rodriquez grabbed a pair of binoculars and began to scan the fray. The rescue boat moved slowly, working against the rush of water. Mackenzie, on the other hand, had already traveled ten yards from the pier where Gideon stood, and she was gaining speed.

Timing wasn't in their favor.

The boat would arrive to rescue him, but she'd be long gone, drowned and swept away to be recovered after the waters receded. There was no other likely outcome. How hadn't she seen that? The woman was obsessed but not suicidal. She was her own worst enemy, and whatever she thought she was doing wasn't going to bring Aaron back.

The cop was still scanning, the boat still churning, the current still yanking Mackenzie toward a watery death. For an endless moment he breathed deep, prayed, and let his decision settle, his mind accept what the next action of his body would be. He tightened the straps on his pack and locked his knees to stop them from shaking.

This is turning into an unbelievably bad day.

He dove into the water for the third time since breakfast.

Like the past two occasions, the temperature hit him like a physical blow. Only now he was weakened from exhaustion and racing toward hypothermia. It took him longer to break the surface after the shock of the plunge. The air he sucked in felt almost as cold as the water.

Mackenzie's orange jumpsuit enabled him to spot her, swimming madly for the column of debris snagged in the roots of an oak tree on the bank. The collection of branches and other flotsam and jetsam was her target, he imagined. A rickety escape ladder.

It was his too. If they didn't make it there, they'd die. If they did make it and the debris wouldn't hold them or they were too tired to climb out, they'd die. If the black truck was stationed somewhere nearby and the driver had seen her stunt and was setting up a neat rifle shot, they'd die.

So where was the upside of this clever plan?

He swam his hardest, kicking with all his might to close the gap between them. He didn't catch up until she'd reached the snag and heaved herself onto a broken two-by-four stuck amid the pile.

He helped himself to the other end, panting and shivering.

Her eyes went wide as she glanced at him. "Why did you follow me?"

"I can only chalk it up to temporary insanity," he growled.

"You shouldn't have."

"One hundred percent agree. But how about we don't talk now, huh? You know, since we're close to freezing to death and all? We have to get out of here."

"No one told you to butt in." Even though she was half frozen, her eyes flashed at him.

A dozen retorts bottled up in his throat as he stared at the infuriating woman. "Just get moving before we can't, okay?" They began to work, seizing slippery handholds and hauling themselves sideways toward the steep bank.

A branch snagged in her hair. She snapped off the offending twig and continued. He kept on, but he could not ignore the fact that the whole pile was vibrating with the shock of the water slamming away at it.

"Mackenzie." He didn't finish as the two-by-four and

the branch that had held it steady pulled loose and were immediately sucked up by the current.

Faster. They had to go faster. He tried to say as much, but he couldn't expend the energy. Mackenzie was moving slower, as if the branch pile was working to hold her in place. He grabbed her wrist and lugged her forward, figuring she'd give him a hostile elbow or at least a serrated glare. She did neither. They kept on.

He estimated they had fifteen feet left to traverse before they reached the muddy edge. How they were going to climb up the steep slope was another problem, but if they could manage it, he might be able to go back for his Jeep. Drive them out. Back to the station. A hospital. Anywhere that wasn't wet and freezing. His body yowled in complaint.

While he was still rolling ideas over, the branch he held was yanked from his grasp by a vicious wave. The whole pile ripped loose, and they were rushing and tumbling, right along with the debris.

Mackenzie's expression was pure terror. Though this was her choice, her decision, and she'd delivered herself squarely into the mess, his heart lurched. He grabbed the front of her coveralls and managed to pull her to his chest. The water hauled them under, dousing them until he thought they were finished, then rocketed them to the surface where they gasped and choked.

"Just hold steady for a minute," he said into her ear. "We're okay." He wasn't sure how exactly they were okay, but panic wouldn't serve. With the network of branches gone, it was all he could do to stay afloat. A thick piece of foam rushed by, and he snagged it, then shoved it under her arms.

When God sends you a flotation device . . .

At least it got her head above the water. He draped an arm around her shoulders and began to try to tow them both to the bank. But as much as he kicked and struggled, they made no progress. He treaded water, panted, searched for the rescue boat, though they were too far out of visual range. Possibly they'd called in reinforcements and decided to get their retrieved victims to safety before returning. He probably would have done the same, rather than risk three people dying of hypothermia while attempting to rescue two clowns who couldn't seem to stay out of the river.

Come on, Gid. Power through.

But the water increased in volume and violence as his muscles began to shut down. The noises seemed farther away. His limbs weren't moving smoothly anymore. Still, he fought on, Mackenzie helping kick.

It wasn't enough.

Should he stop resisting? Let the river carry them where it would, hopefully to a place where they could escape? But it was full of debris and the bank was so impossibly far away.

He hung on to her, and she looked at him.

"I'm sorry." He couldn't hear the words, but the regret in her expression was clear under the extreme discomfort.

You should be.

"Hey!"

Had he imagined the voice?

He whipped a look toward the bank. At first, he didn't see anything. Mackenzie pointed one trembling finger. "There's . . . a man," she said as if she didn't believe what she was seeing.

He didn't dare let go of her as he blinked his vision into focus.

A heavyset man with a brimmed rain cap and a navy slicker stood on the bank, waving a yellow rope.

Not Hairy from the white truck. Possibly the driver of the black truck, but he didn't think so. This looked like a well-meaning local, a guy who might possibly be able to save them. His frozen veins pulsed a tick faster.

The man cupped a hand around his mouth. "Gonna . . ."

Gideon didn't catch the rest of the sentence, but he didn't need to. The man tossed the coiled rope. It unfurled, ribboning down the cliff of mud and hitting the water twenty feet from their position.

"Tread water," he commanded Mackenzie as he struck out hard for the rope that undulated frustratingly ahead of him. He pushed on with his last reserve of strength. This was undoubtedly their only remaining chance to survive.

His fingers touched the wet fibers, but his flesh was so cold he couldn't grip. The surge pulled it farther from him. He thought of the swimming contests he, his brothers, and their cousin had in the lake on their family farm. Who could stay underwater the longest, reach the other side the fastest, make the biggest splash cannonballing off the dock. His cousin Johnny would typically win, which only infuriated Cullen and Duncan. Winning came easily to Johnny, his big size and natural physicality working to his advantage. But all the losing taught Gideon an invaluable lesson that he passed on to his students.

Stay present.

It wasn't about tomorrow, the next hour, or the finish line. It was about now, being focused, deliberate. That was how he'd learned to outlast Johnny and his brothers, to flat-out endure.

Three feet.

Do it. Now.

He concentrated on his arms and cleaved a yard past the trajectory of the rope so he'd be in a good position when their paths intersected. It took every bit of his reserve.

This time, when the rope came within reach, he clasped both hands around it and scooted it to his body, then clamped it under his armpit until he could loop it clumsily around his torso. Elated, he spun. For a moment, his heart almost stopped beating when he failed to spot Mackenzie.

But an instant later, he caught the flash of orange. In spite of her vigorous effort to hold on to the piece of foam, she was barely above water, her face ghastly pale. Nonetheless, at his thumbs-up, she strove to swim toward him, and he met her in the middle.

He wrapped her in a bear hug and looped the rope once more to encompass both of them. The rush of emotion took him unawares. Under pain of death and dismemberment, he would never admit to anyone that he'd longed since he was sixteen years old to embrace his best friend's sister. God had an interesting sense of humor to finally make that wish come true in such a moment, when he was so cold he might as well be clinging to a block of ice. But when she moved and pressed her cheek to his, he felt something flutter through his iced-up interior.

Something other than rage and frustration. An echo of what he'd felt when she startled him with a kiss just before she mugged him.

Nope. No room for teenage daydreaming. *Stay in the moment.*

A tug on the rope informed him the man on the bank was reeling them in. They clung as tight as they could, which was wise considering the way that Gideon had knotted the rope was not up to standard. The speed with which they cut through the water was impressive. The guy couldn't possibly be hoisting two full-grown adults at such a pace. Gideon eventually heard the whir of a winch as they reached the edge, plowing into the mire. They began to slither through the goo until they were pulled above it, skimming the steep bank as they rose, sometimes smacking the earthen wall and at other moments swinging free. They twirled and he did his best to steady them as they were hoisted up the fifteen feet to the top of the bank and delivered, a mucky half-frozen mess, to the top.

They lay tangled together, encased in mud as they panted and shivered.

The man stopped the winch on the back of his vehicle and freed them from the rope. "Town's evacuating. Spotted you down there in the water. What happened?" His brown eyes were wide.

So he hadn't seen the episode on the bridge.

Mackenzie sat up and gave Gideon a warning look. "We had an accident. Went over the side."

The brown eyes widened even more as he threw two musty moving blankets over their shoulders. "Incredible you survived."

Gideon nodded. *You don't know the half of it.*

The man was staring quizzically at them as if he was waiting for more of the story.

Clearly, Mackenzie wasn't ready to trust their rescuer. Because she didn't want to go back to prison or because she feared he might be working with the guys who tried to kill them? The orange of her jumpsuit was almost completely obscured by the muck, but their rescuer might have made note of the color when she was in the water.

He jerked a thumb toward the road. "Got a trailer about a mile from here. You can warm up. Figure out how to get out of town."

"Weren't you evacuating?" Gideon said, finding enough strength to climb painfully to his feet and help Mackenzie to hers. At first he wasn't sure his legs would hold him, but somehow he managed.

"My wife and kids left this morning. I'm staying until I can return a horse trailer to the stables tomorrow. Name's Kevin."

"I'm Zee," Mackenzie said. "This is Gid. Thank you for helping us."

Gideon offered his frozen hand and shook Kevin's meaty palm but could barely feel it. "Yes, thank you, sir. We wouldn't have lasted much longer if you hadn't stepped in." His mouth was on autopilot, his brain foggy and slow.

Kevin shrugged. "It's that kind of town." He unfurled a plastic tarp and laid it across the back seats of his Dodge. A broken cheese cracker fell out and a crayon rolled on the floorboard. The kid thing was true enough. Kevin checked all the boxes so far, but Gideon was barely functioning.

"Okay," Kevin said. "Rain's just gonna keep pounding according to the weather channel. Climb aboard. I got the heater blasting."

Decision time. Once they got into the vehicle, their

choices would be limited. Should they trust that Kevin was who he seemed? A well-meaning family man? Truthfully, there really wasn't a decision to be made. They had to get out of the open to survive. His body was shutting down; hers too.

Mackenzie's desperate nod told him she'd come to the same conclusion.

They climbed in, the mud and river water sluicing off them in puddles onto the tarp. Kevin raised the heat another notch. Though Gideon could hear the air blowing through the plastic vent, no warmth penetrated his frozen hide.

He shot a glance at Mackenzie, who looked like she was trying to stay alert and failing. Her limbs twitched and quivered like his. What was her game plan? He knew what his was. Get warm and dry. Contact the police and share their location. Mackenzie was a detainee, after all, and she would have to face the music.

She steadfastly refused to look at him.

He continued to stare at her profile, the stubborn angle of her chin telegraphing her message.

He beamed his own silent message right back. *Temporary truce. Until we know more, I stay quiet. But if you're running from the cops, you're on your own.*

As they moved off, he forced himself to look at the raging river, which by all rights should have taken their lives. If they didn't stave off the effects of hypothermia, it still might.

God had brought them through it thus far. He was trustworthy, indeed.

The jury was out on Kevin, but Gideon had already made his decision about Mackenzie.

Definitely not trustworthy. Not at all.

Mackenzie forced herself to mentally map the half-dozen turns away from the main road that took them to a wooded glen, where a neat white double-wide trailer gleamed in the rain. She had no doubt Gideon was doing the same mapping, even though he was obviously seething with the unspoken. Demands, likely ultimatums.

She didn't blame him; her last dive into the river wasn't wise. Once their situation settled, he would tell her to turn herself in, which was the logical choice. But that didn't align with her plan. It would have been much less complicated if he hadn't jumped in after her.

Because you'd be dead.

It was a fact, though she hated to admit it to herself. Once the river had yanked her loose from the branch barricade, she wouldn't have had the strength to pull herself out if it hadn't been for Gideon. That grated on her. Even with the shelter of a vehicle and heat, her body was still deadened and her thoughts were slow.

Kevin's trailer home had a fenced yard with a redwood picnic table and a kid's ten-speed bike leaned against the detached garage. Behind the unit was a horse pasture bordered by a split-rail fence. No neighbors.

Kevin's story checked out so far.

But if he was working for Bullseye, there could be a kill team en route. Or maybe Kevin planned on finishing them off himself, though he could have left them in the river if that was his goal.

She found it hard to reason with her muscles quaking and the mud stiffening around her joints like a suit of armor. Hopefully the filth concealed the fact that she was wearing a jail uniform. Her body craved warmth, her mind consumed by the need.

When she recovered, she'd find a way to sneak away from Kevin and Gideon.

She purposefully avoided eye contact with Gideon because she didn't want to think about what he'd risked on her behalf.

But he'd do it on anyone's behalf. He had that hero complex that had led him to the Air Force and SERE training. And yes, she found it enticing. What woman wouldn't? But Aaron's shadow stood firmly between them and always would.

Her memory flashed to an eavesdropped conversation from long ago.

"How can you actually forget to eat?" Aaron's face had looked incredulous.

Gideon shrugged. "Dunno. I guess I just get . . . focused on whatever I'm doing."

Aaron elbowed his friend's ribs. "What's the point if you keel over from malnutrition, you dunce?"

Gideon's laughter was rich and rolling, not something she'd heard often. It sounded almost like . . . music. He was generally the quiet foil to her brother's ebullience. When they were together, most people noticed Aaron, who attracted attention like a magnet to iron.

"I'll survive," Gideon had answered.

Her brother hadn't.

Keep your focus on your goal and don't let Gideon get in the way.

Kevin led them into the cozy trailer, perfumed by pasta sauce that bubbled in a Crock-Pot. The smell almost made her cry. Before, she'd been hungry. Now she was ravenous.

"Shower's in there." Kevin opened a small closet and handed her a towel and a black plastic bag. "You can put your wet stuff in the bag. I'll see if I can get some of my wife's clothes that might fit." He eyed Gideon. "You can have some of mine, but I'm a little broader in the beam. Maybe I can find somehing I squirreled away from a couple of pounds ago." He chuckled, showing a gap between his front teeth.

"I'm grateful for whatever you can spare, sir."

"Lynn left me a pot of spaghetti and meatballs since I can't cook, if you're hungry. I can handle boiling the noodles and making coffee though."

Mackenzie tried to smile, but her face was still too stiff. "That would be wonderful."

Kevin ducked his head. "Ah. Like I said, it's that kind of town."

Supplied with an armful of clothes a few minutes later, she let herself into the tiny bathroom, peeled off the jumpsuit, and stuffed it into the bag. Her reflection in the mirror made her do a double take. The face didn't look like her own. Her hair was plastered down, cheeks scraped, and lip bleeding at the corner. A cut sliced across her mud-spattered forehead. All of it she'd earned with her choices.

As she looked at the eyes staring back at her, she considered how close she'd come to dying. The tears came then, and she turned on the shower to cover the sound before she allowed herself to remember.

She felt again the sensation of being chained in the van, the water creeping up to fill her lungs and take her life. Her plan to get arrested now seemed like madness. What was she doing? Her mission had been so concrete and thought-out. Hours later, she'd been forced off the road and nearly drowned. How had it all gone so colossally wrong?

She'd been sure, utterly convinced her mission was God-approved, that she was destined to make Bullseye pay for Aaron's death and prevent so many others from suffering. The confidence she'd had was shaken. Without her wallet, supplies, even a purse, how could she embark on the next steps?

Panic was getting her nowhere, so she gave herself up to the comfort of the shower. At first, her skin ached as the warmth began to penetrate. Teeth gritted under the stinging stream, she let the water wash away the mud and suffuse her body with glorious comfort.

She helped herself to the shampoo and conditioner, hoping Lynn wouldn't mind. The twin comforts of heat and cleanliness almost made her swoon. Never again would she take for granted those blessings.

As she dried herself, she became aware of each scrape and bruise. She wondered how badly Gideon had been battered in their escape. Never mind that line of thinking.

Lynn was a bit shorter than Mackenzie, but the sheer joy of pulling on the dry undergarments, sweatpants, T-shirt, and long-sleeved nylon jacket made it feel like the best outfit she'd ever worn. Even the sneakers fit well enough with the thick socks. Her jail shoes had washed away at some point in the river.

Trash bag secured under her arm, she rejoined Kevin while Gideon took his turn in the shower. As they chatted, he boiled water for the noodles on the small stove.

"I'll just put this on the porch." She wiggled the bag before she opened the front door and tucked it under a patio chair, her arms and legs aching. Again she scanned the pasture and the main road. No sign of anyone approaching. The rain still came down in torrents. "You don't have any close neighbors?" she asked when she went back inside.

"Couple miles away. That's close enough for me. Lynn would like more socializing with the church people, but that's what Sundays are for, right?"

She nodded as though she understood, but she'd never had the desire to live where there was nary another person to be seen. The busier and more bustling the area, the more she could be a part of the energy or disappear into the crowd, depending on her mood. Being this far away from witnesses at the moment, however, felt creepy, as if she could vanish and no one would be the wiser.

And as for church, well . . . Her parents had kept their attendance and received countless casseroles and comfort calls, but Mackenzie knew what the congregants were really thinking. *So sad Aaron got into drugs. Glad our children aren't living that lifestyle.*

It made her want to scream at them, at God, but mostly at Bullseye.

She tried to keep her thoughts to next moves. If Lorraine was right and Bullseye owned plenty of people in the town, she might just be safest here in the middle of a horse pasture. But not for long. Lorraine's terrified expression would not leave her mind. She silently prayed that Lorraine and the other woman were in the hospital and recovering from what happened on the bridge.

The earlier uncertainty she'd felt about her plan evaporated when she remembered the promise she'd made to make sure Lorraine's mom made it to Jamaica. She would succeed and make sure the woman would be safely delivered there or anywhere else she chose to live. Her mind spun forward into other actions. She could make use of her social media influence to bring attention to Lorraine's unjust arrest. When she brought Bullseye down, she'd enlist the help of her followers. Surely there was a lawyer in the batch, hungry for justice and attention. Lorraine's arrest might just be overturned altogether. The new rush of determination was comforting, bolstering, like a fire on a frigid night.

She itched for her phone to make notes of everything she'd experienced since rolling into Oakleaf. Gideon had taken his pack into the bathroom with him, unfortunately—likely still unaware that she'd hidden her phone inside before she'd gotten herself arrested.

Kevin cut into her thoughts, looking up from his steaming pot.

"No phone?"

She jerked. "Um, no."

"Do you want to use mine to call someone to see about your car?"

Her car? It took her a moment to realize he thought her vehicle had plunged over the side of the bridge. She hesitated, deciding on a stall rather than lie. "Gideon's a dedicated camper, so he probably packed his phone in a waterproof case. If it doesn't work I'll let you know."

"Is that what brought you to the area? Camping? In this weather?"

"Uh, no, not camping, exactly. Gideon was teaching a wilderness class. He had this nutty idea that people should be prepared for all types of horrible weather, so rain doesn't put him off, but his only client was turning tail when I showed up." She hurried on. "Do you really think the dam's going to fail?"

He shook his head. "We've lived here for a decade and that topic comes up every year without fail. It's stayed standing, just to spite the engineers." He fetched a green container of grated Parmesan. "But I'll admit this year's storms have been over the top, and the warnings are more doom and gloom than usual. Glad Lynn and the kids are away, just in case."

She inhaled the aroma of tangy spaghetti sauce, and her mouth watered. "It smells so good I can hardly think of anything else."

He rapped the spoon on the side of the pot. "Yeah, it's the family favorite. Lynn left me enough to tide me over and then some."

"Until tomorrow when you return the trailer? Why not take it back today?"

"Had to pick up a tire and change it out. Gonna wait until morning because it'll be a crazy route to avoid the flooded roads. Everyone 'round here with livestock has been cooperating to get all the animals evacuated safely. The farms in the lowlands will be inundated in the next few days, so we've all been taking turns helping each other get those horses to high ground. Got mine out yesterday but the tire blew. Stable owner's a great gal and we'll get her remaining horses out tomorrow when I bring the trailer."

It was good to hear that the locals took care of each other. Bullseye's evil couldn't stamp that out. Kevin had switched tasks and was shoveling some grounds into a coffee filter in the top of a machine and filling the reservoir with water.

The rich scent was finer than the expensive perfume Aaron had given their mother for her sixtieth birthday. Gideon wouldn't be impressed since he was some kind of coffee snob who actually roasted his own beans and infused his milk products with vanilla and cinnamon, but she didn't think he'd complain under the circumstances. Plus, he had manners, even under extreme duress.

"So you've got stables in town? An airport too, I heard," she added casually while she folded paper napkins and mentally urged him to hurry the food along before she stuck a fork in the pot and helped herself.

Kevin quirked a brow, and she knew the comment had struck him as overly nosey. *Watch it, Mackenzie.*

"Yeah," he said. "An airstrip six miles north. Mostly for small cargo planes and such. Some charters and a few fishing adventure flights do a regular business from there. Nothing much that would interest anyone in weather like this." He finished his coffee preparations. "You're not thinking about flying out of here, are you?"

"That seems like the fastest way with some of the roads closing and now the bridge damaged."

"Maybe, but it's heavy weather for flying. Don't think there's much air traffic in and out right now. Not even sure how you'll get your car salvaged from the river with the roads closed."

"It's Gideon's car. I was riding with him." She'd spilled some unnecessary facts yet again, but she had to offer Kevin something.

"He your husband?"

Her face warmed. *As if!* "No. Just, uh, friends." They weren't friends. But if there had been friendly feelings way back in their youth, they would all be blotted away since she'd almost gotten him killed repeatedly of late. She didn't blame him for being angry at her, even if he had inserted himself in her business.

Kevin pursed his lips. "So, you said he was here teaching a wilderness class, and you didn't want to take it?"

"No. I'm a gal who likes her creature comforts. Mints on the pillows, you know." Her joke didn't take him off the scent.

"Then why did you come here if it wasn't for the class? We're a little short on comforts at the moment."

The conversation was definitely becoming more pointed. "Meeting another friend." Which was actually the truth . . . sort of. "But I heard Gideon was here and I stopped to see him."

"What friend?" Kevin pushed the button to activate the coffee maker. It gurgled and spat. "I probably know them. Small place. Everyone knows everyone else."

There was no way she was going to risk Lorraine's safety any further by revealing her name. She was saved from having to answer when Gideon emerged, limping, hair curling slightly from the moisture, clad in a pair of jeans that hung low on his narrow waist, and a tee with a bowling ball and pins on the front. His eyes sparkled as he inhaled deeply.

"Did I miss dinner? It smells amazing."

Kevin brightened. Maybe he was merely a typical nosy small-towner. He certainly seemed welcoming, but she'd come to suspect everyone. What a way to live. She felt a sudden longing to let it all go, put her roots down again in a locale like this where people looked after each other.

You don't have any roots left. You're adrift.

Kevin's expression was dreamy. "Yep. Lynn's an incredible cook. I don't like much fancy food, but she can make a pot roast that would bring tears to your eyes. And her mashed potatoes . . . She adds something to them, I dunno what it is."

Mackenzie felt as though she could easily weep over the meatballs and sauce.

They took places at the table. Gideon let out a groan as he lowered himself into the chair. Kevin said grace.

He plopped large portions of pasta and meatballs onto their plates, served with buttered white bread and mugs of coffee.

"Dig in," Kevin said.

They needed no urging.

All three focused on the meal, and Mackenzie was sure she'd never eaten anything so delicious in her life. Saucy, savory, warm perfection. She fought to keep herself from flat-out gobbling the food. The pleasure of the feast spread through her stomach until she felt almost thawed, except for her toes.

Gideon was making a point not to look at her. Suited her just fine. They all had seconds on pasta and bread and refills on coffee.

Kevin finally pushed his plate back, and they thanked him again.

"What a meal. Your wife is a winner," Gideon said.

"Yes, she is. She's my better half." Kevin tipped his chair back and folded his hands over his padded belly. "And since she's not here to correct me on my manners, I'm free to ask."

"Ask what?" Gideon said, wiping his mouth with a scratched hand.

Kevin's eyes narrowed. "When are you two going to tell me the truth?"

FIVE

GIDEON TOOK ANOTHER SIP OF COFFEE as he considered how to respond to Kevin's question. Caution was the first rule when interacting with potential enemies. A careless answer could sink them. He wished the ache in his shoulder would ease up. He'd washed down a few aspirin in the bathroom after his shower, but they hadn't made much of a dent in the pain. Mackenzie appeared to be struck silent, which was a point in their favor.

"The truth?" Gideon said. "Don't know what you mean, Kevin."

"Yes, you do. I'm plain country folk, but I'm not stupid. People don't go visiting an area where others are evacuating, so I don't believe that's the reason you're here." He looked at Mackenzie. "Also, before I noticed you two in the river, I pulled over to adjust some gear in my back seat, paid attention to the flow of the water and such. Didn't notice any car floating by. Couple minutes later you two came along, and boy, was I surprised. You'd been in the water for a while, clearly. Something happened on the bridge, maybe, but there was no breach on the nearer side from what I could tell. Can't really see how you'd have ended up where you did."

Mackenzie's jaw was tight. She was about to make things worse, Gideon could feel it.

He spoke quickly. "Mackenzie's vehicle went over, got caught on a piling. I parked mine and dove in after her." Facts, which was the second most important thing in dangerous territory. Stick to the truth as much as possible to avoid contradictions and snares.

Mackenzie went pale, and Gideon tried to decipher the look she was telegraphing. He'd said something wrong, clearly.

Kevin shook his head. "Didn't have time to practice your stories, did you? She said she was a passenger in your car when it went over."

Gideon bit back a groan. He put down the coffee mug. "Okay. Kevin, I'll be honest. Mackenzie is running from some people."

He frowned. "People, as in the cops?"

"The cops would like her to come in, yes, but the bigger problem is the people who tried to murder her. I can't tell you the particulars because we don't know you. You don't know us either, so I understand the mistrust. The truth is that neither of us has hurt anyone, and we didn't cause the accident. I can promise you that tomorrow we are going to report to the nearest police station that isn't underwater and explain exactly what happened. One cop already knows most of it, so it's been communicated." He ignored the raised eyebrow from Mackenzie.

"Are you spinning more lies?" Kevin said.

"No, sir. But it's all I can tell you. We're grateful for your help, we'd probably be dead if you hadn't stepped in. You didn't have to get involved, but you extended yourself for two strangers, and we can't begin to repay that. We aren't a danger to you or your family. If you want us to clear out now, we'll do so, but I can't tell you anything more than that."

Kevin tipped his head back and examined them over his mug of coffee. "My wife is the kind of person who feeds everyone, helps them. Know anyone like that? Heart bigger than their body?"

Gideon smiled. "My mom. No question. My brothers say she'd feed the world if she could get them around her kitchen table."

"My brother, Aaron," Mackenzie said after a moment.

True enough. Gideon remembered when Aaron met an elderly lady down the street from his family home while he was delivering the paper. Mrs. Chavez invited him in for a soda, crying because she'd lost her cat and couldn't walk well enough to look for him. With two phone calls, Aaron had organized their entire baseball team to do a neighborhood search until they found the cat and returned him to a joyful Mrs. Chavez. The lady had cried so hard they'd had to make her sit down to prevent her hyperventilating. Aaron had been simultaneously the most selfish and selfless person Gideon had ever known.

He covered his surprising rush of emotion by focusing on Kevin, who was toying with his napkin.

"My wife's that way," he said. "She's one of those types that shows up when there's been a tragedy with a noodle casserole, and she's the first to bring a cake if it's a happy occasion." His expression was soft. "That's why I stopped to help you. Because that's what she'd want me to do."

Here comes the message. Gideon waited.

Kevin pushed the coffee away. "I'm the sole support in this family. If they were home, I would not hesitate to jettison both of you because I wouldn't risk their safety on a couple of liars. Do you understand what I'm saying?"

"I do and I completely respect that," Gideon said.

Kevin turned to Mackenzie, and she nodded.

"We don't want to make you uncomfortable, Kevin. Come on, Zee." Gideon got to his feet. He dreaded going out into the storm when they'd finally gotten some respite, but there was no choice now. "Thank you, sir, for everything. There's no way we could ever repay you. We'll see ourselves out."

"One night," Kevin said, stopping him.

Both of them stared. Gideon was sure he'd misheard. "What's that?"

Kevin finished his coffee. "You can sleep here until morning and that's all. There's a couch in the living room and beds in the kids' room that are too small but better than nothing, so you've got a choice."

"Why would you allow us to stay if you think we're lying?" Mackenzie said, brows drawn in confusion.

Kevin shook his head. "My good deed for the day. Don't get it twisted. I got me a shotgun next to my bed. Keeping prepared in case we attracted any looters. I'm a good shot and I have no problem dropping either of you where you stand. I'll explain to the cops it was self-defense. My home and my family come first."

Gideon looked to Mackenzie, who assented with a small nod. Though he wasn't exactly easy in his spirit about the arrangement, he didn't like their chances of traveling at night in torrential rain. "Much appreciate your kindness, sir. We'll take off at first light, be out of your hair."

"If there is any light. Storm's not expected to break. If the dam does finally give out, this valley is a disaster waiting to happen. Like I said, after tomorrow I'm out of here too, but I'm leaving for the stables at sunup. Main road's right there anyway. I'll give you both a lift."

That would save them hours of arduous hiking. "That's very generous. We'll take you up on your offer."

"Okay. It's settled then."

Gideon carried his and Mackenzie's plates to the sink, where he started to wash them.

Kevin began to protest as Mackenzie cleared his.

"Let us," she insisted, picking up the dish towel. "It's the least we can do."

Kevin yawned. "Okay. Twist my arm. Lynn would box my ears at letting a guest do the clearing up, but I won't decline the offer. Put the leftovers in the fridge. I'll take 'em with me tomorrow. Gonna hit the sack. Sunrise is at seven. Cordelia's expecting me at the stables by eight to drop the trailer."

"We'll be ready. Thank you again, sir," Gideon said.

Kevin lumbered off to his bedroom.

They heard the door shut and the lock engage. Gideon pondered what had just gone down. Kevin could have ulterior motives for encouraging them to stay. But what choice did they have but to accept his hospitality? They were battered, bruised, and desperately needed rest to keep their wits together. Hairy and his cohort were still out there, unlikely to stand down until they were certain they'd done their job.

No phone signal at the moment saved him from the prickly decision about contacting the police. He knew what Mackenzie would say about that.

The soapy water stung the cuts on his fingers as he washed. Mackenzie stood next to him and dried. Such a tranquil domestic scenario on the heels of all that happened today. From near death to dish duty. He tried not to feel strange about having her pressed against his shoulder, but all manner of feelings surfaced and disappeared inside him like the soap bubbles. She was alive, here, next to him, and they were united, for the moment, instead of enemies.

Post-traumatic reaction, Gid. She was stubborn and unpredictable, and he still had a full head of steam about her diving off the pier after the trouble he'd had getting her out the first time.

Best for him not to forget she was dynamite with a lit fuse.

When the dishes were done and stacked neatly on the counter, they moved to the sofa under the window. It wasn't yet fully sunset, but it felt much later. Exhaustion nibbled at the corners of his conciousness.

Mackenzie peered at a stylized framed map on the wall. The town of Oakleaf. She stood and fingered the mountains in the distance, following the river back to the point where they'd fallen in, then skimmed over the Cotton Flower Dam. Kevin's trailer, labeled "The Homestead," was drawn on the map with a heart around it.

Gideon could practically see her wheels turning as she spun her plan together. His anger returned. Not done scheming? Their nearly fatal adventures hadn't been enough? Was there more she needed to endure to describe to her podcast fans?

If he didn't unclench his jaw, he was going to crack a molar. He tried for a calming breath. What was the best way to make her see reason? Commands didn't work. Suggestions wouldn't make a dent. More facts about the danger they were facing? He gave that less than fifty-fifty. He prayed for patience and readied himself to start in. "Zee . . ."

"This is my fault," she blurted before he could say more, flopping down next to him.

"Completely," he agreed with surprised gusto. At last. She was taking responsibility.

She frowned at him. "Well, maybe not absolutely completely. I didn't want you to go after me and I told you as much. Repeatedly."

Commands didn't work on him either, not when they came from her. Go figure. He glared right back at her. "Barebones truth. You'd have drowned without me and you know it."

"I'm stronger than you think."

"And more reckless."

She huffed out a breath and rubbed at the bruise on her forehead. "All right. That's a fair point, but I didn't want an escort. And I certainly don't want *your* death on my conscience."

"More like you didn't want anyone around calling you out on your ridiculous choices." He heard the quickening of her breath. He felt more at ease when they were sparring. That was infinitely better than the feelings that crept up when he allowed himself to consider what he'd experienced when he couldn't locate her in that raging river.

He focused on the angry crimp of her mouth, but the slight curling of her hair still damp from the shower drew his attention. He wondered how soft it would be to his touch.

"Gideon, you butted in."

He waved a careless hand. "Sue me."

She rested her head on the back of the sofa and emitted a long-suffering sigh. As if she were the one being put upon. A piece of work, as his father would say. But his father would likely know how to approach Mackenzie with more tact and grace. Gideon was not overflowing with tact, as both his brothers regularly reminded him. What was the right approach here?

Rain pummeled the roof, echoing like mini explosions.

"You think Kevin is going to call the cops?" she said.

"He might have already, but I doubt they have the manpower to make it here to arrest you at the moment, especially in light of having to evacuate the station and deal with the river incident. Bigger problems. You're likely going to enjoy another night of freedom, at least."

She smoothed her borrowed clothes. "You know I can't go to the police tomorrow."

And there it was, the pronouncement he'd expected. He kept his tone level and sure. "Yes, you can, Mackenzie. When Kevin leaves us at the stables, we'll make our way back to my Jeep if possible. Ten miles, max. I'll give you a ride to Clover, drop you at the police station there. I'll see to it you get there safely. We can explain the delay, no phone service, et cetera. Get you a good lawyer. They may drop the whole thing at some point if you turn yourself in."

She shook her head, and he resisted the urge to thunk his skull on the window behind him. Through gritted teeth, he tried again. "All right. Why don't you explain to me your big plan, then, huh? How do you see this thing playing out? Are you proposing to live like a fugitive for the rest of your life?" He let the arrow fly. "Disappear and have your parents wonder what happened to their only living child?" He saw his words hit their mark as she paled, and he felt sick with shame. She was a piece of work, but bringing up Aaron was a low blow.

Her nostrils flared, fury painted on her face. "Don't talk about my parents."

He held up a palm. "I'm sorry. That was crossing the line, and I shouldn't have said it. But the question is valid. What is your plan, Zee? You have cop training, you're not naive. You know what happens if you run from the law. A fugitive life? That's no life at all."

She cocked her head, and the lamplight caught the delicate curve of her cheeks and lips, at odds with the ferocious gleam in her eyes. He'd blown it with his earlier comment, and whatever chance he'd had to convince her was gone.

"Of course I'm not going to live as a fugitive. I'll go to the cops as soon as I've done what I need to."

"And what exactly is that, now that your contact is out of reach?"

"You don't need to know," she said coldly.

"Humor me."

"I don't think so. Go home to your parents and your brothers and enjoy the rest of your leave. I'm not your concern any longer. I appreciate what you did for me, and I'm sorry I used you to get to my informant in jail, but we're done. Tomorrow we part ways at the stables, and I don't expect we'll see each other again."

Surprising how the words hit him hard. It was what he wanted too. Wasn't it? To say goodbye for the last time to the passionate, furious woman who'd pretended to steal his wallet and almost gotten them both killed? Repeatedly?

Her gaze drifted again to the framed map. What was she planning? He had to know.

"But have you thought it through? What are your options if you don't go to the cops? You can't return to your hotel. You won't be able to talk further to your informant." An idea surfaced. "Wait a minute. She shared something with you, didn't she? In the van maybe, before the crash? Some type of lead here in town and you're determined to follow it." She didn't react, but he knew he'd hit on it. "It's a bad idea, Zee. A real bad idea."

Her face was stony and she allowed him only a brief glance. "Like I said, Gideon, you don't need to know. I'm not your concern."

The unspoken swirled between them like a poisonous mist, and he couldn't stand it another moment. "Since we're about to part ways, then why don't you just say what's on your mind? Get it off your chest."

"Say what?"

"You know what. We won't have another opportunity. Now or never."

The seconds passed between them, their gazes locked.

"Okay, I will." Her chin raised a half inch. "Like I said, I'm not your concern, but Aaron was. We both failed him."

Failed him. The blow cut into him, deep to the core where the reservoir of darkness pooled. He was suddenly desperate for her to understand. The words flowed out before he could stop them.

"I didn't have the conversation with Aaron that night. You're right. And I'll feel the guilt of that for the rest of my life. But even if I had, I couldn't take responsibility again." The last word slipped out before he could stop it.

She jerked. "What do you mean, *again*? What are you talking about?"

With great effort, he rose from the sofa and straightened the chairs around the kitchen table. "Nothing."

"It's not nothing. What is it you don't want to tell me? What happened between you and my brother?"

The throbbing in his shoulder worsened into a pulsing river of pain. He poured the last of the coffee from the pot and slugged it down, even though it was only lukewarm. Then he washed his mug and the pot and grabbed a towel to dry them. "Not important. Not anymore."

"I think it is." She got up and faced him. Arms crossed, she kept her voice barely above a whisper. "When exactly did you accept responsibility for my brother? When he got drunk on the base and you couldn't wait to turn him in? He told me."

"Is that how he explained it?" Salt in the wound, but not surprising, he supposed. Aaron hadn't told her or his parents what really happened their senior year either—the fire he'd caused that led to Gideon's injury. He hadn't revealed that Gideon's lie to protect him had cost the Landry family dearly. Acid churned in his stomach. That one small deceit had ballooned into a catastrophe. On some sleepless nights, during the long, cruel hours before dawn, he wondered if that was the reason Aaron had never grown up—because Gideon had not allowed him to way back then.

He'd had the sneaking suspicion that Aaron decided to enlist with him because he didn't know what else to do. The thought bothered Gideon then, still did—along with the invisible distance between them bookended by that day in high school and the moment Gideon found Aaron in the ditch.

He folded the towel into a neat rectangle while she stood there, waiting. She wasn't going to let it go.

He considered telling her everything. Why not? If her plans worked out, he'd never see her again. But what would that revelation accomplish? It couldn't bring Aaron back, and she most likely wouldn't believe him anyway. Her brother was her hero. The truth would only cause her more pain. At least he could save her from that.

"I loved Aaron like my own brothers," he said slowly. "I wasn't the friend he needed. Let's leave it at that."

She stood there in the weak light, her skin luminous, hair a dark cloud, waiting for more. He couldn't give it. Not now. Not ever.

"Gideon . . ."

"Get some sleep. Sofa looks more comfortable than the kid zone, so you take it," he said, picking up his backpack and heading for the cramped bedroom across from Kevin's.

Bunk beds beckoned. They were pint-size, covered with rumpled checkered bedding. Toys were dumped in a crate in the corner, and a small table housed a scattering of crayons and pieces of coloring paper. The photo on the wall showed Kevin and a smiling blond-haired woman and their two children, all standing next to a brown horse.

"My home and my family come first," Kevin had said.

Gideon thought about his mom, the cancer treatments that had weakened her, the small farmhouse his parents shared clamoring for repairs and modifications. His mind drifted back to his high school years.

"He needs a complete shoulder reconstruction," the doctor had said. After gently clearing his throat, he'd added, "And I'm afraid the cost far exceeds your insurance coverage."

His mother's mouth had quivered as his father took her hand. "Whatever my son needs, he'll have."

And Gideon had indeed received the procedures necessary to rebuild his joint, then gone on to the military career he dreamed of, but the expense of the surgery, the extended hospital stay due to complications, and the physical therapy after had drained his parents' bank account.

So now it was his turn to step up.

Whatever you need, Mom. He'd be there to pay for it if necessary, and provide support physically, do the remodeling on the house. Rope his cousin Johnny into helping him. Four more months of service and he'd have his discharge and his wilderness classes in place. Four more months and he'd finally be able to put his family first like he should have done so long ago.

He dumped out the contents of his backpack and arranged the items in a neat row on the floor to dry. His shoulder complained, as did his banged-up shins. From a plastic pack, he extracted a cord to charge his cell and one to replenish the external battery pack.

Backpack empty, the weight felt wrong. Something still inside? He rooted around, then lifted the flap at the very bottom.

A cell phone in a waterproof bag. Mackenzie's. A slow smile spread across his face as he realized that she must have stowed it in his backpack when she was making small talk in his Jeep, waiting to stage the mugging. She knew that after each mission he would completely empty the pack and clean it down to the last square inch—at which point he'd no doubt discover her cell phone. Crafty woman.

She probably expected he'd have it sent to her place after her arrest, and it would be waiting for her when she posted bail. He chuckled. Too smart for her own good, that one. No news there. She was the "always do the bare minimum required and still ace school exams" kind of person. Gideon was the "study until his eyes bled and out-prepare everyone else" type. They had little in common, so naturally he'd been fascinated by her. Aaron's baby sister, always dancing in the wings of his attention—a rare butterfly he could never catch but only admire.

He fingered her phone, fighting against a killer wave of fatigue that dulled all his senses.

Mackenzie believed her mission to bring Aaron's killer to justice was what her family needed. She was dead wrong, especially if it cost her parents the life of their other child.

Don't you see that you won't fill the hole, Zee?

He'd learned that lesson the hard way. Sometimes, no

matter how mighty the struggle, people were lost, a fact he detested and fought against his entire career. There were circumstances when "return with honor" meant accepting the end of a life, and admitting that allowed families to heal and go on.

Maybe not exactly move forward, but at least live their lives as best they could. When had he gotten so philosophical?

During hours of lying on his back in a sleeping bag, staring at the sparkling universe?

Could be he'd picked it up observing his older brother Cullen loping around with a toddler on his shoulders, telling her stories about the brave mother she'd never know. Because that woman's life mattered, even if it was gone.

Or it might be due to the fact that his parents had never once complained about all they'd sacrificed to rebuild his shoulder, never ceased thanking God that Gideon was alive. That was honor, he thought, the simple act of carrying on.

Mackenzie was headed for a terrible fall. Smart woman, gifted, charismatic, and completely oblivious.

Underneath the frustration, he felt a twinge of something he finally identified as admiration. Outside of a select few, he'd never met anyone with her level of drive and fearlessness. In her misguided way, she was as committed to her family as he was. And she had way more grit than her fair share.

A clap of thunder split the night, followed by a fresh roar of falling rain.

Would she be there in the morning? He wanted to stalk back out to the sofa and keep watch like the proverbial hawk.

But if she was going to sneak off again, there wasn't much he could do about it. His body was shutting down, spiraling him toward the sleep demanded by his pounded flesh.

Since the kids had taken their pillows, he rolled his extra jacket into a bundle and covered up with the checkered blanket. Feet sticking over the edge of the mattress, he closed his eyes and prayed that Mackenzie would not disappear into the howling storm.

SIX

MACKENZIE DOZED FOR A WHILE, then woke with a jolt from a nightmare of rising waters and indescribable cold. For a moment, she didn't recognize her surroundings and sat up with her heart thumping. Her aching bones quickly reminded her of the previous day's trauma.

The quiet trailer still smelled of spaghetti and meatballs as she took it all in again. Gideon. Kevin's trailer home. Her mission. The danger. The gold anniversary clock on the coffee table told her it was almost 4:00 a.m.

She hurt. Everywhere.

Gideon was no doubt asleep after the day he'd experienced. She wished she was too. Since Aaron died, she never slept well, and her mental gymnastics and aching body hadn't lent her any deeper rest than she usually experienced.

Phone. First order of business was to retrieve it from Gideon's pack. She got up, padded across the kitchen in socked feet, eased as slowly as she could down the hall to the kids' room. She paused, listening to the snoring coming from behind Kevin's door. No sound from Gideon's temporary quarters.

Slowly, ever so slowly, she turned the knob, then paused in the doorway to let her eyes adjust. A meager gleam came from the dinosaur night-light plugged in the far wall. A quick look showed Gideon covered in a kid's blanket. On the floor was a collection of neatly laid-out devices and charging cords. His backpack was open, drying nicely next to the heating vent.

Bingo.

She tiptoed over, darting a glance at Gideon. He lay on his back, one bruised arm thrown above his head. The sight momentarily stopped her. His face could have been sculpted of stone, and she could not ignore the fact that the man was simply beautiful with his chiseled features, dark wavy hair, and lips so prone to that sardonic smile. A less attractive mug would better match his pugnacious personality. Then again, maybe that side of him only came out when they were together.

She'd had a puppy-dog crush on him back in the day. Made excuses when her brother and Gideon hung around together to cross paths with the lanky, serious man-boy. His quiet self-confidence was startling, fascinating. If only she'd known how things would turn out.

The floor squeaked the tiniest bit under her foot and she froze, but he didn't stir. She waited a full minute before she eased forward again. Her phone wasn't there with Gideon's cell and battery. Maybe he hadn't looked at the very bottom of the pack. Uncharacteristic miss for a guy so thorough he carried spare shoelaces in his glove box, but he'd been through a lot since she drove off his wilderness client.

The notion to hide her phone in his backpack was the

best way to ensure she got it back. If not, she could acquire a new one at the nearest store, since most of her files were coded and stored to the cloud for recovery, but the way things had turned out, she needed it. Now.

She reached into his pack and felt around all the way to the bottom, below the flap where she'd secreted her cell. No phone. She turned the pack inside out and shoved her fingers into every crevice. Still no phone. As quietly as possible, she shook it.

"Missing something?"

Gideon's whisper made her yelp and sit down hard.

He was still lying there; to all appearances he hadn't even moved, but he now held up her phone in the plastic bag.

Mortifying, but she refused to be cowed. Awkwardly, she brushed her hair back. "Yes. Thanks," she whispered, reaching for it.

He dangled it out of range. "Your birthday as your password? Weak, Zee. Thought you were a savvy crime podcaster."

She fought to keep to a whisper. "You snooped on my phone?"

He shook his head. "Relax. I have better manners than that. Just wanted to be sure it was yours." He arched a brow. "After all, some strange phone appears in my pack on the very same day I get mugged. Can't be too careful, right?"

She clamped down on her retort. "May I have it now, please?"

He yawned and winced. "In the morning."

"Now," she insisted through gritted teeth.

"You need some shut-eye. Sleep is crucial. Did you know that humans are the only mammals that willingly delay sleep? Doesn't say much for our species, does it?"

"Give me my phone, Gideon."

His smile was sly, the curve of his lips reminding her of the unexpected warmth she'd felt when she kissed him in the parking lot. "What are you going to do about it if I don't?"

A great question. He was strong and skilled. What could she do? She considered and then shot out a hand and tickled his ribs. He squawked, and she clapped a hand over his mouth, still tickling.

"Phone," she demanded.

Rolled into a ball, he continued to writhe.

"I'm not stopping until you give me my phone."

Defeated, he went still. She removed her palm from his mouth, and he slung the bag around to her.

He glared. "That was playing dirty."

She couldn't hold back a smile. "I know your kryptonite, Landry. Don't you forget it." He'd always been so ticklish he couldn't even have sunscreen applied to his back without collapsing in gales of laughter.

Triumphant, she tiptoed to the door with her phone.

"Don't do it, Zee," he murmured. There was a tenderness threading through the words that made her slow, almost stop at the threshold.

Again her soul rang with a deep-down yearning to turn away from the plan she'd set in motion. But she knew what she had to do, and Gideon wasn't going to be a part of it. She kept going and shut the door softly behind her.

She plugged in her phone next to the living room sofa,

and while it charged she pulled up maps of the area, the latest weather report, and the safety alerts about the dam. The airstrip was indeed six miles to the north. That was where she prayed she'd find Lorraine's boyfriend, Cal, who could tell her what she needed to know. And if he wasn't there? If he'd left, she'd find out where he'd gone and follow. All she needed was his phone number, an email, an address—any lead that would take her to the next one.

Normally she'd post an episode on her podcast, updating her followers about her investigations, but that was out of the question. Even if she could, it would be dangerous, maybe deadly, to reveal what had happened at the river, the help they'd received from Kevin. She wouldn't put anyone else at risk—not yet—but when she exposed Bullseye, she'd make sure the world saw what he'd done. God would help her make it happen.

The stream of internet news was dismal. The storm was expected to dump several inches of rain in the next four days on ground already dangerously saturated. Engineers were completing another last-minute assessment of the Cotton Flower Dam, but the authorities had begun evacuations of the town closest to it. Oakleaf was under a voluntary evacuation notice, but it would be mandatory soon.

Just hold together for a couple more days, old Cotton Flower.

She found no mention of the accident on the bridge. Not an accident, she corrected. Bullseye's men, sent to kill her and Lorraine. Again she recalled the freezing water creeping up to fill her lungs, her desperation sharp as a blade. And if Gideon hadn't unlocked her restraints . . .

She imagined the self-assigned mission he'd put into place to keep watch on Bullseye's men at the bridge. And he hadn't shrunk away from the mess that unfolded. Witnessing the attack from some position he'd chosen, diving from the bridge into the water, swimming to the drowning women and the cop.

He'd obviously been worried enough to start surveillance in the first place. Worried, because he was fond of her to some small degree? Purely for old time's sake? Guilt over Aaron? His odd comment poked at her.

"I couldn't take responsibility again . . ."

What did it mean? She wanted to hold his words up to the lamplight and turn them around until she saw the truth hidden inside the syllables.

Didn't matter. Things to do. People to find.

Her backpack was in the property room at the evacuated police station, but Kevin had rummaged in a hall closet and produced a cheap nylon bag with a wrench emblazoned on the front. Oakleaf Auto Repair.

"When you're a mechanic with credit card debt and two kids, you collect all the free loot you can," he'd said.

The bag had black rope threaded through the grommets so it could be carried as a backpack. Flimsy, but it would do. Into the pack went her phone. A few granola bars from the snack bowl Kevin had offered and a bottle of water. Slim pickins. The name of her father's favorite performer. Her throat clogged. Since Aaron's death, Dad's smile was different, vague, as if his mouth knew what to do but his heart couldn't remember why. She'd caught her mother's worried gaze on occasion when her father stared too long out the window, the watering can forgotten in his grasp. Mom's look seemed to say, *"Don't you leave me too."*

Undoubtedly her mother would worry herself into an early grave if she knew what her daughter was up to.

"We have to move on, together," she'd say through her tears.

But Mackenzie simply couldn't because Aaron was dead and Mackenzie wasn't, and the man responsible was going to be stopped before his drugs destroyed anyone else. Simple as that. She snuck outside to the porch, and with the drumming rain in the background, recorded a podcast and saved it.

Back inside, she quietly prepared for the day ahead. She was tightening the cords on the pack when Kevin padded on socked feet into the kitchen.

She plastered on a smile. "Morning."

"Not yet, but I couldn't sleep." He yawned, looking her over. "Fixin' to leave before dawn?"

"Uh . . ."

"That'd be a mistake." He pointed to the window. "Pouring, and I heard on the radio the river's flooded over the road. Gonna have to use the mountain trail to reach the stables. That's a steep three-mile trek, and you'd be hard-pressed to do it in the dark on foot. It'd take hours."

She flicked a look into the howling void. Hours in the freezing cold, soaked and struggling.

"Best to hold until morning."

Her nerves were taut bundles. How could she afford to delay?

Kevin scratched his stubbled chin. "You were going to leave without tellin' your boyfriend?"

"Like I said, we aren't together."

"Oh. That's right. Seems like a good catch, though. Capable. Military man, huh?"

"He's a SERE instructor for the Air Force. On leave."

"That explains it."

To her dismay, instead of heading back to his bedroom, Kevin began to prep the coffee maker. "Dawn in a few hours. Might as well start loading up the caffeine, huh?"

She nodded weakly, considering her plan in light of Kevin's revelation.

As much as she detested delaying, she couldn't afford to spend hours hiking unfamiliar terrain. Lorraine's boyfriend might be departing anytime, or maybe he already had, but she had a better chance of hitching a ride to the stables and sneaking away from there than traversing flooded territory she'd never clapped eyes on.

Before she'd quite finished mulling it over, Gideon strolled down the hallway, appearing as fresh as if he'd slept a full eight hours, except for the slight favoring of one shoulder. He draped his backpack, neatly restored to order, on a chair.

"We're all early risers, I take it," he said with a nod to Kevin. His gaze sought hers. "Good to see you, Zee."

Did he think she had listened to his sage advice and changed her plan? Let him think what he wanted. At the stables, they'd part ways. For good. "Kevin says the main road is flooded so he's going to have to take us another way."

Gideon didn't comment. "May I handle the coffee preparations, sir? I noticed when I put the dishes away that you have a French press and some coffee beans in the cupboard."

"I do?" Kevin shrugged. "Don't even know what a French press is, but have at it."

Mackenzie sat on the sofa. She didn't want to show any interest in the man who'd tried to hold her phone hostage as if he was protecting an ignorant child, but Gideon's movements as he prepped a cast iron pan drew her in.

When he'd gotten it hot, he dumped in the beans. "Just a quick re-roast."

She suspected the coffee had been in the cupboard for a long while. He stirred them with a wooden spatula as they heated up.

The aroma grew even more enticing as he used a small grinder to process the freshly roasted beans into a coarse, glistening pile. He boiled some water and poured it into the press and swirled it.

"To warm it," Gideon said before he added the coarse grounds and the rest of the boiling water to the press. "Four minutes," he said and gave Mackenzie a wink.

She hastily averted her gaze, annoyed that he'd caught her watching him.

At the end of the allotted time, he pressed down the plunger and poured them each an almost full mug. "This should get us started while I prep another batch."

Kevin sniffed his suspiciously. Mackenzie sipped and almost closed her eyes in pleasure at the rich, full-bodied coffee that tasted a world apart from Kevin's brew.

"It's . . . good," she said.

Gideon grinned. "No, it's way better than good, and you know it."

She rolled her eyes and continued to savor.

Kevin gulped his down. “Er, thanks and all, but I’ll stick with the regular stuff.”

Mackenzie didn’t decline a second cup of Gideon’s amazing coffee. Who knew when she’d next have access to a warm beverage?

She should contribute somehow. “I could make French toast,” she found herself saying. “You know, to go with the coffee.”

The two men agreed with enthusiasm, and she whipped up a batch that they ate with syrup and Gideon’s third round of pressed coffee. They talked mostly about the weather, and Gideon pressed Kevin to show him on a map the route to the stables. Taking notes, she thought. Gideon always knew where he was geographically and the best way to get to his point B.

It must be nice to have such certainty about your future plans. Hers ended with Bullseye’s fall. What would her life be like after? It was a nebulous, impenetrable void.

At the agreed-upon departure time, the sky was still dark, an unrelieved black made gloomier by the steadily falling rain. They climbed into the same vehicle, now with a horse trailer hitched to the back. Kevin took off, following a road that was so muddy in spots she feared the wheels would get mired or the trailer stuck. The sunrise eventually revealed a wall of clouds the color of steel wool.

Kevin wasn’t exaggerating about the topography or the steepness of their route. He gripped the wheel, creeping at a sober pace that made her want to leap out and walk. Gideon, she noticed, checked the side mirrors at regular intervals, but the road was so wooded and uneven she didn’t see how anyone would stage an attack.

"Cordelia's gonna be fuming that it took us so long," Kevin said. The morning passed into early afternoon since they had to stop and pry the vehicle out of the mud, and finally, they dropped down into a small valley. The few houses they passed looked empty, the residents having evacuated.

The dirt road led them to a graveled one and Kevin took a final turn.

"Here we are," he said and pulled up a paved circular drive that fronted a barn with a Cotton Flower Stables sign nailed to the red-painted wood. The two adjoining corrals were soaked, water pooling in both. The barn itself was under attack from water, several accumulated inches already creeping up the walls.

"Barn's flooding," Kevin said. "Hoped we'd have more time." He hopped out and quickly unhitched the trailer with Mackenzie and Gideon's help.

They'd just completed the job when a young woman sprinted out from the barn in jeans and a soggy long-sleeved shirt. Her long dark hair was caught up in a tight braid.

"What's wrong, Cordelia?" Kevin called.

"I need help with a horse. Hurry." Then she abruptly changed course and returned to the barn.

Kevin chewed his lip. "That's Cordelia. She owns the stables."

"All right." Gideon motioned to Mackenzie. "Stay here," he said. "Lock yourself in the car."

Kevin shot a look at her. "Right. We'll go help."

She nodded and watched them jog away after Gideon had slung on his backpack. They disappeared into the barn. This was her opportunity to run, bolt from the car and sneak away toward the main road. A clean break, the best kind.

But she hesitated. Gideon had no experience with horses. As a matter of fact, he'd always had kind of a phobia around them. Her horse-loving brother had dragged his best friend to the stables in their neighborhood at every opportunity. Mackenzie tagged along so many times the stable owner allowed her to ride the animals that needed exercising.

"*Gonna get me one someday,*" Aaron had said, fawning over every horse he saw and engaging their owners in his chatting.

In spite of cajoling that bordered on harassment, Aaron had not convinced Gideon to ride, not even once.

And Aaron never got the horse he'd pined for.

With an endangered horse, she'd be a lot more help than Gideon. A quick assessment of the situation would only take a few minutes. Then, if they had it well in hand, she'd hurry away and take off.

She grabbed her pack, splashed through the ankle-deep water into the barn. At the far stall, she heard the sound of a horse in distress, fearful snorts and whinnies, hooves striking against wood. There had been a partial collapse, the water funneling down.

"Roof failed." Cordelia jutted her chin at a hole in the ceiling that had allowed in a torrent of water that left the horse knee-deep.

Cordelia pulled hard at the sliding door of the stall while inside the horse battered and struck at it. Gideon and Kevin helped the woman.

A section of wood had fallen in and bent part of the stable door, keeping it from sliding open.

"I can't get her out and she's freaked," Cordelia called over the rush of water.

It was only a matter of time before the horse broke a leg or impaled itself on the torn wood beam.

As Gideon and Kevin hauled on the door, Mackenzie climbed into the next empty stall, overturned a feed bucket, planted it in the murky water, and scrambled atop to look over. The mare was indeed panicking, eyes wide and rolling, the lead rope whipping her neck as she thrashed.

"I'll get an axe from the tack room," Kevin shouted as he splashed away. "We'll cut through the door enough for her to get out."

Gideon remained with Cordelia, shouting as he heaved on the stall door. "It's starting to give."

He and Cordelia focused their energies on yanking the weakened board, crashing it back and forth to encourage it to break.

But the mare was growing increasingly manic, and Mackenzie was certain she was going to be gravely injured. She leaned over, talking low and calm.

"Hey, sweet girl," she started. "Come here, baby."

Gideon jerked a look at her. "Get out of there, Zee."

She ignored him, bent farther into the stall, and reached for the lead rope. Her fingers grazed it, but the mare jerked away, front hooves smashing against the wall. When the horse came close a second time, she tried again.

"You're all right," she said softly, touching the horse's neck with delicate pressure. "I'm here, and you're going to get out of this mess."

One touch, and then the mare allowed a second. Still stamping in agitation, the horse accepted a small stroke of her back before huddling close to the wall, where Mackenzie kept talking to her.

Continued touches, a calming voice—her tricks were beginning to work. When the horse quieted enough, Mackenzie grabbed the lead rope and eased her near enough to caress her trembling side. She kept her as close as she could. Without the thrashing mare working against them, Gideon and Cordelia heaved once more, and the fallen board gave way with a mighty crack.

Cordelia leapt immediately into the stall while Gideon ripped away more of the board and wrenched back the damaged sliding door. Cordelia took the lead rope from Mackenzie.

Her dark eyes roamed Mackenzie's face. "Thanks." She looked back at Gideon. "Both of you."

Mackenzie nodded.

"I'm Cordelia."

"That's Gideon and I'm Zee," she said.

"You two have good timing." Cordelia guided the shivering creature out of the stall, crooning softly to her.

Kevin returned then. "I'm too slow, huh? Well, let me help you get her into the trailer and hook it up to your vehicle." He followed Cordelia and the mare.

Gideon panted and wiped his sweating brow, and Mackenzie climbed down from the bucket and joined him. They sat for a while in silence. The whole adventure completely delayed her plan, but the horse was safe and Gideon hadn't been clobbered. Maybe they were even now.

A clump of hay stuck in his hair. "Have I mentioned I don't trust horses?"

She reached up and brushed away the hay. His hair was full and thick, coiling with moisture. "That's because you have the horsemanship skills of a city slicker."

His grin was so boyish it took her back to the days when she'd pined for him, hung on every syllable, followed him around like a duckling. He laughed, and she found herself joining in.

This man would do everything in his power to stop her from getting justice for Aaron, yet she couldn't deny that something about him felt like peach ice cream on a blazing summer day.

He massaged his shoulder. "You know, back there at Kevin's car, I had this crazy idea that you were going to take off when you had the chance."

"I was."

"But you came in anyway. Why?"

She shrugged. "The horse needed help."

The corner of his mouth lifted, and it was as if he sensed her confused feelings about him.

That wouldn't do.

"Anyway, I'm—"

He stopped her with a finger to his lips, his playfulness suddenly gone.

"What?" she whispered.

His serious expression told her he'd heard trouble coming.

Fast.

••••••••••••••••••••••

Vehicles. Two. Gideon heard them rolling up the road to the barn lot simultaneously. There was no mistaking the urgency.

He grabbed Mackenzie's hand, and together they ran toward the rear door of the barn, freezing water splashing them up to their knees. He waited, listening as the cars drew close.

Slammed doors, running feet.

A woman shouted. Cordelia. "You won't go near my barn, do you hear me?"

He took Mackenzie's hand and gestured. Out the back. No other option. Before they did so, he risked a look through the barn, where he could see a man standing next to a white truck, his beard gleaming silver, a dark-haired man at his flank. An angry woman's voice, Cordelia's, echoed indistinctly in the background.

"I'll go around the back, Al," the second man said.

"Let me flush 'em out for you." Al pulled a weapon from his belt and blasted blindly into the interior of the barn. Bullets carved splinters from the weathered wood and more followed as Gideon tugged Mackenzie to the exit. Right or left? Which way would the second guy go to cut them off?

With a muttered prayer, he pulled Mackenzie to the left. Tarp-covered crates holding saddles and bridles were stacked and ready for loading, providing some cover. Heads low, they raced along the perimeter toward the front of the barn and stopped just before they rounded the corner to the parking lot.

Gideon darted a look, hoping Al wasn't there, poised to blow his head off. In the half-flooded lot sat Al's white truck, engine running, and next to it a smaller black one. Kevin's vehicle was still there too, farthest away under the trees. He hadn't made an escape.

Another engine rumbled, and he saw Cordelia at the wheel of a truck attached to the small horse trailer Kevin had returned, the mare they'd just freed loaded safely in the back. She shouted something out her window at Al, who stood there staring up at her, gripping his gun.

"This has got nothing to do with you." Al pointed to the road. "You clear out and mind your business, girl."

Cordelia snapped something back, but Gideon couldn't make it out. Finally, she stomped the gas and drove past the stable, her expression one of absolute fury, a phone clamped to her ear.

Calling for help.

At least she'd gotten away, but it would be too late for him and Mackenzie. And Kevin? Where had he gone?

Al advanced into the barn, gun aimed.

Jerry called out to him. "They're on the east side. Heading for the front."

Caught between Al and Jerry closing in from the side.

Options, Gideon. He grabbed a couple rocks from the ground. He'd lay down some cover and Mackenzie could run. Before he could get the plan out, she seized his arm.

"Look. Kevin's in his car."

Gideon looked closer. Kevin was indeed crouched low behind the wheel, face white as paste, knuckles gripping, his mouth open in shock. Gideon signaled him.

Kevin saw. He froze for a moment, then leaned toward the passenger door and pushed it open.

"He's calling us over," she said, starting to move.

But he held her tighter, thinking. Jerry was close, and he could hear Al retracing his steps through the barn, the fastest route back to the parking lot.

If they tried to get to Kevin, they'd be cut down without question.

"We won't make it," he said.

"There's no choice."

"Yes, there is. Al's truck. Keys in the ignition and running." The driver's door was facing them. So close.

Al emerged at a run, scanning the lot, gaze fastening on them.

Mackenzie took a long look at Kevin and then at Gideon.

He counted down on his fingers. Three, two . . .

They bolted.

SEVEN

GIDEON ENVISIONED EXECUTING a smooth dive into the driver's seat like some Special Forces hotshot. Instead, he stumbled in a submerged pothole, slowing him just enough for Mackenzie to reach Al's vehicle first. She launched herself behind the wheel.

With no time to navigate around to the passenger seat, Gideon hurled himself into the bed of the truck seconds before she stomped the gas.

Al roared with rage and let loose another hail of bullets. One shattered the side mirror as Mackenzie sent the truck flying through the stable gates and out onto the dirt road. He clung with all his mettle as the truck tore over the ground. He didn't have to see to know that Al and Jerry would pursue in Jerry's vehicle, but the surprise had provided them precious minutes for a getaway.

It would give Kevin a window to escape, as well, and Cordelia if she hadn't cleared the property yet. They weren't the targets, but then again they might have helped set the trap. Yet Cordelia had been on the phone with utter rage in her expression. *Don't mess with a woman and her horses.*

Kevin could have acted alone to betray them.

Mackenzie took a hard turn that sent him rolling over and slamming into the other side of the truck bed.

Then she barreled over a ditch with only a slight adjustment in speed. He landed hard on his shoulder and bounced back up into the air, where he got a glimpse behind them. The black truck had just made it past the stable gates, a sizable distance between them, thanks to Mackenzie's edge-of-control speed. Ahead was a blind turn that would take them out of sight of their pursuers for a few moments. It might also result in him flying out of the truck altogether. He pounded on the roof of the cab.

"I'm gettin' in!" he hollered.

Hopefully she wouldn't run over him in the process.

She made the turn and stopped, allowing him to scramble into the passenger seat, feeling as though he'd just been churned in a cement mixer.

"I'll—" He was going to say "drive" but she didn't let him. She took off again before his buckle clicked.

She stomped on the accelerator until the vehicle shimmied and shook. "They know this area way better than we do. Finding a place to hide is the best option until we can plan something. Agreed?"

"Yes, I—"

"All right. Then you might want to hold on."

He braced himself with his boots, clutching the armrest as she jerked the wheel and took them at teeth-clenching speed straight off the road and down a grassy hillside stubbled with old-growth trees. "Look out!"

She swerved around one oak and then the next.

"Slow down or you'll do Al's job for him."

"Don't be a backseat driver," she yelled back.

He wished there was a back seat for him to hunker down in as she plunged the vehicle deeper into the tree line. Branches smacked at the sides and the shrubbery grew so dense he lost orientation to the road. A flying rock shattered the right headlight, sending glass ballooning in a sparkling cloud. Ahead the trees thinned and patches of landscape showed through. He blinked and blinked again because it sure looked like—

Ahead the mountain abruptly gave way to a precarious slope.

He shouted over the engine.

Mackenzie sucked in a breath as she practically stood on the brake.

Dirt crumbled under the tires.

The truck continued moving, wheels sliding ever closer to the drop that would tumble them straight off a cliff.

His body was fully taut as he prepared for the inevitable crash.

Twigs raked the windows, as if they were trying to slow the vehicle and prevent it from hurtling into the abyss, but momentum and gravity were working against them.

The precipice loomed ever closer, yards, feet, then inches.

"Come on, come on." Mackenzie's forearms tensed as she worked the brake with both feet. With a groan of protest, the truck shimmied to a stop at last, inches before they would have gone over.

He was pretty sure his heart had stopped beating a few feet back. They both sat motionless, panting.

"Unexpected," she finally said.

"That about sums it up," he managed to say.

Still breathing hard, she rolled down the driver's side glass. They listened to the sound of a truck hurtling past on the road above them.

"They didn't see us turn off." She slapped the wheel in satisfaction. "Smooth, right?"

"Oh yeah. Smooth as silk," he said weakly. His heart was threatening to crack through his rib cage. How they'd survived that escapade had to be purely an act of God. His stomach was still inside out.

Mackenzie, on the other hand, seemed to be unaffected by their near-death experience. She unbuckled and made sure her pack was still on the passenger floor where she'd thrown it. His was mashed between his shoulders and seat since he hadn't had a spare second to take it off.

Every muscle and joint complained thanks to the battering he'd endured. Being around Mackenzie Bardine was hazardous to a man's health. At least this time they hadn't ended up in the water.

"You okay?" she asked. "You look pale."

"Peachy. You?"

"Okay." She craned to see through the branches. "Can you tell where we are?"

"Give me a minute." He climbed out, shoulder complaining along with all his other parts. After plowing through loose dirt and foliage, he found a spot where he could use his phone's compass to get them an orientation before he returned and climbed back in.

"That way's Kevin's trailer," he said, jutting a finger.

"The other way's town and at our nine o'clock is the stable."

She thought it over. "So take back roads to town then? You can report to the cops."

He shook his head. "Al and Jerry will figure on that. I'm sure they've got eyes all over, people on the lookout to find us. Could be Kevin and Cordelia are out searching too."

"But we have to go in that direction somehow. Your Jeep's there. And . . ."

He huffed out a breath. "And?"

"And I can get from there to my next destination."

He rolled his eyes. "You're not James Bond. I know you're headed for the airstrip to get the info your contact gave you." She paused, probably waiting for him to argue against it. No point. If she was going to throw her life away, he couldn't stop her. But if they stayed alive long enough, he could try to lobby for her to change her mind between here and his Jeep.

"We don't have to stay together," she said quietly.

Survival protocol dictated otherwise. It was always better for isolated personnel to stick together. But it was more than his training causing his immediate rejection. The thought of leaving her rubbed him raw inside. Why? Worry? He frowned. Guilt?

Because he'd walked away from Aaron?

The gray of her eyes held streaks of silver as she watched him.

"We stay together. That's the best way to survive," he said firmly.

She folded her arms and thought it over. "Much as it pains me to admit, you're more skilled in this wilderness survival stuff than I am. How about we stay together just until we get back to civilization?"

He nodded, relieved.

She reached for the ignition. "We'll reverse then. Drive out the way we came in, peel off on the first back road we come to that leads north, stick to cover as much as possible. Get some distance from good ol' Al and Jerry and regroup."

He didn't answer as she carefully backed the truck away from the precipice and out of the leafy cover. The ascent back up to the road was much less terrifying than the descent, but the tires fought for traction in places.

When they eventually rattled and banged onto the paved surface, there was still no sign of the shooters' return. She kept her speed slower but maintained a brisk clip nonetheless.

He replayed their morning, the trip to the stables, the ambush. He'd been on alert during their drive from Kevin's and he'd seen no sign that they were followed.

Mackenzie glanced at him. "You've got that lip thing going on."

"What thing?"

"You purse your lips when you're thinking."

He blinked. "I do?"

"Yes. Spill it."

He would have to work on his steely airman persona if she could read him so easily. "Bullseye's guys. The ambush. How did they know where we'd be? Cordelia or Kevin must have tipped them off."

"Cordelia maybe. She's a stranger to us, but I doubt she'd have had time, unless Kevin told her he was bringing guests. Why would Kevin help us in the first place if he was going to hand us over at the stables?"

"We're worth more alive than dead?"

He clung to the dash as she hit a pothole and his skull smacked into the roof. Was the woman actually aiming for them? He considered offering to drive again, but he acknowledged that they were still alive, undiscovered, and the truck was intact, so he checked himself.

"They could be working together for a bounty, or Cordelia might have spotted us as we headed down that last stretch of road. She could have called and alerted Al and Jerry so they could arrive for the ambush."

Mackenzie frowned. "In other circumstances, I'd agree, but she was furious when she drove away. Even you could see that, right?"

"What do you mean 'even I could see that'? I'm a sensitive guy."

She laughed. "Don't I know it. One round of tickling and you collapse. Very sensitive, indeed."

He found himself chuckling too, and aside from his throbbing shoulder, aching head, and tense gut, it actually felt good. Her hair that had come loose from the ponytail blew around her face in the breeze from the open window. Even tired, banged up, and on the run, she was undeniably attractive. He'd dated plenty of strong women who could put him in his place, but he hadn't found one with the combination of strength and faith and . . . What was it? The indefinable something that intrigued him about Mackenzie. He squirmed on the seat and rubbed his chin. "Still visit Aaron's Landing?"

She stiffened and he couldn't quite figure out why he'd brought it up. So much for sensitive.

"Not for a while," she said after a moment. "It's still the best fishing hole ever. Trout as big as my arm. Aaron used to say the fish congregated there on a weekly basis to commemorate the hilarious day he fell in."

"I remember. It was a knee-slapper moment except that he took our bag of lunch in with him." That felt good too. Just for one small tick of the clock to revisit a happy memory of the three of them. Just a trio of friends enjoying a summer day, innocent of the future grief that would forever mark them. "You caught more fish than any of us, yet you never ate a single one, did you?" A fact he'd teased her about relentlessly. "Why?"

She shrugged. "I dunno. They just look so beautiful with their iridescent scales and all. They fight with everything in them to breathe and get back to the water. I just can't bring myself to kill them." She shrugged. "Silly."

"Not silly."

She yanked a look at him. "No?"

"Life is precious. Not silly to remember that."

She smiled, a lovely, warm, radiant smile that erased the defiant lines around her mouth. "I suppose a guy who jumps in to rescue a floundering deer and then a drowning lady on the very same day would understand something like that."

"Yes, he would."

"Rescue is your life?"

"It's my job." Her pack shifted on the seat, and he set it straight again. "But I'm glad I was around at the right place and time, for the deer, and for you." *Why all the honesty, Gid? Why now?* He had the sense that the moments with Mackenzie were about to expire.

Her lower lip wobbled. Suddenly he was taking her hand, cupping his palm over hers. He squeezed her fingers and she returned the pressure. Oddly, he found himself wanting to reach for her, ease the pain from that broken place that refused to be mended. For a moment, he thought she might let their hands stay joined, but with a shake she let go, pressed the gas harder, and sent the truck rattling over his tender thoughts.

An electronic pulse buzzed from the glove box.

She stared. "What was that?"

He pulled out a cell phone as it continued to ring. The number on the screen said "Unknown."

She stopped the truck and snatched the phone from him, flipping it to speaker mode before he could decide whether it was wise to answer or not.

"Ms. Bardine, you need to go home." The voice was low, male, hard-edged.

Electricity jolted through his battered muscles.

"Who is this?" Mackenzie snapped.

"You know."

"Yes," Mackenzie said. "Bullseye, right?"

The voice dripped with disdain. "That's your nickname for me. Clickbait for the social media trash who follow you like pigs after slop."

"How do you know I'm in this truck?"

"A famous podcaster like yourself? I've got eyes on you."

Gideon grew cold. Bullseye knew about Mackenzie's online crusade. Had it allowed him to pinpoint when she would arrive in town? Helped him conclude she'd be meeting Lorraine?

Bullseye continued. "Like I said, you should go home while you can. It's dangerous here. You've noticed?"

She stared daggers as she clutched the phone. "I have, particularly since you keep sending goons to try to kill me."

"They're loyal to me. Everyone in this town is. That's the part you don't understand yet. You won't find anywhere to hide or anyone to shield you from me. This is your one chance to get out alive. It's a gracious offer. You should take it."

Mackenzie's eyes flashed. "I'm not going until you're punished for what you did to my brother."

"You need someone to blame, but Aaron did it to himself."

"You peddle death. You profit off people's misery."

"The opinion is irrelevant to the issue. Your brother's choices got him killed."

Mackenzie's face went white and Gideon grabbed the phone from her.

Rage painted his vision red. "Enough," he snarled.

Bullseye's tone remained calm, clipped. "Gideon Landry, isn't it? Inserting yourself into a situation that doesn't concern you. This is not your fight. Mixing yourself up with her is going to get you dead."

"You don't get to exterminate everyone who crosses you," he said through gritted teeth.

Bullseye laughed. "I don't bother. I have people to do that for me. You'll never get near me. You'll die long before you see my face. You can't win. Go home. The offer extends to you too. I'll forget I ever knew your name."

Gideon looked at Mackenzie and saw the mountain of rage and hurt and pain she was trying to contain. Too much for her to live with, too much for her to let go. In that moment he knew she was trapped, unable to free herself any more than her brother could from his torment. She was bound to this man by her need for revenge. It would blind her.

It would kill her.

His blood pounded through his veins and coalesced into a rush of conviction.

Before he could speak again, she grabbed the phone. "You're scared of me. That's why you sent your men, why you're calling now. You're scared that I'll expose you to the world and upset your business."

"You've annoyed me, is all. With your podcast. Your deal with Lorraine."

Mackenzie bit her lip. "I have an episode loaded already. If anything happens to Lorraine or me, it goes live to my followers." It was all unproven, of course, about Bulleye's responsibility for what happened to them in the police van, how Lorraine said Bullseye was targeting her and what her boyfriend knew about his business operations. Enough to get the authorities to investigate, though.

"She's not my priority. You are." The silent pause crackled with tension. "Listen, because we won't talk again, Ms. Bardine. This is my promise. You'll die if you don't go home, both of you. Your parents can bury you next to your brother."

The phone beeped. Connection ended.

She stared at the cell and then at Gideon. "He knows about you."

Gideon nodded. "His message was pretty clear, Zee. He's giving you a chance to get out, walk away, or he's coming at you with both barrels."

"Us. He's coming at us." Her eyes sparkled with tears. "Gideon, I'm sorry I brought you into this, but it's what I've told you from the beginning. I don't want you here. You have to go or you'll get hurt."

He grabbed her hand and held it up. Palm to palm, he locked fingers with her and would not let her look away. The pressure of their entwined hands infused his words with intensity. "I have a choice in all this too. I choose to stay."

She shook her head. "You can't."

"I'm staying."

"Why, Gid?" The question came out like a whisper. "Why stay? Aaron's dead."

He squeezed harder and cut her off. "This isn't about Aaron. It's about you, and I'm not letting you do this alone."

Her eyes glimmered like smoke rising in the sky. He couldn't help himself. He kissed her. For so many years he'd wondered what it would be like to kiss Mackenzie Bardine. He'd gotten a taste when she surprised him in his car. A real, unhurried kiss, he'd imagined, would be tender and soft and it would light up part of his heart that beat in shadow. He'd been right, about all of it.

The kiss went on for a few seconds, sending sparks through his bloodstream. She might have warmed to it, leaning in for the barest fraction, until she drew away and they sat in awkward silence.

He struggled to catch his breath. "I don't know why I did that."

She shrugged, looked away, and pulled in a shaky breath. "An impulse, just like, um, before. Forget it. Get out of this town as quick as you can. Please, Gid." She reached for her pack.

"Are you coming with me?"

She shook her head.

"All right. Then if you won't leave until you talk to the guy at the airstrip, we'll go there."

Her eyes narrowed. "Why do I hear a catch coming?"

"After you get what you need, we leave. Go to the cops. You sort out your evidence when you return home, where it will be harder for him to reach you."

Her gaze grew curious. "And you're so concerned about this why? To make sure my parents don't lose another child?"

"Not only that."

"Guilt is a bad reason to risk your life."

He bristled. "Do you think it's the slightest bit possible that you don't know me as well as you think?"

She considered for a moment, then shook her head, dismissing the kiss, dismissing him. "I'm going to the airstrip, and if you insist on coming, I can't stop you. What you do is your business."

Frustration banged through his nerves. Why was it so hard to be her friend? "You sound just like your brother."

She flinched. "What?"

"He was Mr. I'm Gonna Live My Life Any Way I Choose.

Always after whatever made him feel good without considering the consequences. It was fun when we were teenagers, but he never grew out of it." His words were bitter, but he was too tired and irritated to regret them.

Rage blazed across her face. "My brother wasn't your kind of person. And I'm not either, so please excuse yourself. Glad that's cleared up." She grabbed her pack and yanked the strings tight to be sure it was closed.

He wasn't sorry he'd said it, but he'd touched a match to the gasoline. If he didn't get himself together and rein in his emotions, there wouldn't be a next step or even a next hour for either one of them. He cleared his throat and focused, then pointed to the cell phone from the glove box.

"The phone no doubt has a tracker. There's a possibility the truck does too."

She allowed him to take the phone, and he opened the window and hurled it as far into the trees as it could go. The truck was an older model, might not have GPS built in, but it wasn't inconceivable that Bullseye had a device installed to keep tabs on his employees. No way to know for sure.

"We should ditch the truck."

She glared at him. "I'll say it again, Gideon. I don't want you around."

"And again, I don't really care what you want." Just the right mix of cocky and certain. He rubbed his chin. "Did you really make a podcast to protect Lorraine?"

"Yes. In the middle of the night, after I got my phone back that you withheld from me."

He didn't take the bait.

"I've got it scheduled to post if I don't return. The police will see it. I tagged an officer I trust."

"High-tech vigilantism."

"If it's the only way to protect Lorraine, call it whatever you want."

No sense creating another argument. It was going to be tough enough to get back to his Jeep and from there to the airstrip. She could be as furious as she wanted, but he intended to be a barnacle on her back until she was safely delivered to local police or, best case, got back home to Seattle.

He grabbed his pack and plumbed the deep recesses of the glove box. "Might as well see if Al left anything helpful before we ditch it."

Giving him the silent treatment, she looked under the seats to do the same.

He located a slender packet. "Score. A stick of beef jerky."

She held up the bounty she'd found. "Two old saltwater taffies and a visor."

"We'll write him a thank-you note later."

There was nothing else of interest in the truck except for tools. They didn't need any extra weight to carry, and he had a bare-bones assortment in his backpack already.

As they exited the truck, stinging needles of rain drilled down on them. Mackenzie zipped up her jacket while he stripped away the truck's spark plugs to disable the engine. "If we can't use the vehicle, neither can they." A small satisfaction, but he'd take what he could get.

"How long to your Jeep?" she asked.

"We can't travel at night, so I'd say we've got about five hours of hiking today and another two in the morning."

"If we're not caught by then."

"Optimism, Bardine. I'm not going to let us get caught."

Big talk. Would he be able to deliver?

"Your parents can bury you next to your brother."

Over Gideon's dead body.

He marched resolutely into the storm.

EIGHT

GIDEON LED THE WAY in the rain, which had increased to relentless sheets that seeped into the necks of their jackets. They'd found a ribbon of hiking trail snaking away from the road that would take them roughly in the direction of the bridge, but progress was slow. The ground was a bloated morass of grass and mud. As they tried to keep their shoes from sinking into the mire, he reran their heated conversation.

"You sound just like your brother."

Funny, he'd always admired Aaron's sunny outlook, the easy way he attracted others like blossoms enticed bees. Aaron was the jovial one in their friendship, beloved by everyone for his charm and by his peers for his fun-loving nature, by Gideon too. He'd never had the same charisma. Maybe he was envious of Aaron on some deep psychological level. Jealous, possibly, of the way Mackenzie admired her brother so deeply. He tried to swat away the thought along with the gnat that pestered his vision.

He looked from under the dripping brim of his hat at

the landscape, everything strange and unfamiliar, shoving branches aside as they plowed onward.

What was happening between him and Mackenzie?

Nothing. They were trying to survive, pure and simple, thrown together in a bizarre twist of fate.

Water snaked between his shoulder blades, and he cinched his collar tighter. He was moving them in the right direction, toward his Jeep, but there seemed no end to the sprawl of wilderness ahead. They were depleted, physically and emotionally, inhabiting that dangerous mental space where thinking could get fuzzy. This was the epitome of an "isolating event" in SERE lingo. As he routinely taught his classes, *"The assigned mission is to return to friendly control without giving aid or comfort to the enemy."*

At least they'd been successful in that part of the mission so far. Al and Jerry were driving around in the mess too, one of their vehicles disabled and left in the mud, minus a jerky, a visor, and a couple pieces of saltwater taffy. Better yet, the two lackeys had been thwarted at the bridge and again at the barn, where no one had been shot. At least, he hoped not. It appeared that Kevin had been fortunate enough to get away, unless of course he and/or Cordelia had been part of the ambush in the first place.

The "friendly control" they were searching for was going to be hard to find in a flooded town where Bullseye seemed to have an incredible reach. If they did come upon a local who hadn't evacuated, would they promptly be given up to the drug lord? The line between friend and enemy could be impossible to recognize, and it was clear they had a price on their heads.

The only way around was through, so he shook the water from his hat and pressed on. He was never sure if cold or heat was harder to bear, but he was beginning to think there was nothing more miserable than an inescapable chill.

The hours passed in a painful blur as the cold seeped deeper into his bones. His shoulder ached to the cellular level. Mackenzie didn't complain, but she seemed to be developing a limp that worsened as they toiled on along soggy stretches of wooded hillside.

In late afternoon, when their pace slackened to a trudge, they split the beef jerky stick and drank water from their packs. He refilled the bottles they'd emptied earlier from a stream and added purification tablets.

He knew her feet were complaining, blisters forming at the heels from the sodden jogging shoes Kevin had given her. His feet ached too, though his sturdy boots were the best money could buy. Never skimp on footwear, that was a lesson he'd learned the hard way. He'd rather go hungry than wear flimsy shoes.

How much longer?

The desperate question ran silently through him, but he refused to let it take over. Wilderness survival was his life, his career, and he could go on as long as he needed to. But Mackenzie was fatigued, and if they couldn't find shelter soon, he'd need to improvise one. He could use the tarp and supplies from his pack, but there was no way he could risk building a fire. Thirty more minutes, he told himself.

They arrived at the lip of a valley. The view would have been spectacular in other circumstances, the rocky peak on which they stood dropping from a dizzying height into a wooded canyon where two forks of a great river thundered along. No doubt there were cabins and homes nestled in scenic locations alongside the water, but the failing light and oppressive fog hid them. It reminded him that they were two very small people in an enormous wilderness.

"Any homes down there?" Mackenzie asked, voice pitched above the sound of the rain. She was shivering, her hand pressed to her side as if she had a cramp.

"Maybe, but they'd be empty, likely. With the flooding, everyone's been encouraged to evacuate, and most people with good sense have left," Gideon called back. He'd let the irritation slip out a bit there, and she'd surely caught it. *"I didn't ask you to come,"* she'd say.

Truth. He'd made the choice, eyes wide open. And he wouldn't change it, in spite of the unending discomfort. Mackenzie did not have a corner on the stubborn market.

Seeing the topography from above reinforced how dire their situation might become. At the upper elevation, the Cotton Flower Dam bottled the neck of the valley, the cement shoulders holding back the mighty crush of water from the town and its offshoots, like this peaceful vista. If it failed . . .

He shook the hair from his face, the water sluicing off, and raised his volume to make himself heard over the downpour. "Let's get to higher ground. We've got a half hour or so before it's too dark to travel. Looks like we're gonna have to make camp until we get some daylight. Need to find a suitable spot."

"No camping," she called back. "We can keep going."

"Not without busting an ankle."

She didn't argue, a clear indication she was approaching exhaustion.

They struggled on as the trail paralleled the valley's edge. Steep, then steeper. It was necessary to pitch their bodies forward to maintain their progress without tumbling, but their pace slowed anyway as the wind stiffened and their energy waned.

Punishing cold chased them around a slow bend in the trail. *Keep going. Keep pushing.* But they were both fighting for every step as they made the turn. When they trekked past it, he stopped so fast she bumped into him.

"What?" she said.

He blinked, and it was still there. A new rush of hope infused his spirit. He pointed in the misty gloom, almost afraid he was dreaming.

She scanned around him. "I don't see anything."

Because the foundation was tangled in shrubbery and he'd been concentrating on his footing, so he hadn't noticed it at first either. He tipped her chin up.

At the top of the peak ahead of them, a wooden fire watchtower rose into the clouds. The tall, squat structure perched a solid one hundred twenty feet up.

As they stared, the rain slithered down his cheeks, adding more goose bumps to his skin if that was possible.

"A fire watchtower," she said, as if she didn't believe it either.

"Shelter acquired." He waved a careless hand and fired off a cocky grin. "It's like I'm not even trying."

Her laugh was tired and reckless and beautiful as she took in the dizzyingly high ladder they would need to climb. She chafed her palms together.

His hands were just as numb. Would they be able to grip well enough to keep from falling? But it was still respite from the elements, better than the emergency shelter he could fashion on the sodden ground. "You game?" he said above the noise. "There's a bit of climbing required to check into this hotel, but the views will be worth it."

Her smile was forced. "Anything to get out of this rain."

He pulled away some prickly shrubbery and started up the ladder, testing the first few rungs. Could they really have a dry place to rest, safe from Bullseye's men? It was almost too much to ask for. And what condition would the structure be in once they arrived at the top? As long as it was somewhat dry and enclosed, it had to be an improvement. "Feels sound enough, but it looks like it's been out of service for a while. How about I go up first and check it out? You wait here."

"I'm coming with you."

He didn't have the energy to argue with her. The last splotches of gray sky gave way to ebony as they hauled themselves rung by rung to the top, then emerged through a hatch onto a wooden platform that wrapped around the entire building. Calf muscles quivering, he surveyed the structure while she clung to the railing. The paint had long since chipped away from the exterior, but the silvery boards were intact, the glass windows too, except for a few cracks and one small broken pane. The wood planking under their feet was solid.

Gideon tried the door. It opened. He kept his cool. Barely. "Unlocked, because who'd arrive uninvited?"

"Except us? No one," she said through chattering teeth.

They stepped into one large square room that smelled

like the interior of his grandma's old hope chest. Rainwater poured off them, rapidly forming a puddle on the floorboards. In the center was a small stove, and against one wall a set of narrow bunk beds, bare of bedding. A circular map underneath a dusty sheet of glass was centered on a table in the middle of the creaking floor, and a telescope was positioned in the corner. Certainly not high tech, but serviceable.

"All the comforts of home," he said.

"Except your fancy coffee."

"We'll see what we can do."

He stopped her when she reached for her flashlight. "Can't risk it. Penlights only and shade it with your hand. Light shines for miles from this height." And there were two men combing the soggy terrain for their prey. They'd have found the vehicle and possibly narrowed down the direction he and Mackenzie had taken.

Her shivering was impossible to ignore, his just as violent. The space was cold, extremely so. They had to get dry quickly. "Got any spare clothes in your pack?" he asked.

"No. The jail has all my worldly possessions except this outfit Kevin provided. I left the prison uniform on his porch."

He pulled a tight bundle from his supply. "Put these on. It's all gonna be huge but maybe adequate with some extreme measures."

She hesitated. "Are you sure? What will you wear?"

"I've got something to use until Kevin's borrowed clothes dry. Go change."

"Uh, where do I . . ."

He pointed to the corner and turned his back, studying

the old firefinder and the map. "No peeking. I promise. I'll just finish exploring the supplies."

She scurried to the bunk area, and he took the opportunity to poke around. God might have provided some useful items along with the lifesaving shelter. He prowled, elated to find a few things that would help with survival and comfort. He moved on to what served as a kitchen area. He discovered a plastic baggie full of sugar and salt packets, which he immediately secreted in his pack. When he looked in the box by the telescope, the next prize had him almost crowing aloud.

Mackenzie approached and he did a double take, his find hidden behind his back. His sweatpants engulfed her slender legs and she'd taken a hair elastic and cinched them tighter around her waist. His sweatshirt was massive too, so she'd rolled up the cuffs. The crew socks puddled around her ankles, and she rested one foot atop the other. But her smile was so warm and lovely he felt transfixed by it.

"What?" She pirouetted. "I'm not doing your clothes justice?"

"They've never looked better," he said, hand on his heart. Honest reaction he'd forgotten to suppress. He recovered. "And I have a gift for you. Here." He produced the battered pair of stained leather hiking boots.

She gaped. "Boots? You found these here?"

"Previous tenant left them. Maybe a little too big, but . . ."

She stared at them as if they were rare jewels. "Are you kidding? They're perfect." Flinging her arms wide, she hugged him. She might have meant it to be a momentary action, but his arms went around her and he held her close and she let him. Her body was soft against him, her hair smelling of rain and the curve of her cheek pressed to his chin. His heart lit up like a beacon. *What? Why?* He couldn't explain the wild firing of emotion, but when she pulled away, turning to scurry to the lower bunk bed, his cheeks felt hot and his balance a little off.

Trauma bonding. Simple as that. Two people struggling to survive, emotions heightened due to the circumstances. Totally understandable. He wouldn't let it get out of hand.

The bootlaces were stiff and the leather too, but the super thick socks helped take up the extra space and he watched in satisfaction as she took some tentative steps in the new footwear. "Jimmy Choo has nothing on these babies." She took them off and put the wrecked sneakers with the rest of her clothes spread out to dry.

With his heart still racing, he pulled himself together. "I'll change quick, and then I need to do some maintenance. Can you be my assistant?"

She laughed. "I guess you don't have any other candidates, so sure."

After he'd pulled on the remaining dry clothes from his pack and spread his wet garments next to hers, she followed him to the broken window. With her palm shielding the beam of her flashlight, she provided enough illumination that he was able to fit a black plastic bag over the missing glass with the roll of duct tape from his supplies. It stopped the cold wind from rushing in. Helpful, since he could see his breath puffing in the frigid air. He would have given a month's pay to be able to light the small stack of dry wood in the stove, but that would be too much of a tip-off to their pursuers.

He then whacked the dust off the bunk mattresses, which caused them both to sneeze. Dusty or not, he couldn't wait to fall into a much-needed sleep. Every muscle was crying out for food and rest and his rebuilt shoulder was clamoring. The telescope was crooked, but Gideon straightened the tripod and reattached it, then peered into the viewer before he gestured for her to look.

She squinted into the eyepiece at the sprawling countryside below them. A glimmering necklace of lights eastward caught her attention.

"The dam," he said.

"Still holding."

But for how long? The rivers were already close to capacity, overflowing in some places.

While she continued to scan for any sign of pursuit, he went on with his search. Below the telescope was a cabinet that he opened.

"Well, lookie what we've got here."

"Blankets?" she squeaked.

He cheered as he pulled out two musty-smelling wool blankets. "Sure as shooting. And they're nice and dry. You take them. It'll help you sleep."

She pushed one back at him. "Nope. Even stephen. One for each of us." She wrapped hers around her shoulders. The fabric smelled of mothballs. He flung his on the top bunk.

The night sky grew impenetrable as the darkness became complete. With the illumination his penlight provided, Gideon locked the hatch through which they'd entered. Secure, a hundred-plus feet in the air. It would afford them an excellent view of anyone pursuing, but it created other problems too. If Al and Jerry or any of Bullseye's people found them, would they have time to get down from their lofty perch, or would they be easy pickings? Pluses and minuses. Right then, the biggest plus was the fact that they were dry and out of the elements.

They each discreetly used a waste bucket, which had been a must for the fire-watchers since there was no plumbing.

He checked his phone. It was nearly six thirty, but it felt like midnight. No bars, which meant no messaging or calling. Hers wasn't any better.

"Here." He handed her a portable charger. "At least we can keep them juiced up and ready for the moment we have coverage."

She plugged in and slumped on the lower bunk.

He longed to do the same, but if he lay down he'd be out like a blown candle. He stretched his depleted limbs. The moment had arrived to apply the old razzle-dazzle. "I'm hungry. You?"

She closed her eyes and moaned. "So hungry."

"While I'm preparing our meal, can you see if there's anything helpful in that box under the lower bunk?"

She sat up. "There's going to be a meal? You better not be teasing about a thing like that."

"Patience, young grasshopper."

While he made his way to the tiny kitchen corner, she pulled out the darkened metal trunk from under her bunk. "Some maps, a flashlight, minus the batteries. An empty tin of cat food. And, oddly, a cookbook titled *Three Hundred Sixty-Five Soup Recipes*."

"Excellent," he said. "I only know how to make chicken noodle. I could use more ideas. Like how do you make that onion kind with the melty cheese on top?" The thought made his mouth water.

"No idea, but chicken noodle sounds divine right about now. Or really any kind at all." Her stomach growled loudly to underline the point. His was complaining too. If only he'd known he'd be going from his survival class to diving into the freezing river, to climbing to the top of a fire watchtower in a matter of two days, he'd have done a more thorough job fueling up. And laying in supplies. He was carrying only the basics, and that wasn't enough for two people. The list of items they were lacking was endless. But they'd enjoy one good dinner at least, and he found himself looking forward to her reaction.

"If you'd care to join me, madam," he said grandly, "your dinner is served."

She moved to stand at the small table. He gestured her into the rickety wooden chair, while he balanced on an upended crate. The tiniest sliver of moonlight sliced through the clouds and illuminated their dinner spot.

"I didn't find any plates, so this will have to do." He put a piece of tinfoil in front of each of them along with foldable metal forks from his camping kit.

Her brow quirked. "You have a burger and fries hidden in your backpack or something?"

He beamed. "Nothing so fancy, but it's hot."

The word made her eyes grow wide, and the thrill inside him blossomed.

"Hot? How did you . . ." she started, dropping off as if she were witnessing a natural wonder of the world.

He opened a small thermos. The waft of heat felt miraculous as he dumped half the contents onto her tinfoil. The smell made his mouth water.

"Kevin's pasta?" she said, incredulous.

He smiled. "Uh-huh. Last night I asked him if I could have some, and he said yes."

"Unbelievable." She put her face close to the noodles. "Oh my stars, it's still steaming."

His smile widened. "The trick is to warm the thermos with hot water and then dump out the water before you fill it. Retains the heat better."

She sat back with a shake of her head. "You are a wilderness wonder, Gideon Landry."

He laughed. "I'll put that on my business card and expect you to post a Yelp review of my class, even though you tanked it by scaring away my only student." Emboldened by her praise, he reached out and took her hand. "For grace," he said quietly, and she nodded.

With her cold fingers clasped in his, he prayed. He'd said grace thousands of times, mechanically, but now his words rang with a deep sense of humble gratitude. He sensed the same emotion in her amen. God had provided and they were still alive. She picked up her fork and twirled up a mouthful of pasta.

The rolling of her eyes in pleasure matched his own as they sampled a bite. He chuckled. "Gonna have to write a thank-you note to Kevin's wife when this is all over. Best pasta on the planet, has to be."

She ate a bite and forked more noodles. "Oh for sure. I

could eat pounds of it." She gazed in wonder at the next mouthful. "What do you think happened to Kevin?"

"If he was smart, he left town, unless Bullseye commanded him to try to trap us again."

She shook her head. "I just can't see him setting us up. He looked petrified at the barn, and he was going to help us escape."

"Appearances can be deceiving and alliances can shift, and Bullseye owns the town. Maybe he figured out Kevin was aiding and abetting and reached out with some not-so-friendly persuasion. Kevin might have been going to trap us in his car to prevent us from leaving."

Her expression darkened, and he strove to improve the mood. "But for now, we have hot food and a roof over our heads, so that's a win."

"And dry clothes." She saluted him with her fork. "Thanks for that too."

He ate another mouthful, trying to keep himself from wolfing it down. "Survival is as much mental as it is physical. A warm meal and a change of clothes can go a long way."

She was making his point for him, savoring each bite with such fervor he could not help but smile.

Though he could have happily packed away three times the amount, the noodles and sauce took the edge off and restored his senses. They swigged water to wash the meal down. He found an old bunch of emergency water packets that hadn't yet expired, which gave him the confidence to indulge in more hydration rations.

She went to her pack and produced the two saltwater

taffies she'd taken from Al's truck. "In honor of the occasion, I brought dessert."

"How delightful," he said. "A sure way to be invited back."

They took off the waxy wrappers, clinked the candies together, and popped them into their mouths.

"Mmm. Strawberry," he said. "Perfect."

"Root beer for me. Remember when my class sold root beer floats at school? You bought one every day."

He had, but not because he enjoyed the soda and half-melted ice cream. It was because he'd wanted to see her, something he'd never admit. He shifted on the seat and let the sticky candy dissolve on his tongue. "I think this will go down as a most memorable meal. Right up there with the carpenter ants I ate on a training mission. You have to eat a lot of those to make a dent, let me tell you."

She giggled. "And catching them must be a chore."

"Patience is required, but I prefer them to praying mantis any day."

She gaped. "Now you're just pulling my leg. A praying mantis cannot be edible."

"Kid you not. They're 58 percent protein, twelve percent fat, three percent ash, with a dash of vitamin B complex and vitamin A tossed in. The outer skeleton is a compound of sugar and amino acids. They taste okay, but man, you gotta get past the crunch factor."

She shook her head. "You really do have an encyclopedia in your head, don't you?"

He tried to appear nonchalant at the praise. "Only about survival stuff and college basketball stats."

"You've studied hard."

"Harder than anyone else." He realized it sounded arrogant. "I never wanted anyone to suffer or not make it home because I didn't know what to do."

Her hair was drying into soft waves around her cheeks, curly like she'd worn it in college. He liked it that way.

Her eyes locked on his. "And that's how you live your life, taking responsibility for people."

Her demeanor was difficult to read. Was it a dig? "No, just for myself. Everybody makes their own choices."

"And you're really choosing to leave your career behind soon. Returning to civilian life and building a business. I can't picture it."

"It's time. My family stepped up for me. So it's my turn to do the same. I'll get my survival classes started. Help my parents with the farm. Take care of Mom." He pictured his mother's worn face, the cheeks that had never regained their plumpness after the cancer treatments, the energy in her movements that had also diminished.

"How is she doing with the cancer? My mom filled me in. She said the surgery was successful and she tolerated the chemo."

And Mackenzie'd been interested enough to remember the details? "Mom's doing well. I'm going to make sure she can take it easy so it stays that way. My brothers and cousin handled things all these years while I've been in the Air Force. They made sacrifices so I could have my career."

Her smile faded. Thinking of Aaron? The military career he had and lost? The tech company he talked about constantly but hadn't lived to nurture? The drug culture he'd become prey to and part of? Anger prickled his belly. Aaron made his own choices and he'd paid for them. His sister didn't have to, and Aaron wouldn't want that anyway. Why couldn't she see that?

Don't die for his choices, Zee.

She balled up her tinfoil and put the candy wrapper in her pocket, then pushed her chair from the table. He didn't know how to make her stay.

He wanted to keep the conversation going, restore them to the easy banter that had delighted him, but he felt it slipping away. "Anyway, my days of eating praying mantis are hopefully in the past now," he said hurriedly.

Her smile returned. *There you go, Gid.*

She tapped the tinfoil ball. "I've never eaten mantis, but this has to be better."

"No question."

"Tastiest meal I ever ate." The watery moonlight plated her eyes in silver. "Thank you, Gideon." Her tone was humble and sincere with a hint of tears.

"My pleasure." And it was. He didn't remember the last time he'd felt so happy to cook for someone, if dumping and cooking could be considered the same thing. Maybe the chicken soup he'd produced for his mom after her first cancer treatment when he was on leave had come close. Every mouthful she swallowed, he counted as an enormous win, his father hovering anxiously over the process as much as Gideon and his brothers. His gaze drifted across the room to the cookbook. At present, he believed he could cheerfully polish off 365 bowls of soup. When they made it back, he'd try each and every recipe.

Mackenzie yawned, which made him do the same. Fatigue rolled over him like a landslide. They had to rest if they were to keep going. He heaved himself to his feet. It was cold, still, uncomfortably so. He chafed his arms and moved around to warm himself.

Mackenzie did a few laps, too, until they met at the map ensconced under the glass sheet.

"Some sort of terrain mapping tool?" she guessed.

"It's an old firefinder." He grazed a finger over the topographic map centered on the table. A circular rim rose up around it, marked in degrees. "You move these sights, look through the hole, and view the crosshairs in the farther sight aligned with the fire. Back in the day it was used to pinpoint the location of the blaze before there were drones and satellites and the like. Old-school but accurate."

She bent closer.

His finger tapped on a point on the map. "Here's where my Jeep's parked on the bridge."

She indicated another location with her forefinger. "And here's the airstrip."

His gut tightened. "All roads lead to Rome," he said lightly.

She stared at the two points. "With Al and Jerry on our trail, it's smarter to split up, isn't it?"

"Disagree. Never the best option for IP." He waved a hand. "Isolated personnel. We'll stick together and I'll get you to the airstrip like I promised."

"I didn't ask for that promise, if you'll recall."

Yet he'd gone ahead and made it anyway. "Like I said, I'll see you to the airstrip." And then he'd figure out how to get her home. "We travel together for now."

"For now."

Until it was all over and they parted ways. Permanently.

He put batteries in the small transistor radio from his

pack and tuned into the local weather, keeping the volume lower than the raging storm, then carried it up the bunk bed ladder with him.

The mattress was thin, the springs creaking and groaning as he settled, but his limbs were immensely comforted by the six inches of lumpy foam. Didn't matter that there was a dip in the middle from the previous occupant. There was no more comfortable bed anywhere, he was sure. He wrapped himself in the wool blanket and silently thanked God for bringing them to safety.

But if they could find the fire tower, so could Bullseye's people. They'd know their quarry would have to secure shelter.

He wondered if they were closing in right then. He set his watch alarm. He'd give himself an hour of rest and then do a security check.

And just what are you going to do if you spot Al and Jerry with guns pointed? Waiting for you and Mackenzie to come down?

One problem at a time, Gideon.

The rain pummeled the glass windows, mirroring his turbulent thoughts as he tried to force his mind away from the killers prowling below.

* *

Mackenzie expected to fall asleep in a flash. Instead she found herself staring at the bunk above her. She was amazed that Gideon had provided a hot meal. Her body still tingled with delight at those precious, succulent—and most of all, warm—mouthfuls. And the man knew the nutritional makeup of a praying mantis. Who stored that kind of information?

"I never wanted anyone to suffer or not make it home because I didn't know what to do." This from the man she'd judged for refusing to help her get justice for Aaron and failing her brother as badly as she had herself. Nothing seemed to make sense anymore; the pieces of her long-held beliefs about Aaron and Gideon no longer fit neatly together.

The storm raged, slashing at the sides of the tower. Occasional rumbles of thunder sounded before lightning lit up the space in garish neon slashes. Her thoughts rolled and rumbled too, refusing to allow her to relax.

"Gideon?" she said softly. "Are you asleep?"

"Yes," he quipped. "So don't say anything too important because I can't hear you."

She smiled and took a breath. It had to be asked. This was possibly going to be her only chance because she had no idea what would happen at the airstrip. "What did you mean when you said you couldn't cover for my brother again?" The question seemed to hover in the air, crackling like the lightning that forked the sky outside their haven.

He was silent a moment. "It's not important. Get some sleep while you can."

"I'm wide awake. Tell me. I have to know."

"Not now."

"Yes, now." When he didn't respond, she bumped the bottom of his bunk with her foot. "You must have noticed that our chances of getting out of this are growing slimmer all the time. If we actually manage to survive Al and Jerry, the dam and the wilderness, and get home, we aren't going to be having coffee or bowling together anytime soon, you and me." Especially since she'd probably be in jail. "There are hours until morning and this is the perfect time, so let's have it. All of it. Now or never."

"I don't think so, Zee."

She was going to fire with both barrels, let loose the rage she kept in check as best she could, but instead she swallowed an unexpected lump in her throat and sat up, climbed out of her bed, and rested her elbows on the side of his bunk so she could see him.

"I'm tired, Gid. Tired from everything." And her body felt suddenly as if it would quit on her at that very moment. Each mile in their journey had taken a toll, but so had everything else. The moments that had morphed into days and months and years. All of it. The truth began to pour from her like the storm.

"I've been tired for two years, since Aaron was killed. Tired of hiding and sleuthing and sneaking and cover stories and podcasts." Tired, even, of who she'd become, the avenger, the truth seeker who would use anyone and everyone to get what she was after. "I've gotten closure for others, solved their cases, but not Aaron's. I want the truth. All of it. Please, Gid. Just tell me." Why was her voice so desperate and thin? And why did it wobble when she said his name? She sighed.

There was an extended moment of silence, and she thought maybe he wouldn't speak at all until he rolled on his back, stared up at the ceiling, and cleared his throat. "Our senior year Aaron and I worked at The Dog House."

She waited for a beat when he went silent. "I know. Best gristly hot dogs in the state. Aaron always came home smelling like them. Mr. Hinkle was going to hire me when I was old enough. He promised." The portly Mr. Hinkle and his tiny bird of a wife had seemed like relics from the past. Mr. Hinkle was a giant of a man with his red suspenders, and Mrs. Hinkle hand embroidered the names of all their employees on personalized aprons and baked a cake for each and every server's birthday. She hadn't thought of the couple for years. It wasn't where she'd anticipated Gideon would start his story.

"We worked the after-school shifts."

Something else she'd already known, but she sensed he needed to lay out all the facts, to sort through the details in his mind. She would let him tell the story in his way.

"It was homecoming week, and Aaron was trying to impress some kids from our school. Fooling around, sneaking free food to them."

That was her brother. Rules rarely served him. He was the epitome of the "life of the party" even in the workplace. The trait landed him in regular trouble with teachers, principals, and as he'd aged, the police. Her parents doled out groundings, confiscated car keys, and stripped him of his phone. On each occasion, he appeared to be honestly remorseful, or at least saddened that he'd grieved them. It was difficult to be mad at Aaron for long, impossible even.

Gideon rubbed his forehead as if the memory pained him. "On their way to the big game, one of the jocks snuck into the kitchen and asked for some free fries. Aaron said yes, of course, and set some in the oil. The two of them started tossing a football around right there in the kitchen, and that's when I decided to speak up. I told them to knock it off, but Aaron got angry at me for embarrassing him. When the jock finally left, he lit into me, and things escalated. He was furious and threw a ladle that landed in the fryer and splashed hot oil everywhere. The oil caught a kitchen towel on fire, spread to the old wood cupboards, and exploded from there. Lots of grease to feed it. Everything was old and not up to code."

She tried to picture the scene as Gideon described. The fire, she'd been told, was accidental, a freak occurrence. In reality, it was her brother's fault?

"It all happened in a flash, literally."

She went completely still, listening to the sadness in his voice as he recounted the experience. Knowing Gideon, knowing Aaron, she was certain she was hearing the truth at long last.

"Mr. Hinkle was just arriving with supplies and he ran in, tripped on the threshold, and knocked himself out cold. So there we are, two teenage kids and an unconscious owner with the flames spreading and smoke everywhere. Aaron stared at me, and I'll never forget that look. He couldn't deal with the situation. Total and utter panic." Gideon shook his head. "Maybe that's enough, huh?"

"The rest," she said. "I need to know. What did my brother do?"

A gust of wind howled like a wounded animal. Gideon's next two words fell like boulders.

"He ran."

NINE

"WHAT?" SHE RIVETED ON HIS EYES, wide and solemn. "My brother ran?"

"Yes. At first I thought he'd gone to get his cell phone or the big fire extinguisher, but he didn't come back. He told me later he just panicked and took off. Left me there to deal with it."

Left his best friend to handle an emergency like that? A memory intruded of Aaron in a high school talent show with Gideon. They were performing a juggling act they'd rehearsed for hours in Gideon's parents' garage. She'd been impressed with their intricate pattern of flying bowling pins. But during the performance, Aaron had gotten a whiff of the audience's laughter when he bobbled one of the throws. He'd gone off plan then, let all the pins Gideon tossed to him drop, and he fell down as if in a faint. The audience had erupted with laughter, but she remembered Gideon's expression—startled, embarrassed, uncertain how to behave after Aaron hijacked their act. Eventually he'd offered an uncertain smile and bowed alongside

Aaron, then got offstage quickly. He'd never done another show with or without Aaron.

"Whatever made him feel good without considering the consequences."

She thought of Gideon standing on that stage after her brother commandeered their act. Gideon, left with the fallout of Aaron's decisions. What else had she overlooked, seen through a foggy lens of loyalty?

"What did you do then, Gid?"

"I dragged Mr. Hinkle outside. That was the priority over controlling the fire."

"By yourself? How?" Gideon had been a slender, wiry teen, not the muscled adult he'd become, and Mr. Hinkle was a mountain of a man.

"Not very gracefully, turns out. I fell over a chair and sustained a complex shoulder fracture. Smoke was pretty bad by then. Had to haul him by the feet with my one good arm. Not smooth, not at all. Poor guy earned more bruises than he needed to, but he survived."

Only because Gideon had stayed and helped. She put the information together with the version she'd heard from Aaron, the one he reported to the police, that Gideon had fallen and injured himself during an accidental fire trying to render aid to the owner. Her brother claimed to have been busy in the outdoor storage room when it happened and wasn't aware of the fire at first. She stayed still, willing him to continue.

His face was the barest glimmer. "Fast forward from there. My parents had minimal health insurance, and they used their savings to pay for my reconstructive surgery and a hospital stay that became way more expensive when I got an infection and wound up in the ICU for ten days. They never complained. Not once." He blinked. "Surgery, recovery, physical therapy, they were there through it all, and I was covering for Aaron the whole time. I finally told them and Mr. Hinkle the truth almost a year later, and they didn't complain then either. Neither did Mr. Hinkle. They all figured there was no gain in setting the record straight at that point."

Mackenzie's heart felt heavy, as if it were turning to stone. Gideon had been covering for her brother. The Landrys had sold some land right around then, she remembered. Several acres with one of their favorite fishing holes had been parceled out and bought by a couple for their summer home. She'd wondered at the time why they'd part with such a perfect spot.

Because they'd needed the money. Because of Aaron. She felt sick.

His voice changed. "Everything was different after the fire. For my family anyway."

Was there a hardening in his tone? A shade of resentment? Or simple regret? She couldn't tell.

"My brother Duncan wanted to go to college and play for Bama for as long as I can remember, had a partial scholarship. He delayed enrolling because of the mess I was in. Taking a gap year, he told everyone. He never wound up going. Stuck around. Eventually started working on the farm for our parents."

So many changed plans, altered lives, because of that one moment next to a vat of hot oil. "Why did you lie about it? Cover for Aaron?" She already knew but she had to ask.

"I shouldn't have. That's clear to me now, but I was a lot younger and dumber, and he was my best friend. He begged me not to tell what had really happened. He was on academic probation at school and already paying back your neighbor for sideswiping their car. He knew your parents were having problems, going through marriage counseling, and he said if he told the truth, it would do in their marriage for sure."

He might have been right. She'd heard the fighting too. Her mother and father snarling at each other, both with different ideas of how to keep their rambunctious son on track. Their fighting had reached peak levels the evening the police arrived to reveal that Aaron had smashed into the neighbor's car while driving under the influence and then fled the scene. If he'd been eighteen, he might have gone to jail. She tuned back in as Gideon continued.

"So I told everyone the oil caught on fire but not why. The Hinkles rebuilt with the insurance money, but they sold soon after. It just wasn't the same for them."

Or anybody. The entire community mourned the loss of the iconic diner. "I can't believe I never knew what really happened."

"I thought about telling you after he passed, but . . ." He sighed. "It felt as though it would cause more harm than good."

Gideon reached out a finger and touched a strand of her hair, curly from the earlier dousing. "Zee, I've had a lot of years to think about it, and I didn't do him any favors by keeping the secret. He never stood up and matured into a man who took responsibility. Maybe facing the music back then might have changed the course for him."

She opened her mouth to defend Aaron, but the words died away. Hadn't she had blinders on where her brother was concerned? Made excuses for him when he missed family events? Given him gas money even though they were both working minimum-wage jobs in high school? He'd always been her hero, her funny big brother who would do anything for her. But she'd just discovered she'd never seen him clearly. And she never would, thanks to Bullseye. And rumbling through her soul was the goodness of this man before her, the one who was loyal and loving to someone who had betrayed him. She loved Aaron because he was her brother. Gideon loved him because he chose to, in spite of his failures. Her shame felt like a cold stone dropped into her stomach.

The pain was almost too much. She turned away, staring out the glass windows into the night.

"We stayed close, but there was always that event hanging in the air between us. That's why I didn't cover for him on base when he was driving drunk. I just couldn't do it again." Gideon shifted on his bunk. "It was almost like he was relieved, finally, to be held accountable, or I thought so at first. He said he understood my decision, laughed and joked about it, said he had it coming, but then it led to his discharge, which was hard to laugh off. After that, whenever we talked, it was strained." Gideon sighed. "I should have let him grow up that day the diner burned. Maybe if I had, he wouldn't—"

"No." She cut him off despite the lump in her throat. "Aaron was who he was, even if I didn't want to see it." She took a breath. "But . . . I . . . understand better now. I . . . I'm not sure it would have made a difference in what happened if either of us had confronted him. I shouldn't have tried to guilt you about not talking to him, or into helping me with the podcast." She shook her head. "I'm sorry I dumped that all on you."

Gideon let out a low breath. "Thank you for saying that. I know it wasn't easy." The wind rattled the sturdy roof, and rain continued to assault their pocket of safety. Slowly she reached out her hand.

He took it, squeezing her fingers as they listened to the storm, lost in their own thoughts.

"Zee, I've been wondering if maybe there was more to Aaron's death than a drug deal gone bad."

"What do you mean?"

"I didn't see any signs that he was using, did you?"

"No."

"Physical indications, stealing from you or your parents, loss of motivation."

She pulled her hand away. "But I'm beginning to think I didn't see him clearly at all."

"Did they recover any drugs at the scene?"

"Not on Aaron. Only a small amount on the body of the dealer after he was hit by the truck."

"Was Aaron carrying a lot of cash?"

"No."

"Is it . . . possible he wasn't just looking to score drugs?" he asked softly. "Maybe he was dealing them and the man who killed him was an intermediary? There was some sort of disagreement between them?"

No, she wanted to say. *My brother wouldn't do that*. But she thought about the condominium Aaron had rented, the nice car he'd bought, the presents for Leah, the girlfriend he'd never brought around. They'd all been funded with proceeds from his tech start-up, he'd told her—but he'd still been pulling all-nighters peering at his computer as if he were trying to breathe life into a dead animal. There had been flashes of concern on his face, now and then, that he quickly glossed over—concern that bordered on fear. It was unlike her brother, who always landed on his feet no matter what the situation.

She'd found him on the back patio one night, smoking the cigarettes he'd promised their mother he'd quit. The phone was pressed to his ear, and he hadn't heard her coming.

"I'm a little short, is all. Figured I'd have it covered by now. I just need a few months. My business is so close to taking off, I can taste it. Couple more deals and I'll be there. Then we can make bigger plans."

When he'd heard Mackenzie's approach, he startled like a deer, flashed her a jaunty smile, and covered the phone with his palm.

"Boring business stuff, Zee," he'd said before he walked off to finish his call. But she'd noticed his hand was shaking as he covered the speaker.

The sneaked cigarette, the secrets, the desperation. What was Aaron willing to do to make his dreams come true? Sell drugs? Work for a man who'd polluted a community? The walls seemed to grow closer. She blinked to find Gideon had climbed out of the bunk and was facing her, arms folded.

"Was Aaron dealing, Zee?"

"I'm not sure."

"I think you are."

She looked away. "You don't know what I think, so don't pretend you do."

"You were almost a cop. You saw the signs in your brother's behavior, I can tell by the look on your face. You didn't recognize them for what they were, maybe, but now you do."

She stalked away a few steps. "So what if he was, Gideon? None of this matters anyway. My brother was murdered."

"I know that, but it *does* matter."

She whirled on him. "Why? Are you implying he deserved what he got because he might have been dealing drugs?"

"No, you're picking a fight to derail this conversation."

The blood rushed to her face. "I'm not derailing anything."

"Yes, you are. Know what I think?"

She tipped up her chin. "No, do tell. What does Gideon Landry think?"

He took a breath, his words softer than a caress. "I think you feel guilty, deep down, like his death is somehow your fault because of what you saw or didn't see. You haven't dug into Aaron's motivations with the same vigor you do other cases because you don't want to know."

She flinched. Anger felt like a live wire touching her tender skin. She burned with it as she glared at him. "Really? Well, maybe it's the opposite. Maybe *you* don't want to feel the guilt of not showing up for him."

"I've got my share of guilt. Always will, both for what I didn't do in high school and when I came home that Christmas. I'm not dumping guilt on you, Zee, that's not what I'm after. I just want you to see what you're doing to yourself."

She folded her arms, not trusting herself to speak. She wished she was anywhere but here with the emotions popcorning inside and threatening to break through the thin crust of her resolve. This was about justice, nothing more or less.

"For what it's worth," he said, "it's hard to see the truth about people you love. I didn't want to acknowledge anything bad about Aaron either. I loved him, and nothing he did or didn't do will change that. If he messed up, got involved with dangerous people, that was his choice. But it doesn't have to be yours."

Unable to face him, she stared out the window, his reflection joined with hers.

"This conversation isn't changing anything," she managed. "I'm sorry my brother behaved badly during high school. I'm sorry he might have been dealing drugs, but none of that earned him a bullet in the head. I am going to make sure Aaron's death wasn't meaningless. I'm going to destroy Bullseye. Nothing has changed."

She was breathing hard, trembling, fighting tears.

"But it could, Zee. You could change things." He touched her shoulder, and she froze. She could not, would not, turn around and look at him.

"Your mission is going to get you dead. Can't you see that?"

Face hot, she gritted her teeth. "I don't want to die, but it's a price I'm willing to pay."

He squeezed her shoulder hard, his breath warm on her cheek. "You shouldn't be. God will bring justice in this world or the next. In his time, not yours. You weren't responsible for Aaron's death. I wasn't either. Don't let your guilt cost you your life. It's not worth it."

His hand dropped away, and she stood there in the dark and frigid space, mind reeling, spirit crushed. It was as if she hadn't grieved her brother until that moment, until she'd learned the truth of who he was and what he'd done. Maybe she'd only grieved the caricature of Aaron, the funny little sketch of him she'd allowed herself to see. Happy, bubbly, amusing, generous, drug-dealing Aaron.

Above anything else, she felt a terrible pain that Aaron hadn't shown her who he really was, the insecurity that made him need friends so badly, the desperation that caused him to seek out Bullseye's easy money.

Why didn't you let me in, Aaron?

I loved you. Why didn't you let me help?

She didn't realize she was crying until she felt Gideon drape a blanket around her shoulders and hold her close.

She let him, for just a moment, until she curled in on herself and he guided her to her bunk.

"Get some rest, Zee," he whispered.

She didn't have the strength to resist anymore. Like a child, she allowed herself to be tucked onto the cot, the blanket settled over her. He stayed there for a while, praying, she suspected.

She should pray too, for the agony to diminish, for peace in her soul. For something to make sense to her shredded heart.

But she prayed something else instead.

God, help me find Bullseye and destroy him.

Because the only thing she could feel under the grief was her soul burning for revenge.

It was all she had left.

The only thing that made sense.

••••••••••••••••••••••

Gideon slept some, maintained a recon schedule every few hours, and fretted in between. Why had he allowed himself to get into the weeds about Aaron? And while they were in such a precarious position. Mackenzie thought she wanted the information, but how had that helped in the slightest? Now her image of her brother was tarnished, and bringing up the whole drug-dealing thing? Was it really important for her to know that, even if it was the truth? Aaron was dead. Nothing could alter that awful fact.

Restless, he walked around the tower again, avoiding the squeakiest boards he'd identified during previous rounds, his portable radio pressed to his ear as he listened to reports. There were no encouraging factoids at the lonely hour of four thirty in the morning. The storm hadn't let up and the weather reports called for four inches of rain in the next eight hours. He spent the following hours planning, trying to decide if it was better to depart at dawn or hold out and give themselves another few hours to rest when a new alert came over the radio. He listened, standing at the window, looking down on the valley, his heart sinking with every word.

"*In an effort to avert catastrophe . . .*" He was running for his boots before the report was finished. His pack was already full, organized and filled with his still-damp clothes and the meager items he'd acquired from their hiding spot.

Mackenzie raised her head from the cot, her hair a wild tangle. "What?"

"We gotta go."

She sat up. "Why?"

"Emergency alert. They're going to release water at ten this morning to try to save the dam from crumbling. We've got a few hours to get out of this valley or we'll be swimming."

She hopped out of bed and scurried to pack her supplies.

He tossed her a bundle. "Here. Another fire tower goody."

She hefted the clear rain poncho. "Did you find one for yourself too?"

"No, just the one. My pants are water resistant, but those sweats are going to soak up the rain as soon as we step outside. The poncho will cover down to your knees."

"It's okay, you wear it."

Rejecting it, rejecting him. "Just put it on, Mackenzie." His clipped tone produced the desired result, though she gave him a sour look.

It would be unwise to delay for breakfast or anything else. It would take hours for them to climb down and trek their way out of the lowlands. The whole expedition would be perilous from the get-go, hiking the wilderness in the dark. But if they didn't beat the water, it was lights out anyway. He was sore and tired, but at least Mackenzie had gotten some sleep.

After they each used the waste bucket again, she yanked

her hair back into an elastic, jammed on a baseball cap she'd found under the bunk, and donned the plastic rain gear. The poncho sleeves could be rolled up, which helped, and her borrowed boots would be better than Kevin's wife's sneakers. It would have to be enough.

They didn't need to discuss their goals.

For him, the Jeep. For her, the airstrip.

And he would get her there if she'd allow it. He was no longer sure since their frank conversation. He wouldn't be surprised if she took off on her own at the first opportunity, because in presenting her with the truth about Aaron, he'd broken something inside her.

Lord, I'm sorry. He'd thought the truth would set her free from her deadly pursuit.

Instead, it seemed it had only sped her on her way.

Focus, Gid. For now, they were together and moving in unison. It remained to be seen how long their synchronicity would last.

"Ready?" He grasped the door handle.

She didn't look ready to face the tempest. It struck him how small she was. She looked like a beautiful bird, fragile yet fierce, unable to fly but unwilling to give up. He wanted to slam the door, wrap her in an embrace, and hold her there until they both felt the warmth of it. But there was no affection in her eyes, only stony strength that masked a fathomless pain.

"Yes," she said, and he lifted the latch.

The gust would have ripped the handle from his grasp if he hadn't been braced against it. An out-and-out wail of wind and moisture slashed at them. The trapdoor was next, and then they were climbing down, holding each rung in a death grip as they descended.

He'd gone first, not that there was much he could do to protect Mackenzie if Al and Jerry were waiting in the tempest to pick them off. The skin between his shoulder blades crawled. Nothing like clinging to a ladder a hundred feet in the air to underscore a person's vulnerability.

"Gideon."

He jerked a look up. She clung there with the raincoat flying around her as if she were the figurehead on a ship lashed by a typhoon. Her first attempt at communication was snatched by the wind, but he caught the second.

"Car."

He stared in the direction she pointed, where a slender trail snaked in loops through thick trees. That was all he saw, trees, until a quick flash of movement, the bare flicker of metal mingling with a drop of moonlight. Truck or car, he couldn't be sure.

His chest went tight. The vehicle was probably two miles in the distance, but that safe cushion wouldn't last.

They scrambled as fast as they could down the ladder. It was only minutes, but it felt like days before his boots hit the bottom, squelching into the mud that threatened to grab hold.

She landed next, more gracefully.

They dashed to the slight shelter of a gnarled oak.

Mackenzie's eyes were wide but not panicked. "If we take the trail we planned, they'll catch us."

"Agreed, but deviating will cost us more time in this valley."

She nodded. "We have to risk it. Retrace our steps back to the stable and get to the bridge from that direction."

"You realize we'll be heading right into the path of our pursuers and the people who probably betrayed us."

"That's what you're good at, right? All this tactical stuff?"

He quirked a grin at her. Survive, evade . . . He hoped there would be no need for resistance because on that count they were outmanned, outgunned, and surrounded. Talk about surviving in enemy territory. "Yes, ma'am. That's it exactly. We're going to evade them in the most unexpected way possible."

Onward they trudged, sticking to the woods as much as they could. The sun rose, lifted higher in the sky, but the light was so weak, it was as if it were in a permanent state of withdrawal. Without his waterproof watch, he would have lost all sense of time, but his stomach reminded him that they'd missed breakfast and his feet throbbed from traversing the long stretches of uneven ground. There could be no stopping if they were to outrace the water release.

After they diverted around a partial ground failure, he brought out his compass and surveyed the most direct route. There was no way to tell what specific obstacles lay in their path, topographical or human. One thing was for sure. Time was as big an enemy as Bullseye's men.

He settled his cap more firmly on his brow.

"Let's pick up the pace, shall we?" He'd hardly gotten the comment out of his mouth when everything changed.

TEN

MACKENZIE DARTED A LOOK at the sky, but Gideon was already pulling her toward the shrubs as a helicopter rumbled through the clouds. The machine was light and agile as a dragonfly, dipping to the right and left, rain gleaming on its sides. When it flew closer, she caught a glimpse of a person in the rear, leaning out the open door, tethered, binoculars scanning, a rifle pinched under his arm.

"Bullseye's got helicopters at his disposal? How big is his budget anyway?" Gideon snapped.

"You don't want to know." She scanned frantically for a hiding place as they ran.

The thickly clustered trees at the edge of a hollow beckoned, but the wide oblong of tall grass meant they would be spotted and shot well before they reached it. Gideon was urging her toward a dip in the ground where an oak tree had fallen long ago, the bark crumbling from the decaying branches.

He dove behind the tangle of wood that rose only about two feet above the grass line and she followed. How was this going to help?

"Arms up," he said.

Bewildered, she did as she was told and he pulled off her poncho, rolled it into a ball, and stuffed it under his jacket.

"Scrunch down as much as you can."

Grass and twigs caught in her hair as she made herself as flat as possible on the sodden earth. He flopped down next to her and heaved some branches over them, caging them as they burrowed like forest animals into the crackling debris.

"Close your eyes," he whispered. "And don't move."

That went without saying. She shut her eyes, the darkness more terrifying than the enemies. The rotors spun debris into a whirlwind that spattered her body. Would the air disturbance blow away their sheltering branches and leave them exposed? Had they been spotted despite the last-second hiding spot?

She clung to Gideon's jacket front, his arms holding her tight. The soggy ground underneath them quaked with the force of the vibrations. Judging from the deafening roar, the helicopter had to be directly over them. The noise shuddered right through her, threatening to blast away her remaining self-control.

Just hold on. That's all you can do.

Something moved under her hip. A snake? Her muscles turned steel-taut as she fought hard not to scream. They'd no doubt flung themselves right on top of whatever creepy-crawlies called the decaying tree home. Visions of reptiles and spiders danced in her brain. She tried for calming breaths, telling herself she'd take her chances with vermin and insects any day over the predators in the sky. But the stinging, biting, slithering . . .

The helicopter swooped lower, and the whoosh from the rotor thwapping the air vibrated her teeth. Had their location been pinpointed and the craft was about to land, freeing men to execute them?

Again she felt the movement against her body, but this time she identified it.

Not an animal or insect.

Her phone.

The ringer was on silent, but it could be nothing else pulsing in that regular rhythm. A cell signal was possible? Here? Now? Her fingers clenched, her desire to answer overpowering.

But she dared not. It was too risky even to check the screen because now she heard voices from the helicopter shouting to each other through their radios, cutting in and out.

"Negative, I don't see them . . . but they're close. They've . . . fire tower . . . Soon."

Move away, she silently demanded as her phone vibrated again. *Go search for your prey somewhere else.*

The helicopter dipped closer, and she was desperate to look, but she kept her eyes closed and her face hidden in Gideon's chest. His rapid heartbeat told her he was as stressed as she, but he was motionless, his arms strong and reassuring.

Another pulse from her cell.

The phone went still.

She wanted to scream. Still the men hovered above, scanning for her and Gideon, two rabbits tracked by the falcon.

An eternity later the helicopter roared away. Gideon did

not loosen his grip. "Stay still for a few more minutes, just to be sure," he whispered in her ear.

At last when he relaxed his hold and eased to a sitting position, she did the same and grabbed her phone.

"I got a call. Someone left a voicemail." She peered at the screen.

Then everything felt very far away, as if she'd been snipped from the bonds of gravity, floating free.

"What?" Gideon said. "What's wrong?"

"It's . . . The call . . . It's from Aaron's cell phone."

His shock mirrored her own. "How?"

She had no answer. The call had come from her brother's number. It was inconceivable.

"Was . . . Did Aaron have a phone on him when he was killed?"

"He told us the day before the murder he'd lost his phone. I don't think he had an opportunity to get a new one before the murder."

Gideon seemed to mull it over as he grabbed his own phone. "I can't make an outgoing call. Can you?"

She forced herself to check. "No."

"Texts won't send either, but someone managed to get through to you." He watched as she pushed the playback button and held the phone between them so he could hear too.

Her heart pounded as he pressed close. Aaron's phone . . . his number.

The message was staticky and garbled, indecipherable the first time, so she pressed the button again. "Is that a woman or a man?"

"Not sure, maybe even a teen, but I can't understand what's being said. Only the last two words."

His breath hitched in her ear as the message replayed.

"Trust me."

Gideon frowned as he got to his feet. "Trust who?"

Mackenzie was dizzied. "How did someone get his cell? And why would they call us?"

"If Aaron was dealing for Bullseye, it's possible he got Aaron's phone somehow. Cloned it, maybe."

She stared at her phone as if it could provide some answers. "It definitely wasn't Bullseye in the message." She groaned. "Why can't we get a signal now when we got one two seconds ago? Phones are completely maddening."

"Agreed. Maybe when we reach higher ground." He was scanning the scattered debris under his boots.

"Has the plan changed?" she said.

"Only that we'll have to move slower and more carefully and stay in the trees as much as possible. We'll parallel the trail but keep out of the open." He checked his watch. "It'll be close, because in another hour we have to be clear of this valley."

"Which way?"

He pointed to the steep, densely wooded slope, and her body sagged.

"Straight up and no roads?"

"I'm afraid so."

She bit back a sigh and took off her pack to shake away the debris that had snagged on the fabric as he bent to retrieve something.

"Hold up," he said.

Before she realized what he was planning, he'd scooped a handful of mud and smeared it on her face, then his own.

The cold goop was clammy and smelled of moldering things. It was all she could do to resist a shudder as she glared at him.

"I hope that was a real important survival tactic, buddy," she snapped through clenched teeth.

He smiled and removed the rain poncho from under his jacket. "Same issue as with this. Shine. It's one of the things that gives people away when they're trying to hide. Movement, position, shape, shadow, shine . . . et cetera, basically anything that stands out to the enemy." He fingered the slippery poncho. "Shine where it shouldn't be is like a beacon to point them right to us. Nothing shinier than a beautiful woman."

She blinked. Did he just say she was beautiful? She laughed nervously. "You probably say that to all the girls after you smear them with mud."

"Only when it's true," he said. Was he blushing under his mud face paint? "Um, anyway, so it's, you know, important to work the camouflage as much as we can, now that they're hunting us from the air too."

"Okay. I accept that, but you didn't have to look so happy about sliming me."

His grin was full of the mischief of a high school boy. "Gotta get the entertainment where you can, you know?"

"Right." They'd restored the easy balance between them, but the word still rang in her ears. *Beautiful*. It made no sense that he'd say it, or that it would quiver like an arrow in her heart. She was unraveling, that was it. The call from Aaron's phone had shaken her, left her off-balance.

Gideon busied himself snatching up a leafy branch and scouring the ground with it to smooth over where they'd left boot prints. When he was done, he threw around some twigs to cover those they'd broken in their landing.

"We have to stay vigilant with Bullseye's guys so close. They probably figured out we sheltered in the fire tower, and since we're on foot, it won't be hard to narrow down the search grid."

She groaned. "The current head count is one in a vehicle, two in a chopper, Al and Jerry, possibly Kevin and Cordelia, and who knows how many more out there beating the bushes for us."

"Not to mention the caller. Dunno if they're friend or foe." Gideon walked back over to her and picked a twig out of her hair. "But it doesn't matter how many are looking for us. We're going to be careful, and we're smarter than they are."

"Such confidence."

"That's not usually something you lack." He paused. "Still planning to get to the airstrip?"

She nodded and pulled on her pack. As they hurried through the brush toward a steep, rocky rise, she wondered again at the phone call.

Aaron's cell number on her screen.

"Trust me."

Who?

As the climb became more excruciating, it consumed her concentration. The rocks were slippery, the ground treacherous with protruding roots and mud. In some places, they had to hold on to those roots to haul themselves over places where the ground had washed away.

In other circumstances, the landscape would have been breathtakingly beautiful—verdant, pristine, like an untouched paradise.

A thought hit her so suddenly she almost lost her balance and slid down the slope.

"What?" Gideon said, scanning in all directions. "Why'd you stop?"

"Aaron came here."

"Here, where?"

"To Oakleaf, to this town."

"How do you know that?"

"He showed me photos on his phone. I remember now that one of them showed a slice of valley taken from a dam. Had to be the Cotton Flower."

"So Aaron was here? I'm not sure I understand the implications."

Mackenzie felt her throat clog. "I . . . guess it's more evidence that you were right and he lied to me. He really was a drug dealer, working for Bullseye." The cold and pain and exhaustion felt like an avalanche. "That's the only reason I can think of."

"Likely he never met Bullseye, though, being lower down on the food chain. He might have come here for a vetting process, or maybe to pick up his stashes sometimes." He paused. "Is it possible he got to know people here in town?"

"He was gone a lot. Every few weeks. He said he was away on business, but his car would come back filthy as if he'd been somewhere rural." Here, to Oakleaf. She was sure of it.

"Every few weeks? That's a vigorous schedule."

She fell silent. "I look like my brother."

Gideon gave her a peripheral look. "Spitting image. So?"

"People who knew him would see we were related."

"Yes," he said slowly.

"Kevin stared at me for a long time. I thought it was because of the weird circumstances, but what if he was a friend of Aaron's?"

"Why wouldn't he say so?"

She considered. "If Aaron had an ally here in town, I sure wish we knew who it was, because the forces against us are multiplying by the minute."

He urged them on, up the steep hillside, and she lugged herself after him. What did it mean, that Aaron had been in Oakleaf? *"Trust me."* What if he had a trustworthy acquaintance or friend in town? Someone not loyal to Bullseye? Maybe that was how his phone had changed hands?

Was there someone in this treacherous situation they could actually rely on?

They stopped to drink in the shelter of a pine. A hundred yards from their position, a river plunged along a rocky chasm toward the valley below. It was full, raging even, and she imagined what it would be like to be swallowed up, like she'd almost been in the prison van. She would not have the fight in her to resist next time.

The air had grown thinner as the altitude increased, leaving her panting. Every second was precious. As she stepped over a twisted root, a stream of pebbles shook loose and rolled down the slope.

They both felt the vibrations.

Helicopter, she thought, stomach flipping. But the roar that filled the air was much bigger than the sound of rotor blades. The rumble sounded like the end of the world.

They locked eyes.

"It's ten o'clock," Gideon said, his face pale under the splotches of mud.

Her throat went dry. "Have we made it high enough?"

"We're about to find out."

The situation was bizarre, almost inconceivable. Wordlessly, she moved with Gideon, inching backward until their shoulders pressed against a pine tree with a trunk as big around as a tractor tire.

At first, it appeared only as if the river was bubbling due to a violent wind, slapping and swirling, the incoming flow too subtle to be detected. Moment by moment the level increased along with the turbulence, the volume of water burgeoning as if they were watching a time-lapse film.

The approaching surge gobbled up the streambed and reached almost to the lip. How much more could the riverbed accommodate before it spilled over to devour more ground, including the patch they stood on?

Her nails bit into her palms as they waited. The mass held steady for a moment and she thought they might be okay—until it slopped over the channel, first in a tiny ripple that soon morphed into a wall of water flooding over.

Her brain told her to run, claw her way up the rocky slope, climb the tree, do whatever was necessary to escape the wave of destruction, but she knew it was futile.

She reached for Gideon's hand, their intertwined fingers tight.

Closer the water crept, making the ground disappear. Solid one moment, covered the next.

Like a liquid avalanche it sped toward them in a terrifying rush, pooling briefly in dips of the terrain before overflowing and continuing its mad progress.

Now only yards separated them from the flood.

Now feet.

The relentless progress left them no choices, but Gideon tugged at her elbow.

"Up." His voice was raw as he cupped his hands and bent over. She stepped into his palms, and he boosted her up to the lowest branch. Painfully she hoisted herself over the limb and into a crouch before she reached down to grab for him.

"I'm too heavy. I'll pull you off," he said, refusing. The water was racing toward him, seconds away.

She grabbed his wrist, and before he could protest, began to pull him up.

His weight almost took her over, but she looped an elbow around a side branch of the sturdy limb. Muscles and bones protesting, she held on until he'd swung up next to her.

The water raged higher, gobbling the tree.

Gideon looked above them, his expression desperate. The higher branches were widely spaced, likely too flimsy to hold their weight even if they could reach. Clinging to the rough bark, they watched and prayed as the flood began to reach their position.

She'd thought going over the bridge in the van had been the scariest moment of her life, but this was worse because she was witness to the whole event—the inch by inch march of deadly water. They'd swim, both of them, fight with every last breath, but it was unlikely they'd survive.

She looked at Gideon, the amber of his eyes, the tumbled dark hair.

He'd said she was beautiful. Would he still think so as the water invaded his lungs and stripped his life away?

The pine needles dancing on the surface of the water twirled and tangled, and she suddenly realized the water was no longer rising. Or maybe it was a trick of her eyes? But the wondrous expression on Gideon's face helped her believe it.

"Thank you, God," Gideon said with a pump of his fist.

Her brain was turning in circles trying to comprehend that the massive flow was not going to overwhelm their perch. Her fingers were rigid from her death grip on the branch, and she had to force them to relax their hold.

"I'll second that." She stared at the glittering surface and the circling pine needles. "Is it . . . is the water getting lower or am I dreaming that up?"

"No, you're right."

Gradually, incrementally, the gurgling swirl receded a few feet.

"Finding its way, settling into whatever creeks and gullies aren't already full. We'll wait a little while and see how it all levels out, okay?"

An excellent idea since her body felt paralyzed with the shock of their escape. She straightened cautiously so she could sit with her back against the trunk, astride the branch as if she were riding a horse. He sat opposite her, one hand holding the stubby limb she'd used minutes before to help him climb up.

He carefully maneuvered to extract a packet that he handed to her. "Protein bars. My last two. I was saving them for a special occasion."

She laughed. "We're really going to have a snack while sitting on a branch?"

He tore open his own protein bar wrapper and took a bite. "Really, can you think of a more memorable place to share a meal?"

She couldn't.

"As a matter of fact . . ." He grabbed his phone and extended his arm, leaning his face close to hers.

"Are you taking a selfie?"

"Say cheese."

With a giggle she complied. Was this actually happening? Two days ago she never would have conceived of the things that had taken place, not the least of which was the fact that in that moment she was pleased to be taking a selfie with the man she'd recently detested. Gideon had enabled her to see the truth about Aaron, and though it stung like battery acid, it helped to know that Gideon loved her brother too, in spite of what Aaron had run away from in high school, and regardless of his work for Bullseye.

Gideon examined the photo, pleased.

The words came rushing out. "Gideon, I'm sorry about how I've treated you."

He cocked his head at her. "You've said you're sorry. You're forgiven."

She saw in his face that he meant it. For some inconceivable reason, he actually seemed to have moved past his own anger. He was a better person than she—more forgiving than she'd ever realized, more kind than she'd allowed herself to believe.

How did she feel about him now? He wasn't to blame for what happened to Aaron or for not helping her when she'd asked, and she'd been wrong to pin her fury on him. So what exactly was she doing in a tree, risking both their lives? Everything inside seemed to go wobbly at that moment, and she clenched her fists to remind herself of her mission.

The swirling water offered a distorted reflection back to her. She and Gideon looked like two thrill-seeking teenagers as they sat above the floodwaters, ate protein bars, and tried to figure out what their next step should be.

....

He should have been uncomfortable, concerned, obsessing about their newest predicament, but Gideon felt an illogical sense of euphoria sitting on that tree next to Mackenzie. There could be no stranger situation. Since he'd told her the truth about the fire in high school and they'd voiced aloud their conclusion that Aaron was likely dealing for Bullseye, he felt unburdened, light, that he could share space with Mackenzie with no lies between them.

And she appeared a bit less guarded with him, or so he imagined. Perhaps even welcoming of his presence? His young adult crush, sitting with him in a tree, sharing a smile with him.

Doesn't mean she feels any kind of way, Gid. Don't fool yourself.

He wouldn't.

This wasn't a path forward with a woman he'd pined for in his boyhood.

This was survival. Period. But at least they weren't enemies anymore.

Next steps. He surveyed the submerged terrain. "Water's only a couple feet deep now. We can drop down and veer to the east. It's drier there, more stable."

"Ugh. More water."

"Unavoidable."

"I was hoping you had an inflatable raft stowed in your gear."

"Sadly, no."

She finished her protein bar and shot a wary glance at the clouds. "Do you think they've moved on to search a different area? Or decided we got swept away in the water release?"

"That'd be great but honestly unlikely. They're pretty committed to the cause."

"The cause of killing us."

"Bullseye made that pretty clear. I think he's the type to require visual proof that we've been eliminated. Until then . . ." He let the sentence remain unfinished as he cinched his pack and pointed to the ground. "On three?"

She scooched to the edge of the limb with a shiver. "And I just started to dry out."

"The clothes in our packs should be drier, and if we packaged them well, they'll be okay to switch out as soon as we get out of this valley. The phones are bagged again too."

"Are you always so cheerful when slogging through the wilderness?"

Only with you. He stopped himself a split second before that fell out of his mouth. Bad enough he'd already told her he thought she was beautiful. *Remember forty-eight hours ago when she drove away your client and took your wallet?*

He settled for a shrug. "Doesn't hurt to keep up morale. It's a key factor in survival." That sounded pretentious enough. Before he could add anything else, he jumped off the limb and landed waist deep in water so cold he almost screeched.

"Chilly?" she teased.

"Balmy. For a polar bear."

She splashed down next to him with a squeal. He trudged off and she followed. The watery slog lasted about a half hour until they climbed high enough to leave it behind. On the positive side, the rain had diminished to occasional drizzles as they dropped down onto the other side of the valley.

"The main road would get us to the bridge in two hours, but . . ."

"I know," Mackenzie said. "We have to take the less obvious path."

"Stealth for health."

"I'm beginning to dislike these witty slogans," she grumped.

They stopped to change out their sodden clothes for the almost dry ones in their packs. It was a chilly process, even with the trees for a windbreak. When she emerged from her turn, she shook her phone disconsolately.

"No signal for me either," he confirmed. The journey was taking far too long as the cold sapped their strength.

Their trek felt endless, his limbs wooden. Twice they

feared they heard the helicopter returning, but it didn't come close enough for them to spot it. The trees were working in their favor.

Their rest periods grew longer and longer, and their pace slowed to a creep until they neared the winding road that would take them to the bridge.

Mackenzie brightened. "Almost to the Jeep."

"There's a hiking trail between us and it. One more set of switchbacks and we'll be at the bridge. Probably another two hours."

She huffed out a breath. "Two hours is not 'almost there.'"

"Sorry. Trying to stay positive."

She chewed her bottom lip. "What if they moved your Jeep? Towed it away?"

"I don't think they'd bother since the road is closed and I wasn't obstructing anything. If they did, we'll be close enough to town to get another ride, if there's anyone left to hook us up. What about your car? At the hotel?"

"I left it at the train station in Clover and took a cab."

"Thought you might have grown a tail?"

"Can't be too certain. Lots of people seem to be on the lookout for me." She frowned. Was she thinking about the fact that the cops would be eager to take her back into custody? The thought occurred to him that it might be the safest thing for Mackenzie, if they were to encounter an officer. Hopefully she'd be protected in jail, from Bullseye and from herself.

He was still thinking about the notion when a brown bird streaked from the bushes five feet ahead. He stopped abruptly. "Something startled it."

But the forest again subsided into quiet broken only by the dripping leaves. When there was no more indication of danger, he moved on, but his nerves stayed knotted.

Something didn't feel right.

The moments blended in an uncomfortable blur, their plodding pace making the hour stretch endlessly on. They stopped only briefly for sips of water and sprinkles of quick-energy sugar from the packets he'd taken at the lookout. Neither wanted to prolong the agony by stopping too long.

The Jeep. Once he got it back, they'd have a much better chance at survival.

They approached another switchback, and the faint hiking trail they were following vanished into a turn screened by windblown trees.

When she stopped to adjust her boot, he touched her shoulder. "Wait here. I'm going to check ahead." She nodded wearily.

He hadn't made it more than fifteen feet when an ATV appeared around the turn.

ELEVEN

MACKENZIE'S STOMACH DROPPED. The ATV advanced slowly as Gideon retreated until he'd rejoined her. The vehicle continued toward them. When it was only a few yards away, wheels churning up mud and small rocks, Gideon shoved Mackenzie behind him. "Run," he told her. "I'll try to slow him down."

But the ATV shuddered to a stop and the door was flung open.

Her jaw dropped as Kevin climbed out. His face was sweat-streaked and there was a rip in the knee of his jeans.

He was wearing the waterproof jacket and hat he'd been in when they'd driven to the stables, but he was haggard, dark circles under his eyes, his lips trembling.

"I've been looking for you all night. Thank God you're okay." He pressed a hand to his heart. "Thought those guys got you at the stables."

"We thought the same," Gideon said. "And we figured you'd led us right into a trap."

"I didn't."

"Really? What happened to you after we stole the truck?" Mackenzie asked.

"Soon as they took off after you, I beat it out of there right behind Cordelia and her trailer."

Mackenzie studied him. Friend or foe? She hadn't decided. "If you weren't helping them, how'd they know we were coming?"

"I dunno. Cordelia maybe?"

"Is she loyal to Bullseye?"

He blinked. "Who's that?"

She frowned. "The drug runner who owns everyone in this town, according to local legend."

"Never heard that name before."

He didn't quite meet her eyes. "Well, what name *have* you heard, Kevin?"

"What do you mean?"

Gideon took over. "Small town, like you said. Who's the power player in these parts? You must know."

Kevin shrugged. "Nah. I stick to myself and that keeps me out of trouble, but you got somebody mad at you and that's the truth. Made me feel horrible to think of you two wandering around with no help or shelter, and I decided I'd try to find you if I could. Honestly, though, I was just about to cut bait and get out of town, but I figured I'd wait another hour and see if you showed up here." He smiled. "I knew you'd come back to get your Jeep. You said as much."

Mackenzie decided to try a different approach. "Did you know my brother, Aaron Bardine?"

Kevin rubbed a hand over his stubbled jaw. "Your brother? I don't think so. Why would I?"

She could detect no tell that Kevin was lying. "He visited here."

"Hmm. Like I said, I stick to myself. If he was a young fella, probably popped into the tavern where there's live music, but I wouldn't have seen him there." He laughed. "My wife wouldn't cotton to me hanging out in a place like that." He looked them over. "You two haven't had an easy time of it since you left, have you?"

"No." Gideon was still scanning warily. "We've narrowly avoided a few ambushes like we did at the stables."

Kevin whistled. "Hard to believe."

"It certainly is." Mackenzie glowered at him. "The people trying to kill us seem to be one step ahead. You sure you didn't have anything to do with that?"

"What are you accusing me of?"

"That you know full well the guy who owns this town and you've been doing your best to help him catch us," she snapped.

Kevin puffed up, stabbing a thick pointer finger in her direction. "Like I said, I only have one priority and that's my family, okay? I shared our home and our meal with you and came here to give you a ride out of town because you're gonna get yourself killed one way or the other. If you don't want my help, so be it. At least I can sleep tonight knowing I tried." He spun on his heel and stalked back to the ATV.

Gideon looked at Mackenzie. She knew what he was asking. The same question they'd considered before. Was Kevin a man to be trusted or not? They required additional information, but more than that, they desperately needed a ride.

"Wait," Mackenzie said.

Kevin stopped and turned, his expression stony.

"I'm sorry for accusing you. We've had a very bad couple of days. We'd appreciate it if you could give us a ride to the bridge."

Kevin hesitated for a minute. "All right. Get in."

"Thank you," Mackenzie said.

"I'll take the back seat." Gideon followed her to Kevin's ATV and clasped her forearm. His pressure told the story. *Don't let your guard down.*

A ride to the bridge and they'd separate. It was a risk worth taking, she'd decided, a way to save them arduous hiking.

She climbed into the front and Gideon behind the driver. Her heart pounded against her ribs.

Kevin looked profoundly relieved once he fired up the engine.

"I can't believe I found you. I've been trying to track you since we got separated at the stables." He laughed, which ended in a wheeze. "You've covered some miles, I'll give you that."

Gideon cocked his head. "How did you know where and when to intercept us?"

"It wasn't easy. Cordelia called me to make sure I'd gotten away from those two thugs."

Suspicion threaded Gideon's reply. "Do you know who they are?"

"Uh-uh. Maybe hired help from out of town? You made somebody real mad around here."

Gideon prompted him to continue. "So you and Cordelia talked?"

He grinned. "Mostly I listened. She was steaming mad about the attack near her horses. Probably she'd take it harder if a horse got hurt than a human. Anyway, she took a guess which direction you took. I had to get the ATV because I didn't think my rig could take the terrain, so I lost time. Found a disabled white truck though. Your handiwork?"

"Possibly," Gideon said. "You caught our trail?"

"No. You did a good job concealing your direction, and let's face it, I'm no bloodhound. You said you were heading to town, and of course you'd go for your vehicle. I figured that was the best way to find you. Found it sitting right where you left it, and I've been up on the bluff with my binoculars where I could see the whole approach on and off for two days. I headed for high ground when they released some water, and man, it almost swallowed up the bridge for a minute, but those engineers know what they're doing. I figured I'd give it until afternoon and then assume you'd drowned somewhere along the way."

Mackenzie was relieved to hear that Gideon's Jeep hadn't been moved. The idea of traveling the rest of the journey in a vehicle tantalized her. She was ready to suggest they push the speed before a helicopter showed up, but Gideon wasn't finished with his line of questioning.

"I've never been married, but I can imagine a wife would be pressuring her husband to evacuate," Gideon said.

Kevin's mouth tightened. "My wife is everything to me. She understands what I have to do."

Rain began to drizzle again, but the steel sky promised it would turn into a deluge shortly.

Kevin shot a look at the clouds. "You done with the

questions? Want a lift to the bridge still? If the answer's no, I'm out of here."

Mackenzie replied with a nod.

The ATV seats were unpadded, and every bump and rock jarred her bones, but the progress was encouraging. From her passenger seat, she watched Kevin white-knuckle the steering wheel, tackling each steep hairpin turn with care. Sweat beaded his brow.

"Haven't driven this kind of terrain since I was a teen."

"You're doing great," Mackenzie said, but Kevin looked more nervous with every moment. When Gideon put a hand on his shoulder, he jumped.

"Stop," Gideon said. "I'm going to take a look before we clear these last trees."

"Man, rain's gonna let loose properly in a second. You don't really want to do that, do you?"

"Yes, Kevin. I do."

"I can't stop here." Kevin removed one hand from the steering wheel and edged it toward his pocket.

Gideon dove forward and wrapped his arms around Kevin's neck, while Mackenzie grabbed Kevin's hand, snatching a gun he'd been reaching for.

Reflexively, Kevin clawed at Gideon's hold. Mackenzie quickly took the wheel, guided them to the side, and killed the engine. "A handgun, huh?"

"Can't be too careful. You two are fugitives, after all. Even if you hadn't come clean, I didn't miss the orange jumpsuit."

Mackenzie quickly checked the gun's magazine. "It's not loaded," she said in surprise.

"Lynn never wanted loaded guns in the house. Shotgun

in the trailer isn't loaded either. Didn't have time to go out and buy bullets." His tone was sullen.

"Why don't you want us to see what's down that road?" Gideon said without relaxing his hold on Kevin's neck.

Kevin's eyes were wide. "This is the thanks I get for helping you? Should have just let you fight your own battles."

"But you didn't," Gideon said. "You stuck close, even though you knew we had targets on our backs. Why would you do that instead of letting the police know and then going on to meet your family? Why, Kevin?"

Mackenzie tried to read Kevin's expression. Fear, certainly, and something else? Guilt?

"You're wrong about me."

"We'll find out soon enough." Gideon hauled him from the vehicle. Mackenzie turned and joined him.

"Go take a look, Zee, while I watch out for Kevin. I'll see that he doesn't make any noise, or message a friend."

"Ingrates," Kevin said. "What did I do to deserve this?"

"If I'm wrong, I'll owe you a humble apology, but considering the couple of days we've had here in your happy little town, I'm willing to risk offending. Go, Zee."

She pulled on her hood and hunched down, jogging over the sticky trail until she rounded the turn. Sticking in the periphery where the branches provided some concealment, she crept forward until she had a vantage point and pulled out the binoculars.

Below the plummeting trail, the bridge looked as if it were floating atop the raging river. The tumbling waves were so swollen they brushed the lower edge of the driving surface. Homing in, she located the break where the van had gone over, then backtracked until she saw Gideon's

Jeep, parked at an awkward angle to the side of the roadbed, twenty feet from the breach.

Her stomach coiled at the memory of the van hitting the water, the feel of her wrists straining against the cuffs as the river crept in. *But I survived it*, she told herself.

Because Gideon dropped everything and risked his neck to save you.

The terror of that moment pressed in again, along with the exquisite relief she'd felt when she saw Gideon swimming through that flooded police van to get to her.

She blinked and refocused the lenses.

Nothing untoward caught her attention. Did it mean they had been wrong about Kevin's intentions? Might there really be selfless people in Oakleaf, innocent bystanders oblivious of Bullseye's criminal machine?

She'd nearly lowered the binoculars when something snagged her attention. A shine, as Gideon would say, a shape that didn't blend in with the bushes, someone screening the exit to the bridge.

Eyes burning, she peered through the lenses. Branches, wet leaves, trickles of silver rain . . . there.

The silhouette of a shoulder, an arm, the orange glowing tip of a cigarette, a man with long red hair contained in a braid down his back. A chill settled deeper into her bones. How close they'd come to allowing themselves to be delivered right into the hands of whoever was watching the Jeep. She continued to scan, searching for other concealed men, but found no one.

Quickly, she drew back along the trail until she was out of sight and ran as fast as she could manage back to the ATV.

Kevin was sitting on the ground, his back to the vehicle, while Gideon stood a few feet away.

"There's a guy down there, tucked out of sight, watching the Jeep," she said. "Not Al or Jerry. I think he's alone."

Gideon stared hard at Kevin. "Waiting for you to roll on down there with two little prize pigeons. Nice trap. Almost worked."

"I'm sorry. I didn't want to do it." Tears shone in his eyes.

"Then why did you? Looking to collect a bounty?" Gideon said.

Kevin shook his head. "No. Nothing like that. I helped a couple of strangers out of the river, is all. But after the stables, I went back to my trailer and I got a visit. Al and Jerry. Their message was that I should find you and make sure you reached the bridge where someone would be waiting. I was hoping the other people would get to you first, but I had to make it look like I was cooperating."

"Why? What did they threaten you with?"

His cheeks went ruby red. "My wife and kids. I know what will happen to them if I don't cooperate."

Kevin had proven himself to be a liar, but she could tell this part was the truth. Of course Bullseye would threaten Kevin's family like Lorraine was sure he'd do to her mother.

"You know they're going to murder us. And you'd go back to your happy home life without telling your wife and kids that you delivered us to our executioners?" Gideon's expression was like granite as Kevin sagged.

"I didn't have a choice," he said to the ground.

"There's always a choice," Gideon snapped. "Take his

phone from the ATV, Zee, and our packs. Grab me the duct tape."

She did so.

"What are you going to do with me?" Kevin's voice trembled with fear.

"I'm going to save your life," Gideon said, and before Kevin could answer, he punched him in the jaw. While she stood in shock, he hauled the groaning Kevin to his feet, sat him sideways in the rear seat, and taped his wrists and feet.

"Obviously, you aren't any good at self-defense," Gideon said. "We figured out your plan, attacked you, stole your phone, and tied you up. You couldn't text or call to warn the guy down below, not that there's any signal worth a darn around here anyway. We got away. You're going to explain all this when they find you, and then you're going to leave town. There shouldn't be any reason for Bullseye to come after your family. You cooperated, for all he knows."

Kevin almost sobbed. "But he might track us down anyway."

"Best I can do for you, Kevin."

"Do you know his real name?" Mackenzie said.

Kevin shook his head. Lie or not, she could see he wasn't going to say anything further on the matter. "Don't leave me here."

Mackenzie felt a mixture of disgust and compassion for the man who was trying to keep his family safe.

"I'm going to bring him down," she said quietly.

Kevin started to cry until Gideon ripped off another length of duct tape.

"Can't have you shouting out a warning," Gideon said, sealing Kevin's mouth. He tossed Kevin's phone on the ground out of reach. "Soon as we can, we'll contact the cops and let them know where you are."

Kevin tried to say something, but Gideon pushed him into the back seat and taped his hands around the driver's headrest. "Then again, maybe you'll be able to get free, but not until we're clear."

Kevin was trying to shout something, but Gideon slammed the door.

Mackenzie felt like screaming. Another reversal in a dizzying game of survival. "We have to get out of here."

He didn't seem inclined to want to move away.

"Gideon? What are you thinking?"

"I'm thinking," he said, a muscle in his jaw twitching, "that I'm going to get my Jeep back."

TWELVE

MACKENZIE HADN'T RALLIED MUCH of an argument against his plan to reclaim his Jeep, and he wouldn't have listened anyway. The freedom Bullseye had to terrorize people into complying was out of bounds, and like Mackenzie, Gideon was tired. His muscles ached, his shoulder was screaming at him, and he was cold down to his core. One guy or three, didn't matter. He was going to retrieve his property one way or the other.

He explained how he intended to go about it.

Mackenzie grinned. "I like it. Am I the carrot or the stick?"

Either would carry risks, and he wished she didn't have to be involved at all, but it would take both of them to pull it off.

"What do you prefer?"

"Carrot," she said after a moment. "They won't kill me until they're certain you're apprehended too."

"I agree, but it's not comforting somehow."

"You'll live with it."

He sighed. "I should have figured out Kevin sooner."

"Me too. At least he's got a good reason for his betrayal, and he did fish us out of the river without any coercion, so he gets points for that. Unless he'd been assigned to stay on the bank and watch Jerry and Al run us off the bridge, but that doesn't seem likely, does it?"

"No. I think he intervened not knowing we were wanted people. I'm sure he's a regular stand-up guy underneath the cowardice. We'll send him a Christmas card." The leaves skimmed their shoulders as they pressed through the foliage that bordered the trail, not concerned that their progress would be overheard by the scout since the river was roaring.

Their pace slowed until they were moving at a crawl, practically on their heels due to the decline as they squelched their way to the bottom. The flattened mud trail led to gravel and finally the asphalt road. Just before they reached the paved part, they stopped. One remaining thicket was all that stood between them and the Jeep. Once they committed, there would be no going back. A careful search with the binoculars didn't reveal any other watchers besides the one Mackenzie had already identified. If he was wrong, the consequences would be quick and deadly. One last chance to walk away . . . but he wouldn't, and neither would she. The rhythm of the rain was frenetic.

"You sure you want to be the carrot?" Gideon whispered, his cheek grazing hers, causing him to pine for all kinds of strange things. He wished it was all a game, a survival exercise he was enjoying with her. In his imagination, they didn't have to be adversaries or vulnerable, isolated personnel. If he had his way, it would be a fun adventure like they'd experienced in their teen years with Aaron, hiking in the woods, scouring the rocks for hidden caves, fishing in secluded pools. Reality soured his daydream. This was anything but playtime. If they were wrong and the guy reacted by shooting first, Mackenzie could be dead in minutes.

She combed her wet hair from her face. "I'm the carrot. Ready?"

"Hold a minute." He looked again, panning the binoculars slowly, making sure there was no detectable gleam to give them away. He caught the scent of tobacco smoke. Rookie move. Gideon continued to scan patiently.

The watcher was barely visible in the branches, palm cupped over a cigarette as he tried to keep it alight in the rain and exhaling a stream of smoke while he waited for his prey. He wasn't a professional, by any means, but he looked fit and there was a bulge in his jacket pocket that indicated a weapon.

"Zee, I changed my mind," he said. "Let's—"

But she'd already stepped out from the shrubbery, tiptoeing, shoulders hunched. Tentative steps took her to the bridge approach as if she was making her way covertly, intending to cross the bridge on foot.

He watched the man, who he could now see had red hair under a black baseball cap. The instant he saw Mackenzie, the stranger erupted from his hiding place and yanked out a revolver. Gideon bit back a curse and wormed his way around the shrubs toward his attacker's flank.

"Stop right there!" the man shouted, completely focused on Mackenzie, the cigarette slipping from his mouth to the ground.

Mackenzie screamed, a feigned look of surrender on her face, her hands up. An impressive performance.

"Where's your partner?" the guy said, scanning behind her.

"Kevin killed him, but I got away," she called over the rain. She was convincing when she rattled off the story they'd concocted. "I . . . I was trying to get to Gideon's Jeep. I have to get out of here. Please help me."

The man's eyes narrowed and he moved closer, gun trained on Mackenzie. She stepped backward, and he countered, which put him closer to the dripping shrubs on the side of the thicket where Gideon crouched, a stout branch in his fist.

The redhead grinned. "Sorry to disappoint, but you're not going to make it out of here. I get a nice finder's fee for taking you out. Better payout if I got two of you, but I'm tired of getting soaked, waiting around here until the dam blows up." He was moving into point-blank shooting range when Gideon emerged from the thicket and slammed the branch on the back of his head with a satisfying thwack. The man dropped to the mud.

Gideon chuckled and tossed the branch aside. "Finally, one phase of this plan goes off without a hitch." He patted down the fallen man's pockets, took a pack of gum, his cell phone, and the weapon, which he stuck in his waistband, along with an extra clip.

Mackenzie snagged a plastic bag from under the tree where the man had been smoking. "Things are looking up. Care for half a cheese sandwich, extra pickles?"

His stomach rumbled. "Exactly the way I like my cheese sandwiches, but we'll eat on the go."

They paused long enough for one more sweep to make sure there were no other eyes on the bridge, but he could detect no one. He took her hand, and surprisingly she let him.

"Ready?"

She seemed to understand. There was a possibility that a concealed individual would shoot them the moment their feet hit the paved surface.

She laced her fingers with his and gave him a confident smile, a bright light in the gloom. "Race you."

She let go and took off ahead of him. Two separate running targets would be harder to handle than if they'd stayed together. He couldn't believe how fast she ran, even though the ground was slippery. His body clunked along like a clogged-up engine as he struggled after her.

A few feet apart, they sprinted onto the bridge and moved as quickly as they could to his vehicle. Their pace felt like slow motion as they each fought off their fatigue, injuries, and dehydration. The Jeep was slick with rain, parked in the exact same position he'd left it.

He checked behind them again while Mackenzie looked inside. "Keys still there?" he called.

"Nope," she said with a groan. "I'll have to hotwire it."

"No need. I never go anywhere without a spare set." He pulled the keys from his backpack, unlocked the passenger side, and flung open the door for her before he went around to the driver's seat.

"Chivalry," she said, sliding inside. "Perfect."

It felt amazing to be out of the downpour, even better when the engine fired up.

Before they took off, he examined the phone he'd taken,

which was locked with a security code. "Shame it's probably got a tracker on it," he said, before rolling down the window and lofting it over the side into the bubbling water.

"This town is murder on phones," Mackenzie said, checking her own. "And there's still no signal." She snapped his photo.

He blinked. "That better not be going up on your Instagram."

"Just capturing the moment so I can remind myself later."

"Remind yourself what?" He reversed and guided the Jeep onto the steep trail they'd used earlier, heading away from town.

"Um . . ." She shrugged and looked away. "How you helped me and stuff. You are quite a man."

Quite a man? He had no idea what to say in response.

Mackenzie became very busy keeping watch out the side mirrors. "No one in pursuit yet."

"The farther we get away from town, the better."

"But Kevin knows we were heading for the airstrip."

"And he'll squeal like a pig as soon as he gets the chance, but hopefully we've got enough of a head start."

A flying branch smacked against the windshield.

She fell silent, and he knew she was thinking she should have gone alone. She didn't want the guilt of adding another potential victim. He'd probably have felt the same way in her shoes, but he wasn't going to let her walk into a firing squad by herself, even if she was determined to. She was coming into sharper focus for him, the vulnerability under the ferocious determination, the softness lurking beneath the silvery eyes.

What would it be like to be forever partners with a woman like Mackenzie? Exasperating, no doubt, with her will and her refusal to bend. But if she decided to love someone, there would be no end, or bottom, or edges to it. Fathomless. Wild. Soul deep.

He blinked and squeezed the wheel. This trauma-bonding stuff was really messing with his head. They drove past Kevin, who was still trussed in the back seat, seemingly having made no progress on freeing himself. Gideon gave him a thumbs-up.

Kevin's eyes bugged out.

Mackenzie giggled. "Almost feel bad for the guy."

"I don't, and he isn't trying hard enough if he hasn't gotten loose by now. It would have taken me ten minutes, tops."

"You have an unfair advantage, grasshopper eater."

"Praying mantis," he corrected. "The downside to driving is we'll be easier for Al and Jerry to spot, but it's worth it to be reunited with old Fluff." Gideon grinned as he patted the dashboard and blasted the heater. "Missed me, didn't you, girl? Sorry it took me so long to get you back."

"Wait a minute. You named your Jeep Fluff?"

He arched a brow. "It's short for Fluffernutter if you must know. Named after the world's finest sandwich."

She laughed heartily. "I never understood why you couldn't use jelly on your peanut butter sandwiches like everyone else on the planet."

"Because Marshmallow Fluff is sublime, and I'm not like everyone else on the planet."

"Well, there's no disputing that." She unwrapped the purloined cheese sandwich.

"Too bad he didn't pack two."

Wet and cold as they were, it was also sublime to be in a moving vehicle with the heater blasting, bumping and jolting as they made their way along the trail. His quads spasmed and he wasn't sure how he was ever going to pry his body out of the driver's seat, but for now, it was agonizing bliss.

She divided the sandwich, and they each took half and tried to eat slowly, but the combination of mustard, pickles, and severe hunger had them finishing in minutes. He gulped his like a baby bird after a worm.

"Oh, that was so good," she said.

"Almost as good as peanut butter and Fluff."

She rolled her eyes. "At this point I'd happily eat that too."

"Well, now that you mention it . . . Grab the container behind your seat."

She snagged the Tupperware and pried open the top. Inside were two neatly filled, squeezable condiment containers, one with Marshmallow Fluff and one with peanut butter.

Her mouth dropped open. "Are you kidding me? You actually carry dispensers of the stuff?"

"Yes. Jars are too bulky, and I don't like to get my hands messy. This is my afternoon snack supply." The box also held two sleeves of saltine crackers.

Her laugh was pure delight. "What? No bread for sandwiches?"

"I was traveling light. Besides, I like the crunch and the hit of salt."

She seemed to appreciate the logic. "Shall I fix us an after-dinner treat then?"

"Please do."

With dexterity, she balanced four saltines on her lap and added dollops of peanut butter and a marshmallow swirl to each one.

"Two for you," she said.

He thanked her and ate them both while she did the same, then they chased them down with pouches of water from his emergency supply. They each drained a pouch completely. The water was so cold it made his molars ache, but he relished every drop.

She closed her eyes and sagged against the seat. "I stand corrected. I've been a PB and J fan all my life, but marshmallow and peanut butter really is the world's best combination."

Exactly the reason he gravitated to the wilderness—it concentrated blessings down to a strength that could not be ignored. The simple provision of food, water, warmth, companionship. He silently thanked God for it all.

He laughed. "Nice to know I'm right about that at least." He wondered if he should seize the moment to suggest she change her mind about the airstrip, but he remembered how she recoiled at the fire tower when he'd last brought it up. At least their route was getting them farther away from the prying eyes of any townspeople whose loyalty Bullseye had bought and paid for. A small consolation, since they could be walking right into a lethal snare.

Don't let yourself relax, Gid.

You're not out of the woods yet.

Not even close.

••••••••••••••••••••

Mackenzie licked a bit of sticky marshmallow from her finger as she steadied herself against the bumps. The trail grew fouler as it dipped lower, water turning it into a quagmire. At its lowest reaches, the makeshift road forked into two choices—a soggy path that would undoubtedly get them mired in filth or the paved road.

"No choice," Gideon said.

She didn't reply. The route would take them directly past the western turnoff to town, a main frontage road that would be busy with the remaining evacuees. And plenty of prying eyes. No getting around it.

When they passed a string of vehicles packed to the brim with belongings and people, Mackenzie scrunched down in the seat. Gideon kept his eyes on the road until they came to a tiny corner gas station, the only business that appeared to still be operational.

"Your tank's full. Why are we stopping?"

He pointed to the pay phone. "I have to call Sergeant Rodriquez."

"Why?"

"Because he needs to know what's gone down, more or less."

She skewered him with a look. "More or less?"

"I'm not giving you up, Mackenzie, but there has to be a record of what Bullseye's done. If things go badly . . ."

Then the two of them would disappear into the maw of the floodwaters and no one would ever be the wiser. He was right. The police could carry on the work against Bullseye even if she couldn't.

She looked longingly at the shop. "All right. If we're risking a stop, I'm using the facilities."

"Mind the cameras. I'll keep my head on a swivel until you're done."

Head ducked low, she hurried into the convenience store and beelined to the restrooms. A quick check of her phone revealed there was no service in the mini-mart either. The sheer triumph of indoor plumbing infused her body with happiness. Washing her hands after, she was again struck at the reflection in the mirror. She looked exhausted, vulnerable, hunted. Intentionally she wiped her face with a paper towel, cleaned off a stain from her jacket, and even applied a slick of ChapStick from a tube she'd found in the Jeep and stuck in her back pocket.

Better. She nodded at herself. Still on the ragged edge but slightly more civilized.

Since there were undoubtedly cameras near the register as Gideon had noted, she didn't stop to see if there was anything left on the ravaged store shelves worth buying. It was a herculean effort only made possible by the fact that she'd eaten two of Gideon's Fluffernutter cracker specials.

She'd almost cleared the door when the mouthwatering aroma of coffee hit her nostrils. A percolator was set up on a card table by the exit with a hand-lettered "Free" sign and a few remaining Styrofoam cups. She'd been in such a hurry on the way in, she hadn't noticed.

"Help yourself," the cashier called out. "Trying to keep people warm as they head out of town. You evacuating too?"

"Uh-huh." Keeping her head turned, she waved a grateful hand and filled two cups to the brim. She wasn't going to dilute this precious bitter brew with any sugar or creams.

"Best not dillydally."

"Airstrip's still open?"

"Yeah, but not for long."

Long enough, she thought with a surge of hope. She hurried out before the clerk could start up a conversation.

Was he watching her closely as she left? She didn't dare check. Probably paranoia born of constant danger. There were only two convenience stores in town. Had her brother been a customer here when he came?

To meet with the handlers who set him up in the drug trade?

Outside, Gideon leaned against the Jeep. He, too, wore his hat down low, pretending nonchalance but clearly tracking her every move.

"They have a free table," she said, handing him the coffee.

He held it under his nose and inhaled. "There are good people in the world, even in this town."

"I guess the clerk hasn't gotten the memo we're wanted individuals."

"Hopefully, but he could be sending a message right now if he's got a ham radio or sat phone."

His response sent a deeper chill into her body as she followed him to the pay phone. The receiver looked clunky in his grasp, but the ancient technology worked impeccably well. In a moment, he'd reached an operator who put him through to the officer who'd been driving the jail van when they ended up in the river. Gideon held the phone so she could hear.

"Where are you?" Rodriquez demanded.

"On the road." He told the officer as best he could about the situation and the locations of the redhead at the Jeep and Kevin in case the guy was a complete dufus and still hadn't gotten loose.

"Is Mackenzie Bardine with you?"

Mackenzie sipped the hot coffee. What would Gideon say? She couldn't be sure as she stared into his somber eyes.

He cleared his throat and moved the mouthpiece closer. "Can't tell you anything more right now."

"She needs to turn herself in," the cop said. "We can work through all this but not if she's running. Tell me where you are and I'll try to get someone to you. I can't leave my post, we've got to help with evacuations, but—"

"That's all I can share for now," Gideon said.

Mackenzie felt a lump in her throat. This wasn't Gideon. He didn't hold back or cover for anyone since he'd lied for her brother and paid a terrible price. Yet here he was, putting himself and his career at risk to help her.

"Listen to me," Rodriquez said. "You proved yourself back there at the van. I'll give her as much slack as I can, but you have to come in before you both die."

The coffee burned her lip. If she was in the cop's shoes, she'd say the same thing. Five more seconds ticked past as the line of cars continued to move by them.

"Do you know the identity of the man who's trying to kill us?" Gideon said.

The cop paused. "I have an idea."

She squeezed the cup, listening. He knew. *A name . . . that's all I need.*

"Guy's trying to kill us," Gideon said. "We have a right to know who he is."

The cop lowered his voice. "I can't talk right now. Do you read me?"

She and Gideon locked eyes. The officer's hesitation was clear. Bullseye might have people in the police department on his payroll too.

It suddenly seemed as if every passenger in every car and all the people stopped at the gas pumps turned to stare at them.

Their position had just become even more isolated.

"Thanks for your help, officer," Gideon said. "I'll be in touch when I can."

"Don't—" she heard the cop say as Gideon disconnected.

"You won't listen, but he's right, you know," Gideon said.

She pretended not to hear him, examining the cars as they passed. He wasn't going to be put off.

"Zee, there's a great chance they know exactly where we're headed. We can change the plan." He pointed to the parking lot exit. "Put this town behind us. Get some distance. Lay it all out for the cops when we're clear."

She was so close she could taste it. A name . . . one tiny little name. "I have to."

"No, you don't."

"You don't get it, Gid."

"I do. I lost Aaron too. So did your parents. What about them?"

"They'll understand."

He fisted his hands on his hips. "They lost both their children when Aaron died."

Mackenzie jerked. "What?"

"When he died, you might as well have too."

She recoiled from the lack of emotion, the flat hopelessness in his tone. Anger flashed like a lit match. "Does that make you feel better? Judging me for how I've handled myself since my brother's murder?"

"No, but it's true. You stopped living your own life after the murder, and you rechanneled everything into revenge. It twisted and changed you. You don't allow yourself to receive love or give it. You're just living to destroy Bullseye, and that's not really living, is it?"

"No one else can do it, Gideon. If they could, I wouldn't be here."

"Wouldn't you? Kind of your identity now, isn't it? Crusader? The only one who can get justice. Never mind the law enforcement departments who are designed for this. Only you, right?"

"I'm the best shot. And I'm almost to the finish line."

"What if you fail? Or you don't even get the chance to confront him? Are you going to spend the rest of whatever life you've been given hating yourself because you couldn't do it?"

She hadn't allowed herself to consider the stretch of road beyond her destination. "I don't know."

"What if it costs you everything to succeed? Your life. That's worth the price? For you . . . and your parents?"

Tears burned. At that moment, she despised Gideon, could hardly keep herself from lashing out at him with balled fists. "You don't get to talk about my family, my choices, anything."

"I don't recognize you anymore, Zee." He paused and added softly, "Do you?"

The comment took the breath from her.

"The Mackenzie I knew was a giggler, a crier, a dancer. When was the last time you did any of those things?"

"You've made your thoughts clear, Gideon. Just drop me at the edge of town, okay?"

Her reflection in the window glass as she stared at the Jeep was unrecognizable. She didn't know the hard-eyed, gaunt face that looked back at her. She did not know herself. She only knew the ache of an empty space inside that threatened to gobble everything, her personality, her heart, her soul.

Was that the price for punishing her brother's killer? To lose herself too?

And was she willing to pay it?

After an endless pause, he shook his head. "I'm going to call my brother. He—"

She grabbed his arm as a truck appeared on the road. Not Jerry and Al, she didn't think, but not loaded down like the evacuees either.

Trouble or not, she couldn't tell, but they hustled into the Jeep, and pulled out onto the road before weaving themselves into the line of traffic.

Two lanes allowed them to pass a station wagon and a four-door sedan. Mackenzie strained to get a look at the driver behind them in the truck.

"Do you recognize them?" Gideon asked.

"No. I can't make out who's behind the wheel."

Gideon edged around a camper full of people. The driver shouted something at him about being patient, but he kept on, providing a gap between them and their pursuer. He repeated the maneuver until they had several cars as a buffer.

Mackenzie stared in the side mirror. It was possible they'd lost the pursuer, but with the slow speed of traffic they wouldn't be able to outdistance them easily. Another plan was needed.

"There." Mackenzie pointed to a lot filled with forklifts and backhoes. Gideon turned off and skirted the nearest piece of large machinery. Mackenzie grabbed her binoculars and held her breath. A couple minutes later and the ruse worked. The truck continued on, oblivious to their hiding spot.

As it passed, she brought the driver into focus through the lenses and caught a flash of long dark hair, a delicate profile. It was the woman from the stables, scanning back and forth in search of the Jeep.

"It's Cordelia," she said in surprise. "Kevin said she urged him to find us. I wasn't sure he was telling us the truth."

Gideon rubbed his chin. "She could be in Bullseye's pocket just as much as Kevin. More. Or he's threatened her too, in some way. We don't know anything about her except that she was angry at the intrusion to her stables. With Bullseye's killers and Kevin out to get us, seems pointless for her to add herself to the mix, though."

Unless she has ulterior motives. Mackenzie considered the anonymous phone call she'd gotten as they hid from the helicopter. *"Trust me."*

"Friend or enemy?" Exactly the question they had about everyone in town. Kevin had turned out to be acting for Bullseye, and Rodriquez indicated some of the police could be too.

"Some locals might seem cordial, but no one's our friend in this town," Gideon said, brows knit. He turned to her, and she could see his thoughts as clearly as if they were ink on a page.

"Clerk said the airstrip's still open. I'm going," she said.

The rest was unspoken. *But you don't have to. Leave me*, she pleaded silently. Deep inside, she was terrified he actually would depart. At what moment had she come to rely on him? To trust him?

Without a word, he put the Jeep in gear and rolled out into the stream of traffic where they would stay until they reached the turnoff to the airstrip. After everything, he was still choosing to stay by her side.

She twisted her hair into a neater ponytail and shoved it under her cap. Cordelia. Kevin. Jerry. Al. The redheaded guy at the Jeep. Cops. So many people might be caught in Bullseye's web.

When Bullseye fell, so would they.

In between sips of the coffee she was trying to make last, she began to tap notes into her phone. Gideon's mouth tightened, but he didn't say a word. Every last fact she could gather would be uploaded, and eventually one of two things would happen. She'd produce the podcast that would expose Bullseye to the world. Or she'd die and the file would be delivered to the police. The cops would have to start from scratch, using her information as a diving-off point to secure their own, which would take time. Her way, he'd be exposed immediately, his mask ripped off, his operations sent skittering off track. Lives saved, perhaps.

The taste would be sweet, satisfying, and worth every risk.

To you, Mackenzie. But what about Gideon?

She watched him drive, the concentration evident in his tense shoulders, the pursing of his lips. If he paid for her choices? What then? More guilt to add, like the pile she already felt because she hadn't recognized what her brother was doing?

But it would be more than guilt if Gideon was lost.

She wondered suddenly how Aaron's girlfriend, Leah, had felt about his murder. Mackenzie hadn't enough to go on to find her, no contact info or even a last name. Did Leah wonder what happened to Aaron? Or had she decided he'd ghosted her?

Gideon drove on, his mouth in a grim line.

She wouldn't let Gideon get hurt—but with the enemies piling up, how could she protect him?

Cordelia's dark hair and flashing eyes popped into her mind.

It was strange that a woman would insert herself into a deadly cross fire, unless Bullseye had a hold over her too.

Her heart squeezed until the pulse pounded in her throat. It was too much. Enemies everywhere. No one to trust.

Gideon stared grimly at the road.

No one but the person who was facing death because of her.

THIRTEEN

MACKENZIE WAS HOLDING her jacket cuffs to the heater vent so the warm air would blow up her arms. She looked like a kid, and Gideon suppressed a chuckle. Considering that the tension was still simmering between them, she might take that the wrong way.

Why couldn't she hear what he was saying? It had to be crystal clear that she was heading for disaster. Out of pride? No, the need for vengeance had obscured everything else.

They finally edged past the glut of traffic and turned onto the only remaining passable road that would take them to the airstrip. Gideon mused as the Jeep's wheels sluiced along the sodden asphalt. Clearly this was not the preferred route, as it was cracked and marred with submerged potholes. No matter how carefully he drove, he seemed to hit every one, which reminded him his shoulder ached like mad.

Was the airstrip really still open, or had that been a comment dropped by the clerk to encourage Mackenzie to go there? Great place to murder someone, seemed to him.

Too many witnesses to complete the job in town. Could the assembled force of enemies be lying in wait at their destination? The thoughts did not help him feel better in any way, but the heater and food were blessings. And the company, even though she was fuming.

The farther away from town they got, the worse the conditions. The route was flooded in some places, and he gritted his teeth as he sailed the Jeep on through, praying the tires wouldn't lose traction or the engine sputter.

They continued their climb. While he drove, Mackenzie kept watch for Jerry or Al in places that looked suitable for ambush points. What they would do in such a situation, he wasn't sure. He was armed now with the redhead's weapon, but a revolver would be a poor defense against a long-range rifle. The seat belt strained to keep him in place as he navigated around mucky holes and spots where the road had begun to slough away at the edges.

"Clerk say anything else that might lead you to believe Lorraine's boyfriend is still at the airstrip?"

She shook her head.

So they were still working off a very slim lead. Gideon held on to the hope that if the guy wasn't there, Mackenzie would consent to depart with him. There would be no other reason to stick around unless she came up with another scheme.

"I'm beginning to get real sick of rain," he said.

"Me too."

At least on one small point, they agreed. He sensed a thawing in the air between them. If he could just maintain the peace. *Step one, keep mouth firmly closed. Step two, avoid driving into an ambush.*

The precipitation alternated between drizzle and downpour at any given moment, burdening the already stressed dam. He could practically feel the floodwaters hovering, ready to swallow them up.

The road dropped to one lane as it twisted along. One side was a sheer cliff that had already dumped piles of stone and dirt in spots. The other was a wooded slope. A chunk of rock the size of a bread loaf suddenly broke free and rolled in front of the Jeep. He hit the brakes, and it missed the front fender by inches as it hurtled across and down into the trees.

He slowed to a crawl, trying to examine the trajectory the rock had taken, but it was all a swirl of rain-washed brown. A sound, or maybe it was a vibration, had him rolling down the window.

Mackenzie gripped his arm. "Did you hear something?"

He listened. "I thought I did."

She craned to see out his window, her damp hair brushing his chin. "Helicopter?"

"Nothing, I guess." He rolled the window back up.

But he heard her soft breathing, felt the warmth of her shoulder against his chest, and for a slender moment he forgot their perilous situation. Mackenzie Bardine had some sort of hold over him that he'd be hard-pressed to explain in any rational way.

She returned to her position and sighed. "Is it too early for more Fluffernutter crackers?"

He opened his mouth to reply when a rumble shook the car.

The dam.

It must have failed.

She gripped the armrest. He pressed the gas, waiting for the wall of water he knew was coming, and clutched the wheel against the vibrations.

The flood didn't appear.

His mind was still groping for explanations when the landscape around them shuddered. The cliff to their right was changing.

A giant mass of brown mud and rocks broke away from the face and moved as if it were a single unit.

"Landslide!" he yelled.

Mackenzie paled, mouth pinched in fear.

There was nowhere to turn off. On one side a sliding mountain, on the other a steep grade interrupted by thickly clustered pines.

Gideon stomped on the gas. Outrunning it was their only hope.

The liquified ground rolled toward the Jeep with sickening speed.

They weren't going to make it.

Grimly, he kept going as the rush swallowed them, inch by inch.

• •

Mackenzie felt a scream bubbling up, but the onslaught impacted the Jeep like a detonating bomb.

Stunned, she held tight to avoid having her head slammed against the door. Through a curtain of brown debris she was able to discern the Jeep was being swept sideways off the road. Gideon still held the wheel in a vain attempt to control it, his arms iron taut, jaw clenched.

In a whoosh of movement the slide picked up the vehicle and sent it tumbling sideways over and over as they were pushed into the trees.

Leaves, branches, mud, and sky whirled. Her vision blurred and she lost all sense of equilibrium. Gideon reached for her hand and she clutched at his, the torrent raging around them until her ears rang.

They'd be buried alive. How long before their bodies would be discovered?

Her mother's face appeared in her scattered thoughts. Another child to mourn. Or maybe one who would simply disappear. An even greater anguish for her parents to live with. Questions that would never be answered added to the ones they already had about Aaron's death.

A great smash to the front slapped her hard against the seat. The airbags deployed with a pop.

Without warning, all motion stopped. The sound continued, growing fainter and fainter until it tapered off.

Mackenzie found herself staring into the sky, the Jeep having come to rest on the driver's side.

She struggled for breath, and when she had the strength, she turned her face and whispered.

"Gideon?" Her sight was fuzzy from the violent shaking, the deflating airbag filling her view.

Was his hand in hers? For a moment, she couldn't be sure. His squeeze to her palm left her giddy with relief. "Gid, are you . . ."

"Present," he croaked. "Status report, Zee?"

"Give me a minute."

"Yeah. I need one too."

They held hands and breathed, taking stock as their

faculties returned. Gideon's window was shattered, the needles of the pine they'd impacted poking through the fractures, cold air numbing her cheeks. If she craned her neck, her sideways view framed a canopy of overhead branches and a patch of steely sky.

"I don't think I'm injured much," she said finally. "Just put through the blender. You?"

"Fit for duty, ma'am." He let go of her hand and unbuckled his seat belt. With a lot of squirming and batting at the airbags, he positioned himself to unbuckle her and help her into an awkward crouch on the passenger seat. No unusual pain to any body part, she noted. Yet.

Gideon peered through his broken glass. "My door is crushed flat to the ground. We're going to have to exit via yours."

She tried the handle and shoved with her shoulder. Gideon helped but it was a wasted effort. The door was immovable, having been smashed and bent out of shape.

"Window?"

He confirmed with a nod. Reaching around her, he used the hand crank to lower the glass.

"Perks of an old-school car," he said.

When it was opened, she stuck her head out like a gopher scenting the air. The oozing ground had settled all around the Jeep, filling the space and cementing the vehicle in place as if it were a brick mortared into a wall. She swallowed, feeling suddenly very small in the upheaval, and very grateful not to be dead.

Thank you, Lord.

She uncoiled herself and threaded her torso through the open window. If any more of the mountain came down, they'd be smothered. She decided to move slowly, which worked fine since her legs were quivering.

"Watch yourself," Gideon called. "Everything's unstable."

"Story of my life." When her pack was on her back, she put a foot on the open window edge and eased herself upward.

"I'll grab whatever essentials I can reach and follow you," he said.

She hoped the peanut butter and marshmallow supplies would be on the essentials list. It required all her power to heave herself from the Jeep and onto the most stable surface she could find, an overturned maple tree that had broken off and lay like a bridge atop the sludge. She shimmied along its length. Gideon followed and joined her there, frowning at the landscape. All around them was oozing, bubbling mud.

"Upward is no longer an option," he said.

That was an understatement. What had been a steep hillside was now an even sheerer drop that looked as if it would unload more material at any moment.

She followed his pointed finger in the other direction.

He swiped at a pine needle that floated down into his hair. "I don't see that we have much choice. We'll have to skirt the debris as best we can and recalculate once we're clear since we don't have access to a vehicle anymore." His gaze drifted to the smothered Jeep behind them.

She saw the sad pinch of his mouth. "I'm sorry about Fluffernutter, Gid."

He shrugged. "Just a car. I'll get another."

A lie, of course. It was most definitely not just a car to

his mind. What had she cost him? Too much. She touched his shoulder. "No, she was a special car, and I'm sorry you lost her trying to help me." On impulse, she leaned over and pressed her lips to his brow.

He sighed and nestled closer, and it was the most comforting sensation she'd experienced since before her brother was murdered. Her mouth drifted to his temple. How easy it would be to kiss him properly, to let the feeling seep into her fragile glass heart that hadn't beat right for a very long time. But there was such a thin coating around that battered organ. One crack, one tiny fissure and it might disintegrate into a pile of useless shards.

She edged away, patting her pockets to be sure she had her phone. "I really am sorry," she mumbled.

He caught her eye, lifted his chin, and smiled. "Are you kidding? Nothing to be sorry for. All this is fodder. My wilderness classes are going to love hearing about this."

The bravado didn't quite cover his regret at losing his beloved Jeep. In silent agreement they crawled the entire length of the fallen tree, which took them to a cluster of firs that had formed a blockade against much of the landslide flow. The trunks had allowed a mass of rock to collect in a haphazard swath, which would enable them to climb farther away from the sticky mess.

To make it to the rocks required them to step off into the ooze, which mercifully only rose to their knees. Thick mud rushed to encase them. Each step required enormous effort as the muck weighed down their legs, but they soon cleared the worst of it.

Upon reaching more stable ground, they supported each other and used sticks to scrape off the mud as best they could. Her jeans were sodden and stiff, encasing her in a freezing sludge. The clock on her almost useless phone added to her worries by showing that they were heading into late afternoon. Another evening was approaching, and now they had no shelter and no vehicle. The idea of enduring another frigid night, wet and exposed, was almost unbearable, and her body began to tingle with fear. Weak, hungry, cold, shelterless.

She also had no idea in which direction they were moving.

Gideon does.

He was the only thing keeping her from outright panic. After checking his bearings on the compass from his pack and a printed map he kept in a plastic bag, he led the way farther down into the glade. She couldn't hear over the crunching of twigs under her feet, but she thought he said something about a trail.

Twenty minutes of walking warmed her only slightly, and Gideon stopped at a marker she hadn't even noticed. No words, just the universal hiker logo, an arrow, and the ominous numbers 15.5. She prayed they wouldn't have to cover all those miles to achieve Gideon's purpose.

"Will it take us around the slide to the airstrip?" she said, chafing her arms.

Gideon stopped and wiped a streak of mud from his forehead. "Zee, gonna be honest with you. The airstrip is a solid ten miles from here, and the only two direct routes are off the table now. We're wet and it's going to be full dark soon. Our primary goal right now needs to be finding shelter and warmth. At least someplace where I can build a fire and pray we aren't spotted. Shelter and warmth aren't optional. If we don't acquire them, you won't live long enough to see tomorrow, let alone an airstrip."

The frustration in his voice prickled her own. She wanted to answer, provide a plan, another option, a way he hadn't considered, but there was nothing. He was right. Maybe he'd been right all along about her plan. Everything seemed suddenly unimportant under the weight of her discomfort and fear.

Her fingers were so cold she couldn't hold her phone, and the trembling in her legs increased. The mud had hardened into armor.

"All right," she said. "The trail's the answer?"

"I hope so. There might be a campground along the way or a backpacker's respite of some kind."

That didn't seem likely to her with the unkempt condition of the trail, but she held her tongue and followed Gideon. At this point, *maybes* were the best they could do. He'd slung the backpack over one shoulder, and she realized he was favoring the reconstructed one.

Her heels were already blistered and raw and her legs might as well be two pieces of wood, but they limped along, shivering as what sunlight there was sank low behind the trees.

Faster, her mind urged, pushing her on toward some phantom place where she wasn't permeated with cold and misery.

When he slowed, she pulled alongside to find another trail marker, but this one pointed the way to someplace called Boatyard at Lake Louise.

She brightened. A boatyard meant walls, didn't it? And

walls meant relief from the biting wind. In unspoken agreement, they pushed on.

What he expected to find at the boatyard, she couldn't say exactly, but her imagination furnished all kinds of optimistic visions. Maybe they could even find a boat to borrow, to motor down the river until they happened upon a waterfront house with someone at home—or not. She'd be happy to accept breaking and entering charges if they could find someplace with a working phone and hot water. Even tepid would do because her extremities were slabs of unyielding ice. A garage? Woodshed? Doghouse? She struggled to match Gideon's pace, though she knew he'd slowed to accommodate her.

Another half hour took them along a wide sweep of riverbank and finally to the inlet where a small boathouse appeared, hovering over the water as if floating there. The water level had risen so that the bottom of the structure was submerged.

With as much speed as they could muster, they hurried toward the neatly painted building. The rear and sides were made of varnished wood slats. The front opened into slips for four boats, the spaces dark like missing teeth. She could see the vague outline of two boats secured as well as possible against the elements. The residents of the river houses, of course, had their own places to dock their vessels. This one probably served several dwellings tucked farther back into the greenery.

A peek inside revealed only an inky dark interior. She paused to allow her eyes to adjust as they entered. Four slips, two boats, and merciful protection from the wind. Gideon bent to examine one vessel.

The sound of an engine made them both straighten. Gideon ran to the entrance, and she followed. *Help?*

To her dismay, she saw an ATV, similar to the one Kevin had driven, but the two men in the front seat were hideously familiar.

She shrank back into the shadows, holding her breath.

"Al and Jerry." Gideon was scanning wildly, trying to figure a way out.

The ATV was parked at the drive, windows open. No chance they could sprint out the way they'd come in.

Jerry's voice cut through the stillness. "I still say the helicopter oughta be up. Why should we have to tackle this area in a crappy all-terrain vehicle?"

"Because we messed up and let them get away at the stables. They made us look like idiots. Now we gotta make it up to the boss or pay. Our necks are on the line, or don't you remember?"

Jerry laughed. "He chewed you out royally, didn't he?"

"Us, man. Us."

The response was indistinct, but Al's angry tone grew more conciliatory. "Clerk in town spotted them. They came this way, all right. They'd have to."

Gideon's teeth ground together. Al and Jerry had made it to the landslide. It wouldn't have been hard to track their direction.

"What happens if that dam lets loose?" Al said. Springs creaked as the two men got out of the ATV.

"Then we're gonna hightail it out of here and let the water take care of business."

"Boss won't like it unless we bring back bodies."

"Well, boss has his house all nice and safe on the

mountain. Not like he has to worry about drowning like us worker rats."

"Let's just disable these boats in case they make it this far."

"All right," Al said.

There was no way out, both entrances blocked. In unison she and Gideon moved to the edge of the slip.

Not in the lake. Anything but plunging into that deep freeze.

But there was no other way. Gideon silently affirmed it with a finger pointed at the water. He went in feet first without even making a splash.

His head bobbed up and he blinked. Behind her the boards creaked.

Every sinew screamed at her not to do it. She looked down at Gideon. He was shivering, jaw clamped tight. He raised his hand to her, urging and reassuring.

Still her body resisted until the voices grew closer.

Do it, Mackenzie. Do it or die.

She stepped off as quietly as she could.

The cold hit like a hammer. Gideon grabbed her wrist, and they swam under the wood of the docking into the dark shadows. The smell of diesel and tar was pungent.

The beam of a flashlight began to cleave the shadows.

"Look at this," Al said in a whisper.

Mackenzie's heart dropped.

"Wet tracks here," Al said.

The footsteps grew more hurried, and the distinct sound of a gun being drawn from a holster followed.

"They're in here," Jerry whispered. "Go to the other side. We'll pincher them."

Divide and destroy. Jerry's boots scuffed across the planks as he passed their hiding spot, then stopped at the next boat slip.

"Any sign of them?"

"Footprints not showing here. Check the boats."

Gideon and Mackenzie watched, still as they could be, looking up through the skinny gaps between the boards. Mackenzie struggled to keep her panicky breaths quiet and shallow. Her limbs quaked so badly she was making ripples in the water. Al's shadow flickered past, closing in. She saw his rifle held tight.

"We know you're in here," Al said, "and you're not getting out. You think you're real clever, don't you? That's what people believe at first when they cross the boss. Then what happens? They turn out dead. Like your brother, right?"

He continued to prowl, and Mackenzie barely felt Gideon's hands clench around hers.

Jerry stayed in his position, checking the boat next to the slip where they were concealed while Al closed in from his side. Good strategy, she had to admit. Gideon could take Al, probably, if he had the strength to free his weapon, but Al and Jerry had the upper hand in terms of position. Gideon wouldn't be able to subdue them both, not in his present condition.

Feeling Gideon's pressure on her wrist, she allowed him to ease her slowly backward, deeper into the oily water under the walkway, searching for a way out. It was like being dipped in liquid agony.

"Gonna kill you," Al said. "Dam's gonna fail anytime now. After you're dead, you'll be washed away and no one will ever even find your bloated bodies. We'll take a picture first, though. Show it to the boss. Nothing left to chance, right?"

Gideon gave Mackenzie a sign before he dove down. She waited, her body shivering uncontrollably as she prayed for his return. The visibility was nil. Rain began to slash against the boathouse roof. She'd lost track of the seconds by the time Gideon popped up again. Quickly he pantomimed that she was to go down with him.

Go where?

Her brain wasn't working well enough to think out any plans, so she merely took a breath and dove with him. In the murky water he pointed to the pilings, set ten feet apart with a nice gap in between. Plenty big enough for two people to squeeze through and escape the boathouse into the lake.

But she was too desperate for air, so they had to surface again for a quick breath. She had no idea how much longer her body would obey commands.

Al was still talking.

"No way out, but if you surrender, maybe we'll change our minds and take you alive. How's that? Boss would love to meet you, especially the pretty lady who made all those podcasts and raked up trouble. Might want to get your autograph. Gonna be worth something after you're dead, huh?"

Gideon put his mouth next to her ear. "Swim out. Stay under as long as you can to get some distance. Let the river carry you and we'll get to land when we can."

If they could . . .

She prepared to dive again, but as she did so, a nail protruding from the dock caught in her jacket.

She pulled and the fabric tore.

It was a small enough sound, but it might as well have been a siren.

"Down here!" Jerry yelled.

She and Gideon dove, bullets striking the water around them. They kicked hard for the pilings, but her body felt slow and unwieldy. The distance was almost insurmountable, but Gideon grabbed the back of her jacket and propelled her in front of him until she made it through.

Once they cleared the pilings, she tried to stay underwater for as long as she dared until at last she surfaced, begging for breath. Gideon appeared a few yards away and immediately spun to double back to her.

Al shouted. "There! In the water."

Bullets whistled through the air. They dove again, struggling to stay under as they were caught up in the strong current created by the swollen river. The rush carried them along so fast it was all she could do to avoid obstructions.

Gideon's arm broke the water ahead of her, then his head, but the white sprays caused her to lose sight of him.

She called out, but her voice was swallowed by the roar.

A glint of metal caught her attention. A rusted car fender, lying prone across the water, all sharp metal edges. A vision of her body being skewered like meat on a shish kebab flashed in her mind.

Sliced and diced. Morbid humor, the kind she'd learned in cop school.

What a way to go.

She shouted to alert Gideon, but she couldn't be sure he'd heard or seen. A series of hard kicks enabled her to avoid the obstacle.

Beyond it was a half-submerged tree, the thick trunk bristling with long, twisting branches. The water was racing. If they didn't get out soon, they wouldn't have the strength to escape.

She caught the edge of a waterlogged branch. It tore at her fingers as she fought for a grip. Flailing her arm wide, she snatched at another stick of the slippery wood. Enough to hold her in place. Barely.

She screamed again for him.

His dark head plowed the waves until he, too, snagged hold of the fallen tree. They held on, moved gingerly, hand over hand, until they made it to the far side where the water moved more slowly.

She pointed to a brushy section of the bank. "We can get out there."

He nodded. "I'm done with swimming, and I picked the worst time to give up swearing."

She would have chuckled if she had the breath. She labored to swim what felt like the longest quarter mile of her life. Gideon made slow progress as well. They were both nearing the edge of their physical reserves.

When they heaved themselves to shore, she could no longer feel her extremities. Her thoughts spiraled in slow motion as hypothermia began to take hold.

Hiding spot, her addled brain blared.

They needed to find one immediately in case Al and Jerry tracked them with their ATV. Her eyes struggled to focus. Trees, mud, rocks, a graveled pathway . . .

Was that a cabin she saw just next to the hill with a trailer parked nearby? She wiped her eyes and looked again, praying it wasn't a hallucination. "I th . . . think I see a . . ."

"Zee," Gideon said.

She snapped a look, noting his odd tone.

His face was white, his whole body trembling like hers.

Her gaze dropped to his side where a pink blush stained his shirt.

A tear in the side of the fabric was the source . . . caused by a bullet, she realized, just as Gideon collapsed.

FOURTEEN

MACKENZIE BENT CLOSE and checked Gideon's pulse again, still in disbelief about all that had happened in the last thirty minutes. He'd be very surprised when he woke up.

Please, please, let him wake up.

She should have tried harder to lever him into the bed, but the mattress was on a high bunk, and her strength was nearly gone. Instead, she'd dragged him into the motor home and rolled him onto the cushion she'd pulled from the bench seat next to the tiny kitchen table. The agonizing process seemed endless, but she'd persevered, inch by inch, and the effort had warmed her some. He didn't really fit, but at least he was off the cold floor. Once more she prayed, then tucked the blanket tighter around him, willing her fingers to function.

"Please, Gideon," she entreated. "Open your eyes." He was still, pale, battered, and bruised. All the pain she could accept for herself—the catastrophic events, the personal consequences of her choices—but if Gideon didn't survive . . . she wasn't sure she could withstand it.

She chafed his hands.

He twitched, and her pulse raced. She leaned close. "Gideon?"

One eyelid cracked open, and she held back a sob of relief. *Thank you, God.* She pulled the blanket up to his chin and held her breath as he fought his way back to consciousness while she rubbed his tremoring shoulders.

"Hey, tough guy." Her voice broke. "You decided to wake up now that the hard work's done?"

Gideon blinked and opened the other eye, taking in her, the ceiling. "Where are we?"

At hearing him speak, her joy was almost too much to bear. Somehow she managed to answer. "In the most luxurious 1970s RV you ever did see."

He blinked some more, his voice a hoarse rasp. "You're going to need to fill in the gaps for me, Zee."

"Right before you passed out, I told you I saw a cabin, remember?"

He shook his head and winced. "Nah."

"Well, I was right about the cabin, but it's locked up tight and there are storm shutters, so I couldn't get in. The occupants left their old RV in the side yard unlocked, though. Fortunately, it's in a bit of a high spot, but I don't think we'll stay dry for long. Water's mid-wheel right now."

Gideon's expression was still befuddled. "But . . . how?"

She knew what he was driving at. "How did we get here? I dragged you. You might want to lay off the praying mantis, by the way. It wasn't easy. I used that horrible poncho as a kind of a sled. You aren't the only one with skills." Her comic twist covered the fact that it had been a brutal effort, and her body still sang with pain. But he was alive. Praise God, he was alive.

He tried to sit up, startling her, and immediately clamped a hand to his side and groaned.

"Stay still, would you? I'm no nurse and I can't guarantee my first aid will stop the bleeding for long if you knock everything loose." She checked the bandage, which was showing minimal signs of seepage. "The bullet grazed your ribs. Shallow, much better than lodging in your innards."

"Excellent."

"Yes." So excellent. An inch in the other direction . . . She shivered, her blood demanding warmth. "I'm going to try and hot-wire this thing and get the heater running. It's almost dark. Al and Jerry might have seen us bob up too, so double the urgency."

He sighed. "If we get out of this mess, we're going to have to explain our auto theft at some point."

"I memorized the address on the mailbox. I'll contact them and make restitution for taking the RV."

"Your second crime since you've hit town," he teased.

"Just have to hope they'll be understanding. Kevin says the locals look after each other . . . unless they're working for Bullseye."

He nodded. "I'll help with any restitution. Who knows? We might become the joint owners of this fine rig if they don't want it back." The quip didn't cover the pain in his expression. He was hurting, and they both needed warmth immediately.

She didn't want to leave him lying on the orange Naugahyde cushion. She wanted to hug him close and tell him how scared she'd been when he collapsed—almost paralyzed, in fact. The adrenaline from moving him was ebbing away, and she felt as if her heart was about to cease pumping altogether.

She walked unsteadily to the console and eased onto the driver's seat, where the stuffing showed through a crack in the vinyl. Her hands were tremoring, and she attempted to squeeze her fingers into fists, but they would not obey. She shoved them under her armpits to try to restore some circulation.

Gideon squirmed. "I'm getting up."

"No. Just stay there, and I'll—"

He wriggled and finally sat up.

"Not going to do what you're told?" she said.

"Astonishing, right? Usually that's your MO." He rubbed his eyes and stared at his bare feet. She'd yanked off his boots and wet socks after she deposited him. "Am I looking at orange shag carpet?"

"Yep. And there's a macramé plant holder behind you, so don't knock it down, okay?"

"Okay," he said with a weak laugh. "I love this setup. Shag carpet never should have gone out of style." A glance told her he was too pale, but the color was coming back to his lips, and he was certainly well enough to ignore her directives.

She managed to toss him a pouch of water from his pack, which she'd flung on the passenger seat next to hers.

"I feel like I've had enough water," he said.

"Hush your mouth. What would your wilderness instructor say? Drink it and rest. I've got a camper to hotwire."

"I'll help you."

"Do you know how to do it?"

"No, but I know enough about cars to figure it out."

"Leave it to me." How was she going to fiddle with the ignition? She tried to tuck her hands under her thighs and sit on them, but there was so little of any kind of heat in her body, it was virtually useless. She finally realized Gideon was saying something.

"Visor."

"What?"

"Check under the sun visor."

It took a few seconds for her to understand, but she finally reached up to flip down the visor. A set of keys dropped onto her lap. She gaped.

Though she didn't turn to look at Gideon, she heard the smile.

"Country people are trusting. Easier than cutting wires, right? Work smarter, not harder. That's an unofficial SERE motto."

She pawed the key, and it required four attempts before she got it into the slot. "Start, you awesome camper," she whispered. One attempt, and on the second, the engine coughed to life.

"Atta girl," Gideon crowed. "You got it, Zee."

"And there's a half tank of gas." She hardly dared believe her eyes. She immediately wrestled the unwieldy camper into drive and rolled out of the yard.

"No—"

"Headlights, I know," she said through chattering teeth.

"Sorry, backseat driving." He startled her by staggering

close, sliding the packs off, and collapsing in the passenger seat with a moan.

"You should be lying down."

"I know, but I need to sit up here to avoid being that nagging backseat driver."

She didn't like the gravel in his voice, or his slight breathlessness, as if it hurt too much to fill his lungs properly. But she knew there was nothing short of physical force that would compel him to return to the makeshift cot, and she had no strength to spare.

"Make yourself useful then. What's the best way to get to a passable road?"

He pointed. "Follow the drive and we'll recalculate when we get to a better line of sight."

Sticking to the roads would make them easier to spot, but there wasn't any choice except to keep the unwieldy old vehicle on paved surfaces.

Though she desperately wanted to turn on the heater, neither of them could stand to have cold air blown on them. "In five minutes, we blast it," she said through gritted teeth.

"Four and a half."

The graveled path was the tiniest bit luminous as it wound through the trees, as if it caught and held on to the sickly rays of remaining daylight that managed to penetrate. It was near sunset, so that advantage would go away quickly. At least they'd caught a stoppage in the rain.

But that meant Al and Jerry had too. And they were in an ATV, faster and more agile than an aged RV. *Take it up a notch, Mackenzie.* She tried, but the waterlogged road and gloom made her keep to a crawl.

Gideon reached forward and cranked the heat lever.

"I think that was only four minutes," she said.

"Close enough."

The heater blew the faintest puff of lukewarm air until she'd rolled another quarter mile. Then it blasted out the most glorious warmth she'd ever experienced. The forceful stream of heat warmed her face. A measure of circulation returned to her hands with a mingling of pain and pleasure. Her rigid cheeks melted into pliable flesh again, burning and tingling.

"Should I turn the heater down?" Gideon said.

"Don't even think about it."

He laughed. "I was hoping you'd say that. Whoa." He suddenly clutched the dash.

She slammed on the brakes.

Part of the road in front of them had disappeared into a water-filled sinkhole. The rippling surface made it impossible to judge the depth. Traversing it was out of the question.

"Do I have room to go around?"

He cranked down the window, letting in a cold blast of air as he craned a look out. "Yes, but we're talking inches of clearance, no more."

Would the rest of the road disintegrate under the weight of the vehicle and swallow them? Neither one of them wanted to voice the question.

Jaw clenched, she guided them around in a space so tight the side scraped the bark of the overhanging trees. It was an excruciatingly slow process, but inch by precarious inch they squeezed past the obstacle.

Gideon blew out a breath. "Good driving. They work on that in cop school?"

"My brother taught me."

"I remember. For all his wildness, he was an extremely cautious driver, most of the time." Gideon went quiet. "I offered to help with your lessons, but he declined every time. He said, 'She's my responsibility.'"

Mackenzie's throat clogged. And Aaron was hers. Only she hadn't saved him. There were so many ways she should have tried to pry into his secret life.

Too late.

"I didn't know you signed up to help teach me how to drive."

"Yeah, not altruistic, I'm afraid. I wanted to show off mostly. I had that sweet ride. Figured it would impress you."

"It did." A sleek sky-blue Mustang and a honey-eyed boy who fussed over every inch of it. He was gangly, with the lean physique that would later bulk out with muscle. Maybe if she hadn't been Aaron's little sister, two years younger, Gideon would have taken her for a ride in that gorgeous car, and . . .

The painful what-ifs struck at her heart. It all seemed so terribly long ago, an innocent era when she'd known who she was, or thought she did. Now everything was surreal, confusing, and it left her numb inside. "I thought you were indifferent. Why did you want to impress me?"

He shrugged. "Teenage boy? Best friend's hot sister? What's not to understand?"

Her cheeks warmed. Hot sister? She'd never thought

he'd seen her that way. "I wanted to impress you too, I guess," she admitted. "But I never quite knew how."

He steadied the palm tree deodorizer hanging from the rearview. "Just being yourself was enough."

Being herself? The stubborn, hyperactive know-it-all? She couldn't look at him so she focused on the route ahead. The graveled section ended at a larger paved two-lane road. Decision time. She braked while Gideon consulted his compass.

"Left will loop us closer to the highway."

"So right would be the more direct route to the airstrip," she said.

"That's correct." His tone was carefully neutral.

And there it was, the choice that could not be ignored or put off any longer. Up until Gideon plucked her out of the prison van, it had been Mackenzie versus Bullseye, black and white, right versus wrong. Not anymore.

There was another person in the passenger seat now, a man whom she suddenly realized she hadn't really known properly at all. Someone whose future was riding on her choices.

A man she cared for very much.

She let out a breath, pressed the gas, and eased the vehicle into a wide left turn. She could feel his shocked reaction as he stared at her.

"Left?"

She nodded.

"Why?"

"Because," she said slowly. How could she express all that was going on in her spirit? Her heart? "I've changed my mind."

....

Gideon thought the sheer overwhelming bliss of a functioning heater and the blood loss from the scrape across his side had messed with his mental acuity. "We're not going to the airstrip anymore?"

She didn't look at him, just kept the camper creeping forward. "You heard me."

"Yes, I did. But why, Zee?"

"I'm not totally sure."

He took in her wet hair, the small hands clutching the wheel, the pain in the line of her jaw, and the crimp of her mouth. The choice had cost her. In letting go, she'd also given something up. "How about you tell me what you can?"

She was quiet for a full minute as they rolled along. "I . . . When you collapsed back by the cabin after you'd been shot, I thought you were dying."

He opened his mouth to make a joke but closed it again. *Listen*, his soul whispered.

A few more seconds ticked by. "I showed up before they'd moved Aaron from the shooting scene. Did you know that?"

His mouth went dry. "No, I didn't."

"Since I was in the academy, I knew all the on-duty cops. They called me immediately once they ID'd him. I got to the gas station when the medics were still working on him, but I knew it was too late." Her voice broke, and he put a hand on her knee. She didn't acknowledge his touch.

"I'm sorry. So sorry you had to go through that."

She blinked. "As they took him away, I thought of a

million things I should have done differently. If I'd texted him, if I'd snooped through his room, if I'd pressured you harder to talk to him."

A lump formed in his throat. He hadn't known. He should've.

"I questioned my own actions, wondering if I'd been thinking about myself instead of Aaron. You know what happened after that?"

"No."

"I lost the ability to feel anything. Almost literally. Like, I didn't know what season it was, if it was cold or hot, or if I felt hunger or fatigue. It was as if something inside blinked off, like a flipped switch. I stopped talking to any of my friends and really even my parents. We still spoke about superficial things, but nothing of substance. I wanted to, and they probably needed me to help them process Aaron's murder, but I couldn't deal with anything because I was numb."

"I can understand that."

The RV rolled on through the darkening woods. "The only emotion I was able to regain was anger, at Bullseye." She paused. "And at you."

"So what's changed now?"

"I can feel again." She shrugged. "Maybe all this near-death experience stuff did it. Or . . ." She glanced at him, then quickly looked away. "Doesn't matter, but I can feel again." Her brows knitted. "And let me tell you, most of the feelings are garbage, and I liked it better numb."

He smiled. "I hear you."

"But anyway . . ." She cleared her throat. "It's made me think maybe there are other things to consider."

"Looking at all the factors. That's wise." He was trying not to let his voice echo the cautious cheering in his heart. If she could let go of the vendetta, if she would choose to live, it would make all the agony they'd experienced worth it, every last bit.

"I'm not giving up, though, if that's what you think. I'm going to get Bullseye, but this isn't the way." She swallowed. "Not if you get hurt in the process."

A sense of wonder engulfed him. "You're changing plans, for now, because of me?"

She flipped the hair from her eyes and waved off the question, but he saw her lips tremble.

The space between them was charged with the unspoken. He couldn't think of how to respond.

"Don't get a big head about it." She adjusted the seat belt and disengaged from his touch. "But . . . you said you didn't recognize me."

He grimaced. "I spoke without thinking. Personality trait that definitely needs work. My brothers will tell you I have no filter."

"You don't, but you were right. And I don't recognize me either. I don't know who I am anymore or what I'm supposed to be doing outside of punishing Bullseye, but I know you're not meant to die while I figure it out."

Each word scrolled through his head in slow motion. She'd lost herself, and it grieved him. But maybe, somehow, his being with her and all that they'd endured would help her remember who God had made her to be, regardless of what had happened with Aaron. Mercurial, passionate, loyal, amazing Mackenzie Bardine.

She heaved out a breath. "Looks like we risk the highway

then. Maybe we'll be able to join in a caravan of late evacuees. Safety in numbers, right?"

Back to business. He wasn't sure Bullseye's guys wouldn't take a shot regardless of witnesses, but he didn't say so. He was still marveling at their unexpected change of plans.

When she let out an enormous sigh, he noticed her pallor, the exhaustion tugging her mouth. He touched her hand in a silent question, his nerve endings still dulled.

She surprised him by stopping, leaning her forehead against the steering wheel. "I'm so tired, Gideon."

It was an admission, wrapped in a plea. *God, renew her spirit,* he prayed, holding on for a moment longer. "I'll drive for a while."

When she turned to him, her eyes were dull. "You can't. You're hurt."

"Nicked, but fit for duty, and I'm an extremely fast healer." He touched her mud-covered sleeve, slid his hand down until he found her wrist, barely able to feel the strong pulse that beat there. "Let me take over for a while, Zee."

Without a word she shifted to park while they switched. His side throbbed as he climbed into the driver's seat, but he was careful not to wince or groan. It was a pain he would gladly bear if it meant she could rest. She closed her eyes.

"I'm sorry, Gid," she whispered. "For everything."

"I'm sorry too." *And I'll see you home.* "Get some rest."

The road was clear for the most part, except for the few occasions he had to navigate around piled mud and fallen tree trunks. It was harder than it should have been since he still felt clumsy and slow. He turned the radio on to a low murmur. Mackenzie had curled up sideways into a ball, perched against the door.

The weather report was bleak, but the dam news was worse. Newly appeared cracks had caused expanded evacuation mandates. The intent behind the precise language was clear. Those who chose to stay were making a dangerous choice. No amount of help would be enough if the dam failed. There would be no hope of survival. At least he could hang on to the fact that they were now attempting to depart the danger zone—if they could avoid Bulleye's guys long enough. Could be Bullseye and his team had enough good sense to leave off their kill mission and get out before the dam broke.

After fifteen minutes of driving, he almost missed the last turn that promised to take them to the highway. A half-dozen birds shot across the road. Startled. By what?

He stopped, peering into the gloom.

The source of their alarm whirled into view a moment after, circling in a methodical way.

A helicopter.

He hit the gas.

Mackenzie jerked to attention. "What?"

He pointed.

She gasped. "Oh no."

Their only chance was to make it to the section of road where the woods hemmed in from both sides, which would obstruct the aircraft's view. But they had to get there before the helicopter fixed on their location.

He pushed faster, praying they wouldn't encounter another sinkhole.

The helicopter hovered over a hilly glade in the distance

for a few moments as Gideon neared the forest. The camper rattled and shook. A few more seconds . . .

As if in slow motion the helicopter turned and glided closer, red lights blinking in the gloom, zeroing in on their location.

"Did they . . ."

He cut her off. "They've already seen us, Zee."

"Can we outrun them?"

They couldn't, but he knew they'd both try in vain rather than surrender. "If we make it to the woods up ahead, we could ditch the camper. Slim chance we could outrun them on foot."

Her eyes were hard, expression grim but determined.

She reached out, took his hand, and squeezed. "Let's go for it, Gideon. There's nothing else we can do."

"Okay," he said. "Ready?"

She nodded and braced her boots against the floorboard.

He punched the gas.

FIFTEEN

GIDEON DIDN'T FIGURE the helicopter was weaponized, but it didn't matter. The people in it were locked and loaded, and the pilot would instruct additional ground support to press them in on both sides. What were the escape options? The list was painfully short, only one in point of fact.

They'd have to ditch the RV in the forest, lose themselves in the trees. How long could they stay one step ahead of their executioners? With his wound and both of them running on fumes?

The helicopter roared behind him as they shot into the thicket. He practically stood on the accelerator for a half mile maybe, willing the old clunker onward until he pulled the unwieldy RV to a stop amid the dense evergreens. Mackenzie was ready with their packs, but her expression was void of hope. Once more they were forced to ditch the shelter and warmth they both desperately needed.

No more denying it. The net was being pulled tight on all sides. Their best option—to get to the main road and follow the nearest evacuee out of town—was now off the table.

He thought of survivor stories from soldiers who had been captured after excruciating days and weeks of evasion. The level of defeat they'd experienced, the profound hopelessness, invariably weighed more heavily on them than the physical duress they'd endured.

No. Not while his heart was still beating would he give up and allow that to happen. The last-gasp scenario was his own surrender, but only if it gave Zee a chance to escape—something he'd never share with her. If it came to that, he would make the choice for both of them.

He took the gun and got out, left the vehicle with the engine running, and locked it. The curtains in the back were drawn and would conceal the interior. "They'll have to assume we're barricaded inside. It will buy us some time."

She didn't answer, surveying their surroundings like he was.

One side of the road harbored a mass of young trees crowded together in a shallow muddy basin, pooled with standing water. The other offered denser pockets of shrubbery and trees that would provide more cover but also slow their escape.

Which way? His side was on fire and his head throbbing. *Think, Gideon.*

Ahead they saw the gleam of headlights as a vehicle twisted its way along the wooded road toward them. The helicopter thundered overhead, concealed by the canopy.

"They're coming." She understood they were trapped.

The aggressors were approaching from the air and land

now. The two of them would have to run, but it would be over soon. They could not escape on foot. It would be moments, no longer, before they were captured. His pulse thundered.

Why did it have to end like this? After all they'd survived? And all they had to live for? But for the first time in his life he couldn't think of a single alternative that would spare them.

Defeated, Gid? Had they survived, evaded, resisted, only to find there was no escape? It was a bitter reality. Why couldn't he come up with anything?

He'd let Mackenzie down, and the pain of that was an agony worse than the wound.

He took her hand, but before they could leave the road there was a crackling in the branches. Must be yet another team closing in, cutting off their only avenue of escape. He drew her behind him as the foliage parted and he reached for his weapon. Would it even fire properly after being submerged?

His mouth fell open as a familiar woman appeared astride a horse, another horse following with no rider. It took a couple of blinks to convince himself he wasn't dreaming her up. It really was the stable owner whose horse they'd freed from the damaged stall. Cordelia.

She wore a navy rain jacket and mid-calf boots over her skinny jeans. Her black eyes were smudged with fatigue. Was she working with the others to capture them? He recalled her intensity at the stables, the rage in her features when Al and Jerry arrived and began shooting.

"Come on," she said. "You two can ride on Lady. Hurry."

Gideon finally found his voice. "Why are you here? How did you find us?"

"I'll explain later. Get on," Cordelia snapped. "They're going to be here in minutes."

"We have no reason to trust you."

Her eyes glowed with intensity. "You're worth as much to them dead as alive so they won't hesitate to kill you both. Come with me or die. It's that simple."

He tried to absorb it, to understand her possible motives.

Mackenzie tugged his arm. "No choice."

But would this choice just get them dead quicker? Would it mean hopping out of one grave and into another? Why was she here? And how had she found them?

He could hear the engine noise now and a second vehicle approaching behind the first. Worse yet, he was starting to feel dizzy, sparks dancing across his field of vision.

Mackenzie pulled him after her toward the big mare. She stuck her foot in the stirrup and hoisted herself into the saddle. She held down her hand to him, and he swung up behind her, momentarily dazed by the pain the movement unleashed. He thought he was going to hurtle right over the other side to the ground, but Mackenzie pincered his arm under hers.

"Hold on tight around my waist," she said.

He did, or tried to. His bad shoulder was refusing to function properly, so an awkward grasp was the only thing that kept him seated behind her as they wheeled around. Cordelia urged the horse speedily away from the road. There seemed no extreme urgency in Lady as she moved smoothly after her companion. He, on the other hand, was coiled up with tension as he heard the squeal of brakes. Two cars stopped on the road within shooting distance of the camper.

Running feet. Shouts.

The horses' pace was quick and steady, and soon, the thicket sealed off the road behind them. The helicopter was holding in place, but likely not able to spot their escape under the branches as the dusk deepened, unless they had thermal scanning capabilities. He figured they'd have a few precious minutes while Al and his cronies problem solved how to breach the RV.

When their ruse was discovered, their pursuers would start a search on foot. The forest was a mess of fallen pine needles and leaves that would conceal the fact that they were on horseback and the direction they'd taken. He hoped.

Cordelia led the way into a tangle of blackberry bushes. On the other side was a narrow, almost invisible horse trail onto which she turned. The mare followed, and Gideon was grateful the route required less lurching. Pain made him dizzy and he kept his arms looped around Mackenzie's waist as he whispered in her ear.

"We don't know if we can trust her."

"I trust her more than Al and Jerry," she whispered back.

He did, too, but not much more. "Where are you leading us?" he called.

Cordelia didn't answer.

The nerves in his stomach cinched tighter. The fuzziness in his head grew along with the pain until he was afraid he'd pass out.

He'd lost all bearings as they kept on, one sodden mile after another. As the forest descended into night, the animals navigated by intuition, he supposed. He couldn't see Cordelia or her horse, but the soft scuff of hooves on wet earth reassured him they hadn't lost their guide.

An hour stretched into two. He heard no further sounds of the helicopter or any pursuing vehicles. The ache in his side was rising to intolerable levels, so he tried to keep his mind on other things.

Why would Cordelia take the massive risk of rescuing them from under Bullseye's nose? And how had she found them at the moment they were about to be captured?

He found no answers. An occasional spray of icy droplets kept him alert as they rode on. It was all he could do to maintain his grasp around Mackenzie's waist to prevent him from toppling off. Twice he blacked out for a few seconds, rousing just before he fell.

When he thought he could not stand the discomfort one moment longer, he felt the horse slow.

Mackenzie pointed to something. Tucked between two towering pines stood a wood-sided cabin gleaming wetly at the end of a raised planked walkway. He blinked to be sure he wasn't imagining this fairy-tale cottage in the woods, tucked away from the outside world.

It couldn't have been more than a couple hundred square feet with two windows on each side of a sturdy oak door. A dense canopy overhead would make it difficult to spot from the air.

In the glade next to the structure was a small fenced area with a three-sided shelter, to which both horses immediately turned their noses.

Cordelia slipped easily off her mount and led the animal inside the corral. Mackenzie dismounted, and he pridefully ignored her helping hand, which resulted in him almost collapsing to his knees in a heap.

Mackenzie reached for him, but he forced his spine straight with a grunt. "I'm good."

With a doubtful shake of her head, she led the mare to join her companion.

Cordelia jutted her chin at Mackenzie and Gideon. "Door's open. Go on in. I'm going to wipe the horses down and feed them. Be there in a minute."

He and Mackenzie approached the squat structure, and he did a quick look through the windows. Nothing stirred within. No indication there was anyone inside readying a surprise attack.

Mackenzie clasped him by the arm and helped him heave himself up and over the front step. "We've got to check your bandage."

When they stepped inside, the interior smelled of coffee, which made his mouth water. Nothing fancy in terms of layout, a living space with a worn burgundy-colored couch that had seen better days. The kitchen had no stove, but a small propane burner and a blue ice chest sat atop the narrow counter. He found a minuscule bathroom with a composting toilet, no shower. Behind a folding screen was a bed, neatly made, covered by a chenille spread. There was no bedside table to prowl through that might give him a clue about whether Cordelia fit into the friends or enemies camp. He hadn't the strength to investigate further anyway.

Mackenzie forced him into a chair. In the common

space near the lumpy sofa, he'd seen a small side table with a drawer. He intended to rest for just a moment and then, as soon he could get up, he'd rifle through it, but Cordelia entered before he made his move. She pulled off her boots and dropped them on a mat just inside the door.

Immediately she closed the curtains over the front windows and activated two small lanterns, one on the coffee table and the other in the kitchen.

"Do you have any supplies? First aid? Gideon was grazed by a bullet, and I used up most of his already," Mackenzie said.

Cordelia's brows arched, but she produced a small pouch from her pack. Mackenzie took it and set about rebandaging his wound. Fortunately, his pain threshold had already been breached so he hardly felt it. Now that he was off the horse, his body would rally. Hopefully.

A blue flame sprang to life as Cordelia switched on the propane burner and filled a pot with water from a bottle.

"Coffee in a minute," she said.

The word *coffee* sparked a fierce craving. He forced himself to sit straighter. "First things first. Who are you? Really?"

"The same person you met before. Cordelia Bellamy. I own the stables, remember?"

He paused. "Let me backtrack. How did you know where to find us?"

"I have a friend at the airstrip. He gave me some intel."

The airstrip? Why did that location factor so prominently in their lives? He exchanged a look with Mackenzie. "What friend? And how did he know where we were?"

"He's a helicopter pilot." She adjusted the pot on the burner.

Gideon folded his arms. "Look. If we have to do this question by question, it's gonna take forever and I'm not in the mood. How about you cut to the chase. How'd you find us and what's your stake in all this?"

Cordelia cocked her head and gave him full eye contact. She spoke slowly as if he were dim-witted. "Al and Jerry messaged my pilot friend about your escape from the boathouse and told him to prepare the helicopter for another search. Before he launched, he texted me and told me the area he was heading for. I took some shortcuts because I was on horseback, but even with that I barely made it." She dumped spoonfuls of instant coffee into three porcelain mugs. "You like it strong?"

He ignored the question. "Your pilot friend who is helping the people who want to kill us?"

"Yes."

They were back to one-word answers. Best to unload the big one. "Why, Cordelia? Why would either of you stick your neck out for us?"

Her dark hair shone in the lantern light as she regarded him. "I get an interrogation instead of a thank-you? You're alive, right? You could try being grateful for that. I don't have to explain right now, do I?"

"Yes, you do."

Mackenzie nodded her agreement. "We have been hunted, Cordelia, and I've no doubt there's a hefty price on our heads. Good reasons for us not to trust you."

Cordelia's eyes were smudged with fatigue, her ponytail messy, and her clothes disheveled, as if they'd been worn over consecutive days. Her exhaustion reminded him of his own, but he wasn't going to budge until he understood her motives.

She heaved out a breath. "I've been trying like crazy since the stables to find you. I heard a report that you'd been knocked off the road by a mudslide."

Mackenzie raised a brow, and they exchanged a look. "A report from whom?"

"That's not important."

His remaining patience frayed. "Knock it off, Cordelia. I'm tired, hungry, cold, and bashed up. I got no more patience for talking in circles."

Cordelia took two bottles of water from the ice chest and set them on the table. As much as his thirst clamored to be slaked, he made no move to take one. He glowered at her, arms still folded across his chest.

After an extended silence, she seemed to come to a decision. "Kevin contacted me after he got free of your duct tape and he could get a text to send. He said you'd tied him up and gone for your Jeep."

Kevin and Cordelia were allies. He'd been right to suspect them. Had he and Mackenzie played right into enemy hands by following Cordelia to her hidden cabin? Two against one at the moment, and he had a gun. They could overpower her and escape, if he could get his limbs to cooperate. A few more minutes to keep her talking . . .

"With his information, I tracked you as far as the landslide," Cordelia continued, "and I've been desperately looking for you since then. There are only a few passable roads at this point, and even fewer of them would take you in the direction of the airstrip—which Kevin said was your goal." She paused. "Why are you headed there? Looking to get a flight out?"

Gideon lifted his chin, which hurt, but he did it anyway. "Answer the question, then we'll fill in our details."

She watched them for a few seconds before she went on. "Okay. I see the flow of information only goes in one direction. I've been driving back and forth for the past two days, beating the bushes to find you. No success until the tip-off from my pilot friend just now."

"But how'd you know about the landslide? We left Kevin near the river."

"When Kevin freed himself eventually . . ." She laughed. "That would have been funny to watch. He traced your route as far as that point. He got one more message through to me before he stopped communicating. I don't know what's happened to him. If he was smart, he left town, but maybe his phone died or . . ." A shadow crossed her face. "I'm not sure."

Gideon's rib cage sparked with pain. He gripped the table and gave her no way to evade the question. "Why are you and Kevin working together? He was after us because of threats to his family, or so he says. What's your motivation?"

Her lips thinned into a grim smile and her chin went up. "Kevin helped me because he hopes I'm going to stick it to his boss."

Mackenzie jerked. "His boss?"

Her gaze found Mackenzie's. "On your podcast, you call him Bullseye."

The name seemed to suck all the air out of the room. She

knew about Bullseye and the podcast? He was momentarily unable to rally another question, but Mackenzie wasn't.

"What do you know about Bullseye?" she demanded.

"More than I care to, but the point is I'm aware he wants you two dead and I've been trying to prevent that."

Prevent their deaths? Not looking to collect on a bounty? Alarm bells were clanging so loud they almost deafened him. "Hard to believe. To defy him means risking your life. What's in it for you?"

She looked at the counter, wiped at a scratch on the Formica. "I want to wreck his plans."

"Why?"

"He's a bad man." She stared at Mackenzie. "You know that better than anyone. All your talk on the podcast about bringing him to justice?" Cordelia paused a moment. "You're right about him. He's a killer, and I'm going to get you out alive so you can continue to harass him and maybe even send him to prison."

Gideon held up a hand. "Listen, that sounds very grand and altruistic, but maybe this is all a ruse and you're actually looking to get a payout from Bullseye for taking us down. There's gotta be an extra reward for beating Al and Jerry to the finish line."

Her mouth tightened. "I don't want a nickel from that man, and if my actions make things harder for Al and Jerry, so much the better. They never should have trespassed at my stables. They declared war between us when they brought guns around my horses. My stable, those horses, are an inheritance from my mother."

The silence was broken only by the bubbling of the

kettle. Wordlessly, she poured the steaming water into the three mugs.

Gideon knew his doubt was probably written all over his face. "You want us to believe you're working against Bullseye out of some vague notion of making the world a better place?"

"Believe what you want." Hatred shone in her coal-dark eyes. "He's determined to see you dead, you've got to acknowledge the truth of that. It's why I've put my life on hold to protect you."

Mackenzie was staring at Cordelia. "You're not telling us everything."

She smacked a palm on the counter. "Don't you get it? Everything around here is falling apart. You have to get out. There are too many people in this town on the payroll, and that dam isn't going to hold."

"We were trying to get away when the helicopter spotted us," Gideon said.

"You've got to trust me now. You two are half dead as it is. You'll never escape without my help."

Three days ago, he wouldn't have agreed. Now it was more than likely the truth. They'd come to the most difficult part of the whole survival, evasion, resistance, and escape conundrum. Whom to trust? The environment might be hostile, but it was nowhere near as dangerous as a human enemy, the kind pretending to be a friend.

If his pain would just let up a minute and allow him to think clearly.

Cordelia thrust the mugs of coffee at them. He accepted. Maybe the hot brew would sharpen his senses. Mackenzie handed him a few ibuprofen, which he gratefully accepted.

Cordelia started to walk past him to the living room, but he clasped her wrist. "I agree with Mackenzie. There's more you're not telling us. Much more."

She flinched. "You're right. The stakes are high. There are excellent reasons why I would risk my own safety to help you two, but I don't really trust you either. My reasons are my business."

Gideon's tone was sharp with impatience and the twinges that were knocking at his bones. "It is our business. We've been betrayed at every turn, and you're holding back on us."

She yanked free from his grip, carried her coffee into the other room, and sat on a worn leather chair. He managed to get on his feet, clutch his coffee, and stagger after her, Mackenzie hovering at his elbow.

He sat on the sofa, proud of himself for not spilling a drop of the hot liquid. Mackenzie settled next to him, taut and wary.

Gideon tried again. "You could have alerted Bullseye. He might be on his way right now to get us so you can collect. Maybe get some sort of favor from him."

She appeared to come to a decision as she lasered in on Mackenzie. "I called you."

Mackenzie cocked her head. "That was you in the phone message?"

"I would have explained more, arranged a meeting, but the call dropped."

Mackenzie's eyes widened. "But . . . that call came from Aaron's phone."

Cordelia nodded slowly. "Yes, I have his cell."

Cordelia had Aaron's cell phone. Gideon's brain kicked into high gear as she continued.

"You want me to tell you the reason I'm involved? Okay." She looked right at Mackenzie and pulled a chain from under her shirt. A slender band with a small diamond chip glinted in the light. Her eyes shone as if there were tears collecting under the lashes. "This is my engagement ring."

Engagement ring. Aaron's cell phone.

The jewelry sparkled as it swung gently on the chain. "I'm helping you because I don't want to see my fiancé's sister murdered."

....

Mackenzie felt as if the room were spinning around her. She perched on the end of the lumpy sofa with the mug of hot coffee cradled in her trembling hands. Gideon sat next to her, squeezing her forearm, and Cordelia eyed them from the chair where she sipped her coffee, lost in thought.

My fiancé's sister . . .

Leah. Aaron's tendency to shorten people's names.

Mackenzie had become Zee.

Cordelia was Leah, the woman he loved, whom Mackenzie had never met.

Her heart refused to beat in a normal rhythm as she assimilated the information. *How did you meet her, Aaron? How come I didn't know about the engagement? Why was everything such a secret from me? Your sister.* She couldn't get any of the words out so Gideon took over.

"All right," he said calmly. "This is a lot to take in. Would you mind filling us in on how it all came about?"

So polite. As if they were at a tea party chatting about vacations or hobbies.

Mackenzie almost laughed at the absurdity of it.

Cordelia took a breath. "Aaron came to the stables two and a half years ago and asked about renting a horse to take a ride while he was in town. We hit it off immediately, wound up talking for hours. He's—he was—one of the only people I've known who loved horses as much as I do. He told me he'd come to the area for a job interview, but that sounded pretty suspect. Oakleaf isn't exactly a hot market for up-and-comers. Aaron just wasn't country material either. Except for his love of horses, he was a better match for a city."

That was the truth. Her brother had liked fine dining, luxury apartments where his friends would let him stay once in a while, places with excellent Wi-Fi and plenty of nightlife. He enjoyed foreign films and exotic foods—but nothing outshone his love of horses. Mackenzie held her breath.

"He started showing up almost daily at the stables, and even after he went back home, we talked on the phone for hours. Eventually, I called him out on his 'job interview' cover story, and he admitted he was moving some product for Bullseye." Her face burned in the lamplight as if the memory were branded there. Mackenzie felt singed by the confirmation too.

Her brother had indeed been selling drugs for Bullseye. *Aaron, a drug dealer. Why?* Gideon squeezed her wrist, but she barely felt it.

"Keep going," she said to Cordelia.

"I told him if there was going to be a future between

us, he had to quit dealing drugs. He promised he would, as soon as he had enough to launch his tech company. I begged him to do it immediately." She looked at the ceiling. "I'm proud and stubborn and impatient, but I begged him to get out. We could survive on the income from the stables until he got established, but he was too proud for that."

Mackenzie's heart bent toward this woman who'd loved her brother and tried to steer him on the right path. "Thank you," she said quietly. "For trying to persuade him to quit."

For doing what I should have done.

Cordelia shook her head. "It wasn't enough."

"Why do you have his phone?"

Cordelia smiled. "He lost it when we were out riding. I found it the day after he left, but there was no way to reach him. I knew he was coming back soon, so it didn't seem like a big deal. He had a burner phone for his work things.

"Two days before he was supposed to meet me here, I saw a news headline about a man being shot and killed in Aaron's hometown." Her voice wobbled. "I knew it. Even before they released his identity, I knew it was him."

Mackenzie was horror-struck at the excruciating way Cordelia had found out about Aaron's murder. Cordelia's grief was real, the deep ache close to the surface. "I'm sorry you learned about his death that way. If I'd known about his relationship with you, had some kind of contact information, I would have called."

Cordelia didn't acknowledge the remark. Her throat convulsed as she swallowed hard, trying to master her emotions.

"Why do you think Aaron was killed?" Gideon said.

Her voice was dull. "Because he worked for Bullseye. Simple as that. Drug deals go bad in that business. He should have walked away when I asked him to."

Cordelia seemed to shrink in on herself. Mackenzie gave her a moment before she asked the next question. "Why didn't he tell me about you?"

"Probably because you'd ask all the things you're asking now. How did we meet? Why was he coming to town in the first place? He didn't want you to know about his dealing. He was . . . ashamed. Deeply." Her gaze grew cloudy. "He said his job was to look after you, keep you away from trouble." She shook her head. "Looks like you landed yourself right in the middle of it anyway, didn't you?"

Mackenzie experienced a stab of guilt. She had run into the mess and towed Gideon along with her. And had she dragged Aaron's grieving fiancée into the crosshairs too? She swallowed a sob. "Guess I'm stubborn like my brother."

"Guess you are." Cordelia's gaze drifted over the small space. "We'd meet up at this old place when we both could get away. I guess we were like kids, playing house and pretending he didn't deal drugs, counting the days until we could be together legitimately, go public so to speak, but away from this town. I was going to help him run his tech business and relocate my stables, maybe nearer to where your family lived." She paused. "He told me I'd like your parents."

Mackenzie felt the hot tears trailing down her cheeks. "You would."

"And that I'd like you too, because we were both strong-willed, intelligent women."

It was almost too much to bear, listening to the things Aaron had said to this woman he loved who would have to live her life without him. The vise squeezed her heart.

Gideon cleared his throat. "Thank you for telling us about you and Aaron. There are a few other things I'm still unclear about. How did you know Mackenzie arrived in town?"

"I didn't at first. Even when you two showed up at the stables, I didn't know who you were. There was something familiar about you, Mackenzie, but I was too distracted saving the horses to notice the family resemblance. After Jerry and Al tried to ambush you, I started asking questions and figured it out. I found your podcast, listened to every episode." She chuckled. "Gotta admit, you have some serious nerve to call out a kingpin like that." Her smile faded as she looked at Gideon.

Mackenzie toyed with her mug.

Cordelia shook her head. "Bullseye feels threatened. He's got to be really rattled to spend so much energy trying to catch and kill you. The good guy is much more his preferred persona in town. He fancies himself a Robin Hood type, providing jobs and pouring money into projects and people when he feels magnanimous. It's not comfortable for him to be publicly vilified, I'd imagine. You made an enemy of him and you delivered yourself right into his backyard in the process. What information were you after, by the way? Did you get it?"

Mackenzie frowned. "A lead about his real name, but I lost my contact before I got it. Do you know his identity?"

She hesitated. "Yes, I do. Are you sure you want to find out? After everything that's happened?"

Mackenzie's whole body went slow and quiet. At last, this was the moment. "Yes, I do. Tell me who he is."

She nodded. "Okay. His name's Frank Soliel."

Her heart jumped. *Finally.* "How do you know?"

"Lots of people know, they just don't want to say because they're afraid of him. You can understand that after everything that's happened."

She did. Poor Lorraine, falsely arrested, their van forced into the river. Kevin fearing for his family's safety. Attack after attack on her and Gideon. Bullseye reigned with an iron fist. Mackenzie sat back. A name. She had a name. It was the key that would unlock the rest of the investigation. With her web of shadowy contacts she could unearth his secrets, deliver them to the police along with her other notes, and help them put their case together.

"Why didn't you go to the cops?" Gideon asked. "After Aaron was killed? Tell them he was working for Soliel?"

Cordelia flushed. "What good would that do? There are so many layers between him and his lower-level people, they'd never prove anything."

"Especially since Aaron's shooter was killed shortly after the murder. Not that he would have squealed on his boss anyway," Mackenzie said.

Cordelia straightened and put her mug down. "The best option now is for us all to leave. Soon as we hear from my friend that he's returned from the search, we'll head to the airstrip. He's going to fly us out of here the first moment he can."

"That's a huge risk for him."

"Yes, but I can trust him."

Mackenzie chewed her lip in thought. "When we're clear, we can meet with the police. Together we'd have enough to convince them to look into the case."

Cordelia shook her head. "I don't think so. I'm leaving town all right, but I'm not getting myself involved in an investigation."

Not getting involved? When her fiancé was brutally murdered?

"What's your plan after we get out of here then?" Gideon said.

Mackenzie tried to patiently wait for an answer.

"Why do you need to know?" Cordelia said.

"Why wouldn't you want to share?" he countered. "You're going to ensure that we all get a flight out. Then what will you do?"

"I have a college friend in Oregon. I'll be okay there."

"Safe from Bullseye's reach? He'll put a price on your head too," Gideon said. "Might have already."

Her eyes flashed. "Let him. Most of my horses have already been taken to safety. There's only the two that carried us remaining and I've made arrangements for them. Got a buyer for the stables if there's anything left of them after the dam fails or the town is washed away by the rain." Her tone went flat. "There's nothing here for me anymore, not one single thing." She got up. "I'm going to lay down. I have a radio that my friend's been using to contact me since there's no cell service. Soon as I hear from him, we'll go. You should get some sleep if you can." Cordelia walked soundlessly to the bathroom, closed the door, and ran the water in the sink.

Gideon drank his coffee. "You okay, Zee?" He kept his voice low and soft.

"Honestly, I don't know. That was a shock."

"You can say that again." He finished the last gulp. "I don't know if I believe her completely."

Mackenzie started. It hadn't occurred to her that he might not be as convinced as she was. "Everything she said was right on with the timeline. I know she was Aaron's fiancée. She's not faking that."

"It's not the engagement part that troubles me." Gideon rolled his empty cup between his palms. "I just feel like there's a missing piece, something she's not divulging."

She felt a flicker of irritation. "This is what you wanted all along, to get out. Now that we're doing it, you're upset?"

"Not upset. Wary."

She shook her head. "I'm not. I feel like we finally have the answers. I've got Bullseye's name. I'll convince Cordelia to go to the cops with me eventually. She knows things that will help them nail him to the wall."

"She doesn't want to talk. Can't exactly blame her for that."

"Bullseye won't be a threat for long."

His eyes roved her face. "Doesn't it seem odd to you that her fiancé was murdered and she didn't want to take that up with the police? A tough woman like that?"

Her impatience grew. They had the truth now. Why was he throwing up roadblocks? "He owns some of the cops here, maybe that's the case for other departments. She has a right to be nervous."

He didn't answer, so she touched his shoulder. "Let

me check your bandage again and you can get some rest, okay? We've still got some dangerous hours ahead if Bullseye gets wind we're flying out. His people know we're somewhere in this forest, and I'm sure they haven't stopped their ground efforts."

She led him to the kitchen chair, where she examined his bandage. There was a small amount of fresh blood, but not enough to make her worry. She retaped the gauze into place.

He winced.

"Uncomfortable?"

"Nah. I'm practically healed."

She kissed the lines of pain on his brow, allowed her fingers to graze his temple. He sighed, and his body relaxed. "We're almost clear, Gideon. We're going to return to the land of hot showers, microwaves, and all the praying mantises a guy could want."

He didn't smile and it pained her, so she bent her head and kissed him. His lips were warm and soft and his chin prickly with stubble. She'd intended a quick peck as a friendly encouragement, but she couldn't resist giving him a proper kiss. Then it was all warmth and comfort, and when he eagerly returned the kiss, she couldn't back away for what seemed like forever. When she did, breathless, she stroked his cheek.

"I'll never forget everything you've done for me, and I promise I'll accept my punishment for stealing your wallet as soon as I return."

"You know that's not my concern."

"I do know that."

He went quiet, the tenderness of his expression, the

tingling on her own lips urging her nearer. But this was not the time, nor the place, nor maybe even the right choice, for them to nurture their closeness. This was a terrifying movie that was nearing its end. Soon they'd be safe.

Soon they'd be home.

She forced herself away from him. "I'll take the armchair. You lie down on the sofa."

Gideon's gaze followed her. He needed more convincing. She didn't.

She and Cordelia had both loved Aaron, and that bond would hold them together forever. Cordelia had risked everything, including her own life, to save theirs. It was enough proof of her intentions.

Mackenzie settled into the armchair, prepared for an uncomfortable night.

In a matter of hours their harrowing journey would be over.

And Bullseye's problems were just beginning.

With a smile on her lips, still tingling from the kiss, she closed her eyes.

SIXTEEN

WAKING FROM A DEAD SLEEP well before sunrise felt like trying to swim through concrete. It was only to stop Mackenzie shaking his shoulder that Gideon opened both eyes, more out of self-defense than wakefulness.

"That really hurts, Zee," he said with a grunt.

"Sorry, but you're sleeping like the dead and we need to go."

He couldn't be 100 percent certain he wasn't actually dying. His whole body was one throbbing nerve ending, and his head pounded like a timpani drum. Nonetheless, he extricated himself from the sofa, made it cautiously to his feet, and drank more coffee that someone had prepared as he tried to absorb the details revealed the previous night.

Cordelia appeared. She'd pulled her hair into a long dark braid, and she was dressed in the same clothes, a radio clipped to her belt. "It's all set. We'll ride most of the way until I drop off the horses to a lady I know who will evacuate them. The last quarter mile will be on foot, but Jake will pick us up if he can."

"Jake, the pilot?"

"Yes."

"And you're positive you can trust him?"

"He's sticking his neck out to help me."

Gideon looked over the top of his coffee cup at her. "And why would he do that?"

"He owes me."

"How?"

Cordelia shook her head. "Do you ever run out of questions?"

"I'm just getting warmed up." He had a ton more. Facts he'd like confirmed. Motives he didn't understand. And there was still something niggling deep in the recesses of his brain that he couldn't put his finger on. Getting answers from her was akin to extracting teeth.

Cordelia heaved out a breath. "Jake and his wife, Willa, live on the ranch next to my stables. A couple months ago, Willa was out riding and her horse got spooked. It took off like a thunderbolt. I was setting out on a trail ride, so I intervened before she got carried into a real treacherous area or thrown. Jake says I saved her life, and he's old-school about loyalty. Once he flies us out, his debt is settled."

"A man who loves his wife," Gideon said.

Cordelia sighed. "He adores her."

There was a wistfulness in her tone that spoke of the love she'd lost. This part, at least, he believed was the truth. She'd loved Aaron and she mourned him. On that point, they could all three relate. They'd lost a best friend, a brother, a fiancé.

They took turns in the minuscule bathroom, and the mirror confirmed he looked as bad as he felt. The scruff on his chin was not his style, and he longed for a shave. Cuts and scrapes dotted his face, neck, and hands. He suspected the wound from the bullet might need stitches, and that was only the beginning of a long list of damage. A splash of frigid water infused some energy back into him but didn't stop the myriad aches.

Get yourself together. Head on a swivel. These last few miles might be the most dangerous of all. The threat hadn't diminished, and they were now depending on yet more strangers to enact their escape—strangers who could be bought for a price.

Cordelia provided them each a handful of cookies. "Sorry, I don't have anything else right now."

"This is just fine." Oatmeal raisin wasn't his favorite, but it tasted so amazing he might have to change his opinion. He and Mackenzie gobbled their cookies and washed them down with coffee.

Mackenzie zipped up her jacket. "Ready?"

Were they? Ready to sneak onto an airstrip under cover of darkness, avoiding a team of people bent on killing them, with a woman he believed was not completely forthcoming? He made sure the gun was loaded and easily accessible.

"Let's do it," he said.

Outside, the horses were already saddled, and he needed every atom of reserved strength to once again haul himself up behind Mackenzie. He held her around the waist as they started off through the freezing, predawn air.

A novice horseman, he never would have chosen to ride in darkness with another wave of storm coming, but

Cordelia led the way across some sort of trail he hadn't even noticed. The horses seemed to know it well enough.

"I used to wait at the airstrip with the horses when Aaron would fly in. We'd sneak off to the cabin this way so no one could follow," Cordelia said over her shoulder.

He noticed the way Mackenzie studied Cordelia. Odd, he imagined, for her to suddenly be introduced to the woman who would have been her sister-in-law. Had Cordelia's presence returned Aaron to Mackenzie in some way? After they fled, perhaps the two could somehow stay connected. He suspected they'd find comfort in sharing stories about the man they'd both loved in different ways.

She leaned her head against his shoulder. "You okay back there?"

"Yes." He snuggled in a little. It might be the last occasion he'd be able to hold her close. It surprised him how much he craved the connection that had only grown when they'd kissed the previous night.

Don't get ahead of yourself, Gid. When they returned to the real world, God willing, he had a feeling she'd keep him at a distance while she again took up her mission to destroy Bullseye. But she'd changed, hadn't she? Begun to feel again. He craved the chance to watch her heal. His cheek brushed her damp hair. He'd try, he decided, to stay close to her, if she'd allow it.

His inner pessimism told him his rosy vision wasn't going to come true. A proud woman, she wouldn't want a witness to the messy process of healing. And she wasn't going to want him around reminding her of what she'd lost. Four days ago they were enemies. Now the thought of parting with her made him ache inside.

What is wrong with you, Gideon? His brothers would tell him he'd lost his mind, and they'd be right. Survival should be his chief and only concern at the moment.

The ride became a tedious rhythm of clopping hooves and pattering rain that continued until Cordelia finally slowed her horse. Mackenzie followed suit.

In the distance, headlights revealed a truck hitched to a horse trailer. A figure was silhouetted in the window, the tip of a cigarette glowing.

"That's Willa," Cordelia said. "You two stay back here out of sight. I don't want her to have to lie if she's ever asked about you. Jake's kept her in the dark about transporting us. It's better she doesn't know."

They watched from a distance while Cordelia and Willa loaded the horses into the trailer. After a quick hug, Willa drove away.

Cordelia called them over and they set off on foot. The ground was muddy, but Gideon was so relieved to be off the horse, he paid it no mind. The movement helped warm him too, and an hour later they descended along a pitched trail. At the edge of the woods, across a stretch of flat ground, was a small hangar with metal doors thrown wide and a narrow runway lit by small red blinkers. Behind the hangar he could make out the rotors of a helicopter inside a fenced area.

Their escape was so close he could taste it.

When they exited the woods, Cordelia's friend Jake was waiting in a battered Ford. He nodded at them. "Willa said to tell you she made it to the highway. Glad she's clear of this place. Let's move it."

He was an impossibly thin man whose tall frame seemed

too big for the vehicle. They climbed in the truck and Jake took off. He didn't say another word until they'd arrived and walked into the hangar.

"Bathroom's there if you need it," Jake said, pointing. "I'm wheels up in five minutes and I'll leave you behind if you aren't in the seats." He turned on his heel and left through the back door.

Mackenzie hurried to the restroom while he looked around the hangar. Only one aircraft was present in the drafty space, a sleek Cessna.

Gideon's father had flown as a younger man, taken him and his brothers once or twice. Good memories. He wandered over and skimmed his hand along the wing. "Pretty bird."

Cordelia sniffed. "Should be. It's Bullseye's private jet. He's got too much money to bother moving it out of flood range. That's how rich he is. He can throw things away and people too."

Blood money. The black script painted on the nose caught his attention. He read the name and his heart shuddered to a stop. He read it again.

A stylized heart sketched around one word . . . *Bellamy*.

His pulse slammed into overdrive. Mackenzie opened the lavatory door. He quickly jogged to her. "Change of plans. We have to get out of here. Now."

Mackenzie stiffened. "What's wrong?"

Cordelia was looking at him, puzzled.

"She's been lying to us."

"What are you talking about?" Cordelia said.

"Why don't you tell us the part you left out?" He palmed his weapon, certain there was an ambush coming.

Cordelia shook her head. "I don't . . ."

He pointed. "Bullseye's plane . . . it's called Bellamy. Your last name. There's no such thing as coincidence, so don't even try that one. You're connected to him. Fess up."

Cordelia's shoulders slumped. "Bellamy is my mother's name. I use it as a last name to avoid questions."

The confirmation ratcheted his adrenaline even higher.

Mackenzie's mouth fell open. "Are you saying Bullseye—"

"Is my father, yes," she said.

In the silence, he heard rain start to fall, drilling the roof. He eyed the big metal door. "We go right back out, Zee. We'll get to the woods and regroup." How, he didn't know, but they'd figure it out.

Cordelia shook her head. "You won't make it."

"Gideon." Mackenzie stared past his shoulder. "I see lights."

A set of headlights appeared in the distance. Immediately he hit the button on the wall and the hangar doors began to slide closed.

"Rear exit then." The yard, where the helicopter was their only option. The fence was an obstacle, but it was climbable if Jake didn't interfere. Who knew if the story Cordelia had told them about him was real?

"Wait." Cordelia raised her hands. "You have to listen to me. He's my father and I wish he wasn't. I didn't tell you everything because I wasn't sure you'd trust me."

"You were right," Gideon said. "We don't."

"Everything I told you is true. Aaron and I were engaged. I loved him." Her voice cracked. "I'm getting out of here and never coming back. You have to come with me unless you want to die."

Mackenzie's face was as pale as milk. "Bullseye is your father. Did my brother know that?"

Cordelia's words spilled out in a rush. "When Aaron finally told me the truth about his work, I was horrified. I had to tell him who I was. He promised he'd quit, as soon as he could, and we'd leave. In the meantime we kept our relationship a secret. I knew Daddy would never accept anyone in the business dating his daughter. And especially someone whose sister was going to be a cop."

Mackenzie jerked as if she'd been slapped.

"How's that for irony? We told no one, were never together in public, but . . . but Daddy found out anyway." Tears flowed down Cordelia's face, dripping from her chin. "I was stupid to think he wouldn't."

Gideon stared, willing her to say it, the terrible fact he feared was coming, one that would detonate Mackenzie like a bomb. "Your father knew about you and Aaron."

"Yes." Cordelia looked at the floor. "And he had Aaron killed."

* * *

Mackenzie reeled back into Gideon's chest. She tried to absorb Cordelia's revelation. Bullseye had Aaron murdered because of his relationship with Cordelia?

She was engulfed by a wave of nausea. But was it the truth? All of it? Cordelia was clearly stricken, but there was no way they could trust her with their lives, not now.

Gideon tugged at her forearm. "Mackenzie, we're out of here. Hold on to me and let's go."

She was shaky as he steered her. She heard the sounds of car doors wrenched open, boots pounding toward the hangar.

"You can't get away. The chopper's ready out back. We have to go," Cordelia said.

"We're not going anywhere with you." Gideon urged Mackenzie on. "Faster."

Rifle shots peppered the steel doors. The weapon now in Gideon's hand was hardly a match.

All three of them ran to the rear as more bullets plowed into the metal. The fenced area would provide no protection from gunfire. They had minutes, maybe less.

Her mind cycled through possibilities. Cordelia would get on that chopper and when it lifted off, it might be enough of a distraction for Mackenzie and Gideon to run back into the hangar, open the doors, and tear out the front. Without getting shot? It was no better than a suicide mission, but she could think of nothing else.

Holding on to Gideon, she tumbled past the door and into the fenced yard. He held her close as Cordelia sprinted to the chopper. The rotors were whirling, getting up to speed as the engine whined.

Jake was tight-jawed, working the controls. He called out to them. "Get in! Now!"

Cordelia turned back to Gideon. "You can't stay here. I'm . . ."

Her words were lost in a roar as a surge of water burst from beyond the field and rolled in a tumbling mass toward the tarmac.

"The dam!" Cordelia screamed. Her eyes were wild.

The water moved so forcefully it shook the ground

under their feet. Swirling waves foamed toward them with terrifying speed, engulfing their ankles within seconds.

Gideon slipped and went under, the gun snatched from his grip and sucked away.

Mackenzie yanked him up as the water level rose. The helicopter was their only way out. Cordelia was a pace ahead of them.

Gideon shoved her. "Go, go!"

Mackenzie catapulted forward. Cordelia tripped, splashing face-first near the skids already rising. Gideon grabbed her around the waist and hoisted her through the open chopper door with Mackenzie's help.

Water sucked at Gideon's boots as he jumped in after the two women. The split second he and Cordelia were aboard, Mackenzie slammed the door closed, and the chopper rose straight up at a dizzying speed.

"Buckle in!" the pilot shouted. All three of them took the rear seats and strapped in against the vibrations of the aircraft. Within seconds they were flying into the darkness.

They banked left. She caught sight of the shimmering surface below as the floodwater surrounded the hangar. Al and Jerry were nowhere to be seen. If they hadn't made it back to their vehicles, survival would be out of the question.

She felt unmoored, unable to process what had just happened. Cordelia was Bullseye's daughter. He'd had Aaron executed. Now they were trapped in a helicopter with her and her pilot.

Jake listened on his headphones and turned to report, gesturing for them to put on their own headsets. "It was only a partial failure. The dam's still hanging on, but no telling if it's going to last."

"How long until we get to Clover?" Cordelia said into the headset mic.

"It's forty-five minutes north," he said. "Fortunately, out of flood range."

Cordelia sighed and slumped back on the seat. Was it resignation on her face? Sadness? Guilt?

Mackenzie stared at her, mind still reeling with the revelation. "You are a liar. I don't trust you to keep us alive."

Cordelia's voice through the mic was slightly tinny. "I know, but the important thing is your brother trusted me."

"Did he?"

Cordelia blazed a defiant look at them.

"The two of you aren't dead, so I've done what I set out to do." Cordelia folded her arms around herself. "As soon as we get to the next airport, you can do whatever you want. But if you die, at least I can sleep knowing I tried my best to save you. I'm Frank Soliel's daughter, but I'm not his lackey, no matter what you think."

"So you're going to run away from your father?" Gideon said.

"Yes."

Mackenzie considered. Could she be telling the truth? Why else would she have plucked them away from her father's minions? "Aren't you worried he'll come after you?"

"He will, I have no doubt."

"But you'd still rather face that than turn him over to the police?" Mackenzie asked.

"I know how the system works."

Gideon's disgust was clear. "It's easier to hide than do the right thing."

Cordelia's eyes flashed fire. "You have no right to judge me, either of you. You don't know anything about what I've endured as a Soliel. How do you think it feels to know your father had your fiancé murdered?" Tears sparkled in her eyes. "I'll be in hiding for the rest of my life. Anyone new I meet, anyone who shows interest . . . might be one of my father's spies. I'll never have a chance at a normal existence while he's alive, so you can paint me as a villain if you want, but I'm more of a victim than either of you. Aaron was the only one who ever understood." She gulped back tears.

Mackenzie was stung. Whatever Cordelia had or hadn't done, Aaron had loved her. Her anger began to dissipate. "I . . . can't imagine what it must have been like for you with that man as your father."

Cordelia swiped at her cheeks. "You have no idea. I only figured out what he was into when I was a teen. Up until then, I didn't understand the meetings, the strange people who showed up to our house, the phone calls. I thought it was all normal. When I'd ask my mother what Daddy did for a living, she'd say he was a businessman. She knew, of course, but she pretended not to. I guess it was easier that way."

Mackenzie understood. She'd dismissed aspects of her brother's life that she hadn't wanted to acknowledge. Her love had bordered on hero worship, and it had blinded her. The tight knot of anger in her belly loosened. She and Gideon listened as Cordelia's story flowed out.

"He wasn't always like he is now. Oh, he was overprotective and strict, but after my mom got sick, he changed. He made sure she saw the best cancer specialists in the country, and he flew her all over the world to seek treatment. He wasn't able to accept that he couldn't find a cure to save her. He controlled everything, everyone, but he couldn't defeat her disease."

The helicopter vibrations thrummed through Mackenzie as she listened.

"I remember when I first realized who my father really was. Three men came to our house, Al, Jerry, and someone I didn't know. I didn't understand why the third guy was so scared. He was soaked with sweat and shaking. My dad saw me looking and shouted for my mom, who came to get me, but before the door closed, I heard the man say, 'Please.' I'll never forget the way he said it, begging." She folded her arms across her chest. "Begging for his life, I came to realize. Mom wouldn't tell me anything, but from then on I understood my dad was powerful and people were afraid of him. I listened after that, eavesdropped whenever I could until I was old enough to put the details together. I should have known from the way people treated us in town, like we were royalty or mobsters, which I guess we were."

Gideon nodded, encouraging her to continue.

"My mother died when I was eleven, and he turned into someone else. He wouldn't let me go anywhere or be around other people unless he was with me or his bodyguards were. I wasn't even allowed to go to public school. There were tutors instead. I had no friends, no community. My cell phone was policed, and there was a tracking app on it. My only escape was the horses, if I was accompanied."

Mackenzie forced herself to absorb every word, unbelievable as it sounded. This person sitting before her, the woman her brother had loved, was Bullseye's child.

"I left home when I was eighteen, went to community college. Eventually I bought the stables with the money my mother left me. It upset him so much he didn't speak to me for six months, but he had me watched. I kept my distance, except for one visit. It all came rushing back, and I couldn't stand knowing what he did for a living. I saw how everyone around him looked . . . scared. Scared of what he'd do if they displeased him. I knew I'd disappointed him, but I couldn't be what he wanted. I couldn't fill the empty space my mother had left. A child can't do that. It's wrong to try to make them. Children deserve to be free." Cordelia's eyes blazed with emotion, and her lips trembled.

Her story ended in a breathless rush. "There was always someone spying wherever I went. People knew, and they made sure never to get too close to me."

"Why didn't you move away from this town?" Gideon asked.

"It wouldn't have mattered. He could find me anywhere. At least I had some acquaintances here, and my horses. I lived my own life and pretended."

How incredibly lonely she must have felt.

The helicopter thundered on through the dark sky. A blurry thumbprint of sun shone behind oppressive cloud cover.

"Dad never stopped watching me, even when I was a full-grown woman. He was still watching when I met Aaron," Cordelia said. "I'd let my guard down after so many years. I thought Daddy realized I was an adult who wouldn't take his money, no matter how hard he pressed."

And Aaron had landed in the middle of this fearful clan.

"There. You've got the sordid family history. Satisfied?" Cordelia closed her eyes and leaned her head to the side. "I'm done talking. I just want to sleep now." She turned away.

Mackenzie looked at Gideon, unsure of how to respond.

He squeezed her hand and slid off his headset. She did the same. He put his mouth close to her ear. "Phone?"

She checked. "Still no service."

"Hopefully when we get to the airport in Clover, we can call. They'll have security there that can help in any case."

She nodded, but her thoughts were elsewhere . . . with Cordelia, a woman caught in her father's violent world, his grief over his wife transformed into something ugly and vengeful. Then again, he could have been ugly and vengeful long before the loss.

Ugly and vengeful . . . Mackenzie wondered suddenly if that described her too. She shook the thought away. Maybe it had until Gideon convinced her otherwise. She'd let that be her core for way too long. That wasn't the identity God meant for her, and he'd used Gideon to deliver the message. It eased a tightly coiled place inside her, and for the first time in a long while, she took a full breath. Down below, the hills glittered wetly in the starlight.

Once the waters receded, they'd be back on solid ground again. What would that be like? With all the painful truths she'd learned? She found herself leaning against Gideon, her head on his shoulder.

He wrapped his arm around her, though she knew the motion caused him pain.

"I can't even believe what's happened. I just want to go home."

"Soon," he whispered.

Drowsiness overcame her, the thudding of the rotors a soothing lullaby. Rest was the thing her body craved most.

She wasn't quite asleep yet when a sudden movement from Jake startled her. He clasped his earpiece, listening intently. He gestured for Cordelia to join him in the jump seat where she put on the copilot headset.

Gideon reached for Mackenzie's hand, waiting.

Had the dam finally failed completely? Were there gunmen waiting at the airport?

The message Cordelia listened to was quick, but it hit her like a splash of acid. She ripped off the headphones and flung them at Jake as if they'd burned her. Jake didn't make further eye contact, his fingers white on the controls.

"Gideon, something's going down." Mackenzie's stomach lurched as the helicopter dipped to one side.

"Yes," he said grimly. "We're changing direction."

They were both reaching for their seat belts when Cordelia spun to face them. She held a small gun, and pain hardened her features into stone.

"I'm sorry," she said. "We have to go to my father's house."

Bullseye's home? Mackenzie was too stunned to speak. Again the rug had been ripped out from under them. But surely everything Cordelia had revealed was the truth.

"Cordelia . . ." Gideon started, reaching again for his seat belt.

"No," she barked before her voice dropped to a strangled whisper. She aimed the gun at his chest, center mass. "I don't want to shoot you."

Jake jerked a look, sweat beading on his temple. "You know you can't fire a weapon in here. If you do, we'll crash."

"I know." Her eyes never left Gideon's. "So don't make me, okay?"

"What is going on?" he demanded.

Her lips quivered. "I really thought I could get you out, get us all out, but things have changed."

"What things?" Mackenzie said. "Whatever it is, let us help you. We know you're not a bad person, Cordelia. You loved my brother and he loved you too."

Twin tears coursed down her face as she shook her head. "I'm sorry. So sorry."

There was nothing more they could do but watch as the helicopter completed the turn and spun toward the dark ridge of the mountain.

SEVENTEEN

CORDELIA REFUSED TO ANSWER any questions, no matter how many Gideon threw at her. Whatever message the pilot had shared with her had changed the game somehow, and it was clear events were no longer trending in their favor. Possibly the whole thing had been a clever ruse on Cordelia's part, but he couldn't bring himself to believe it.

Cordelia was delivering them to their deaths, but she appeared unwilling and devastated to be doing so. Bullseye must have some kind of leverage she could not fight against.

Gideon touched his seat belt buckle, ignoring the throbbing in his side. He might be able to unclick and overwhelm her, but her firing in the confines of their aircraft could result in catastrophe for all of them.

Cordelia's eyes burned and she sat resolutely gripping the gun, lips pressed in a grim line as they flew in silence northward. The helicopter lights revealed a rippling series of foothills glistening with rainfall, until they flew toward a fancy mountaintop home with a helicopter pad on the third-story roof. Lights blazed from every grand window, the neat grounds tastefully illuminated as well. To the west of the structure was a luxurious boathouse with slips for four vessels and a dock protruding over a swollen lake.

Bullseye's home.

A picturesque retreat for a monstrous man.

Thus far the floodwaters hadn't reached the estate, but Gideon didn't think the elevation would be enough to protect it if the dam failed completely, especially with the lake already brimming with stormwater. It seemed foolhardy for the kingpin to remain, and Gideon didn't think Bullseye was a reckless man. With an available chopper, perhaps he was preparing to evacuate . . . as soon as he dealt with his prisoners and retrieved his daughter. Cordelia thought she'd been able to evade her father's relentless eye. She'd been wrong. Dead wrong.

He shifted on the seat. So this was it. The exact scenario they'd almost died trying to avoid. Capture. He knew he could withstand whatever punishment was coming without breaking, but . . .

He turned his head to look at Mackenzie.

She stared straight ahead, hands clenched into fists, a vein jumping in her jaw. Probably regretting, like he was, choosing to trust Cordelia. He wanted to tell her that something was at play here; whatever Cordelia heard on the radio caused her to turn traitor. Wouldn't matter much when they were executed, but he couldn't stop wondering anyway. He bitterly regretted that he hadn't resisted more vigorously, hadn't credited his instincts that had screamed at him earlier in the cabin that Cordelia was hiding things. If he'd refused to go to the airstrip until she came clean about everything, maybe they wouldn't be in this position.

Would have, could have, should have. Too late, Gid. Better find a new way.

Jake set the chopper down on the roof and cut the engine. His body language told Gideon he hadn't been part of the double cross that had delivered Cordelia back into her father's custody. Clearly the pilot was terrified.

The red-haired man who'd been guarding Gideon's Jeep was waiting for them at the landing pad, armed. Also nervous. Probably face-to-face executions at the boss's house weren't in his typical wheelhouse, and he had to be eager to leave in the face of a dam failure. When Jake opened the door, the man took the weapon from Cordelia, who made no effort to resist. She hunched her shoulders and stared at her feet. It was as if she was in a trance.

They disembarked.

"You wait here," the redhead told Jake before he turned back to them. "Get moving." He pointed to a stairwell. They obeyed and walked single file down three flights of carpeted stairs to the bottom floor. The gunman remained in the rear to prevent any resistance. He ordered Cordelia through the door to the lower landing.

"Daddy's waiting. You know the way," he said to her with a cruel laugh.

The hallway they entered was meticulously clean, no hint of footprints on the tile. Oil paintings hung on the walls, beautiful mountain landscapes displayed in opulent frames. He remembered the story Cordelia had told them of the terrified man who was dragged in to meet her father, and he wondered if Bullseye used this discreet route to dispose of people who had crossed him.

He catalogued every detail of the corridor—tiled floors

that flowed into plush carpet, almond-colored paint, an aroma of furniture polish. They filed along like sheep headed for the slaughterhouse, past windows that allowed what would be a spectacular view of the mountains when they weren't wrapped in rain clouds.

Any moment an opportunity for escape could present itself, or at least a way to resist. They weren't bound, and that was an advantage. He'd take whatever risk was necessary. Mackenzie would too, if given the chance.

She tried again to speak to Cordelia, who was a few paces ahead. Her voice was ragged with desperation. "So the story you told us was all lies, Cordelia? That stuff about wanting to help us avenge Aaron's death? That was all some excuse to lure us here? You said you wanted to keep me from being murdered like my brother." Her voice broke on the last word. He reached to touch her, but the gunman prodded him in the kidneys with the weapon. "Did you really even love him at all?"

Cordelia didn't turn to look at them, but he heard her broken sigh. "I loved him so much," she said. "So, so much."

"But you sold us out anyway," Mackenzie snapped. "Couldn't walk away from Daddy's money?"

Cordelia bowed her head without a reply as they continued on.

They reached an entry covered in marble tile and lit by sleek brass wall sconces.

The gunman gestured them through into an enormous room fitted out with luxury leather furniture, Persian rugs, and a massive stone fireplace where logs crackled and spit. A carved mahogany bookcase that had to be an antique of some kind held pristine leather-bound volumes. The overhead lighting shone softly from delicate fixtures against pale-colored walls.

Gideon stuck to his recon. A hallway located to the left no doubt led to the front entrance. Another one in the rear showed behind a grand piano. French doors opened to a porch of some kind. The drug business was definitely a moneymaker. The opulent room was bigger than Gideon's entire apartment.

Cordelia gulped as a man entered. A foot shorter than Gideon, he was well-dressed, silver hair neatly trimmed, buttoned shirt open at the neck, stocky but athletic torso. His expression was bland and pleasant. He might have been mistaken for a harmless visitor if Cordelia's reaction hadn't made it clear this was her father. A perfectly normal guy, Gideon mused, the kind who might be your dentist or lawyer, instead of a drug trafficker.

As he came around the side of the massive sofa, Gideon observed in utter shock that he held the tiny hand of a child of perhaps no more than two with curly hair and dimples.

Mackenzie's mouth dropped open as Cordelia's father, smiling broadly now, helped the child up onto the seat.

"Sit here for Pop Pop for a minute, all right?" he told her.

"Mama," the little girl said, stretching her arms out toward Cordelia.

"In just a minute, honeybunch," Frank said. "Mama and Pop Pop need to talk."

The child slid her thumb into her mouth and nodded to her grandfather.

Gideon felt the tidal wave of dismay. The girl had Cordelia's dark hair and Aaron's unmistakable cleft chin. His mind sped through the math. Two years . . . conceived just before Aaron's murder. Cordelia really had no choice about handing them over to Bullseye because she had to protect this little girl, her daughter.

"Children deserve to be free," she'd said.

Cordelia stepped clear of Gideon and held her arms out without looking at her father. "Katie, it's okay. I want to hold you. Come here, sweetie."

The little girl's face lit up and she climbed off the sofa and toddled on chubby legs to her mother.

Frank did not try to prevent the child from running to Cordelia's arms, smiling fondly at her. Cordelia swept her up in a bear hug, whispering brokenly, "I love you, baby. Mommy's here now. It's going to be all right."

"She's been such a good girl," Frank said. "We've had a wonderful time getting to know each other. We've finger-painted, and Cook helped her make a cake before she left. That was fun, wasn't it, Katie, my love? Messy, but fun."

"Cake," Katie said, patting her mother's cheek.

"I think there's some left. We'll take a slice with us so you can have it later when we're in Pop Pop's other house."

"You had no right to take her," Cordelia spat.

He appeared confused. "Of course I did. I'm her grandfather. Her well-being is my top priority. You left her in another state, for goodness' sake. Completely vulnerable."

"I left her with a friend. She's my child, I—"

"You were running around putting yourself in dangerous situations trying to rescue these people." For the first time he flicked a hostile glance at Gideon and Mackenzie before returning his attention to his daughter. "What kind of choice is it for a mother to leave her child in order to protect a couple of strangers?"

Cordelia pressed her palm over Katie's ear. "What kind of choice was it for you to murder her father?"

Gideon saw Mackenzie go pale. He edged toward her, but the gunman stopped him.

Her father shook his head. "That was totally avoidable, Cordelia. I love you enough to call you out on your blame-shifting here. I told you that man was wrong for you, beneath you. It was simply a relationship that would hurt you in the end. I implored you never to see him again, and you lied to me and said you'd broken things off." He huffed out a breath. "There were so many points at which you could have averted the need for his death."

The need to have him murdered . . . Gideon felt his rage building. The ultimate narcissism. He could feel Mackenzie's tension racheting up.

Cordelia's eyes filled, and his tone softened.

"Baby, I told you so often, didn't I? I promised your mother that you'd never be touched by what I did for a living. That was my sacred vow to her. How could I let you marry a man who dealt drugs? Even if he swore on bended knee to step away from it? It showed what kind of man he was, don't you see that? Someone who would stand on a street corner and peddle drugs isn't worthy of you."

Mackenzie's nostrils flared. "This from a drug runner."

He ignored her, gaze riveted on his daughter. "You wouldn't want me to go back on my word to your mom, would you?"

The most frightening thing was that the man obviously

believed his murderous logic. The happy grandpa, Frank Soliel, the doting father, a stone-cold killer.

"What a hero you are. How dedicated to preserving your family while you poison other people's children." Mackenzie's voice swelled with rage. Ignoring the redhead, Gideon put a warning palm on her forearm, but she jerked it away.

"What a fine, ethical man you are, Frank. You had Aaron killed to protect your daughter? To keep a promise to your dead wife? How exemplary. I guess it had nothing to do with the fact that Aaron knew what you really are." Her hands were balled into tight fists. "You couldn't have a son-in-law who was privy to your sordid business dealings. That would give him leverage over you. He could inform on you anytime. You couldn't have that, could you? That would never do."

He turned cold eyes on her. "The sister. How nice to finally meet you face-to-face. But you're mistaken, of course. I wasn't threatened by a peon, low-level nobody who sold drugs on street corners." He paused. "Nor am I bothered by a girl who couldn't even make it through cop school."

Gideon edged a few inches in front of Mackenzie. "Yes, you are. You've gone to a lot of trouble to take Aaron out and then try the same on Mackenzie. You wouldn't expend that kind of energy unless you felt threatened."

"Everything I do is to ensure the well-being of my daughter and Katie. I will not let anyone or anything impact them negatively." Frank's gaze riveted on Mackenzie. "You and your brother have been nothing but a stain on our lives. If I had been able to foresee the damage you've caused, I would have had your brother shot well before he set foot in Oakleaf and saved us all the aggravation."

Mackenzie jerked forward, but Gideon clamped onto her wrist. The gunman clenched his weapon. Tension crackled the air. They needed to stall until he figured out what to do. Frank likely wouldn't have them killed in front of his daughter and granddaughter. Like Cordelia said, he left the dirty work to other people.

Gideon flicked a glance to the rear hallway, the stairwell, the foyer leading to the front door, the French doors. Was there a way out? He had to find one.

"Stop it." Cordelia's body was rigid as she held her daughter. "I don't want to hear any more. I'm taking Katie and we're getting out of here."

Frank morphed back into the cajoling father. "Honey, listen to reason. Oakleaf is on the brink of cataclysm. The roads are flooded, the dam's partially failed, and the only way out is by helicopter." He pointed to the roof. "Jake's not going to disobey my orders again. I know where his wife is, and I included that information in the earlier message. He isn't taking you anywhere unless we're all three going together." His tone was almost jolly.

The perfect family of three. Father, daughter, granddaughter.

Gideon's brain churned up plan after plan. If they could reach it, would the front door be unlocked? If not, how long would it take him to get through it? The French doors would be easy to breach, but he couldn't be certain they wouldn't find themselves trapped in an enclosed patio or courtyard.

Keep him talking.

"You're going to fly off with Cordelia and Katie," Gideon said. "Where does that leave us?"

Frank gave him a disinterested look. "You know where. I warned you what would happen if you stayed. You stubbornly refused to save yourselves. Again, what happens to you isn't my choice. It was yours. You should have chosen better." He gestured to the red-haired man. "Cy, dispose of them after we take off. Take the boat on the landing and dump them somewhere. Doesn't much matter where. The dam is going to collapse and the floodwaters will carry them away from the property. You're free to leave from there."

"No, Daddy." Cordelia's voice was barely a whisper. Katie began to whimper. "You can't do that."

"I'll take care of everything, honey." He held out his arms to Cordelia. "Let me carry the angel. You look so tired. We'll go someplace warm. Wherever you want. This will all be over soon."

Cordelia's sob was swallowed up by a low boom that shook the floor.

"The dam!" the redheaded man shouted. "It's busted."

Gideon's heart plummeted. Their time had run out and there was nowhere to hide from the destruction that was coming.

EIGHTEEN

IT FELT AS IF THE ENTIRE BUILDING had been struck by an invisible explosion. A glass sculpture fell off its pedestal and thudded to the hardwood, splitting into three pieces.

Gideon spun to urge Cordelia and Mackenzie toward the stairs. *Up!* was all his brain could think. They had to get to the highest point possible.

Cy moved tentatively to stop them, but a roar filled the room, shaking the foundation with even more violence.

"Go!" Gideon shouted. "To the roof."

"Cy . . ." Frank started, but a barrage of water shattered the floor-to-ceiling windows and cascaded into the room. The surge took their feet out from under them.

Freezing water pummeled Gideon as he coughed out a mouthful of water and righted himself.

Zero hour. The dam had finally failed completely. They had minutes, maybe less. Mackenzie was already regaining her balance behind him. Cordelia lurched toward the stairs with a screaming Katie.

Frank's henchman stood up with his gun in hand, watching in shock as the water rushed over his shins.

Seizing the moment, Gideon lunged. Cy's gun went flying. Cy immediately sprang up again and readied his fist, but terror filled his expression. He didn't want to die any more than they did.

Gideon jerked his chin at Cy. "You know there isn't room in the chopper for everyone. Think your boss is going to let you aboard? No way. Are you so loyal that you'll drown here so he can fly away to another of his mansions?"

Cy shot a look at Frank, who was clinging to the edge of a chair.

"You know what happens to people who defy me," Frank thundered at Cy.

Cy's face was stark. "I . . ."

Gideon pressed. "You mean nothing to him, and he'll leave you to die."

Still, Cy hesitated.

"You have time. You can get out and save yourself, but you have to go now."

Cy turned on his heel and splashed toward the foyer and out of sight. He wasn't likely to make it to his vehicle, but Gideon couldn't concern himself with Cy's choices.

He dashed the water from his eyes in time to watch the flood wrest the heavy sofa from its position. It hurtled toward Cordelia, who hadn't yet reached the bottom stair.

She screamed and clutched Katie. They both went under as the sofa rammed into them.

Gideon dove for the furniture, gripped one end, and dropped his weight like an anchor to slow it down.

Cordelia bobbed up, coughing and frantic. "Katie!" she screamed.

His stomach plummeted as he realized she no longer held her daughter.

He struggled to hold the heavy sofa in place, desperately looking for the child.

A flash of her pink fleece caught his eye. Katie had been jerked loose from her mother and swept across the space, caught against the wall beside the French doors. He called to Cordelia.

He scanned the room for Mackenzie while Cordelia splashed her way to Katie before he let the sofa go. Cordelia hauled Katie into her arms. The little girl coughed and cried, her small body shaking with cold and fear. He swam to them and took hold of Cordelia's forearm, then propelled them once again toward the stairwell.

Across the room he saw Mackenzie with her back to him, water streaming from her jacket. Beyond her, the liquid splashed and foamed as if they were in a giant washing machine, rapidly filling. Where was Frank?

The water began to pull Cordelia from his grasp. He tightened his grip. "Hold on to me," he called over the chaos.

He was fighting to move them along when he heard Mackenzie shout behind him.

"You're not leaving here, Frank. You're going to pay for what you did to Aaron."

He turned to find Mackenzie lunging at Frank as he tried to rip open a drawer that probably contained a weapon. She shoved him away, sending him staggering to keep himself upright.

With Cordelia and Katie in his arms, Gideon could do little to intervene. He had to get them to the stairwell fast and then help Mackenzie. The room was a swirling mass of debris. He hadn't made it halfway when a second deluge ripped inside, tearing loose one of the floor-to-ceiling bookcases. It toppled sideways, completely blocking the stairwell, books sliding off into the water.

His heart dropped as he anchored Cordelia against the other bookcase, still holding in place for the moment. Her limbs shivered so violently it was all she could do to hold on to Katie and keep from being swept away.

He shouted to Mackenzie, pivoting in time to see Frank throw a punch that she avoided.

Gideon stumbled over something and went under. He got to his feet again, spluttering.

Frank had shifted toward the back hallway to escape Mackenzie, but she seemed to have read his thoughts. She plunged her hand in the water and swept up something in her fist. It took him a moment to realize the glittering, dripping fragment was a piece of the glass sculpture that had broken into a sharp point. She held it like a dagger toward Frank. The water bubbled and gurgled around them.

"I told you, you're not going to get away."

Frank looked behind Gideon at the bookcase and then at Cordelia. "They're going to drown," he said, and Gideon saw fear play across Frank's features for the first time.

Mackenzie looked too, finally becoming aware of Gideon's predicament.

Gideon kept his tone firm and level. "Let him go, Zee. We have to get out of here." He longed to rush to her, but if he didn't unblock the stairwell, Frank would be proven correct. Cordelia and Katie wouldn't make it. None of them would.

Mackenzie took a few steps toward Cordelia until Frank moved and she whirled to face him again.

Gideon plowed to the bookcase blockade and threw his weight against it. He strained every muscle and succeeded only in lifting one corner of the heavy oak. He could not do it alone.

Cordelia clutched Katie as the force of the water threatened to snatch the child from her numb hands. In her panic, Katie was flailing, which made it harder for her mother to hold her steady.

Still the bookcase did not move.

Mackenzie stared at Frank. "You're not leaving here." The water was up to her waist. She stood between Frank and the hallway he'd been heading toward to make his escape, the glass shard gleaming in her hand.

Gideon fought to make himself heard. "Cordelia can't hold on to Katie much longer. You have to come help me."

Mackenzie shot a look at him, agonized. "He can't just get away without paying for what he's done. He killed my brother." She refocused on Frank. "You're going to stay with me all the way into a jail cell or until we drown. Whichever comes first."

Gideon repositioned his grip on the bookshelf. "Mackenzie," he said through gritted teeth, "this isn't who you are."

Cordelia's arms were shaking around Katie. Gideon's repaired shoulder felt as if it was going to snap.

"Please, help me, Zee." And then he let his desperation leak into his voice. "I need you." *In so many ways.*

She shot a look at him, agony painted on her face. His

strength waning, he saw her drop the glass, straighten, and spin around toward him, Cordelia, and the wailing child.

He heaved at the stubborn wood. A corner of Katie's sleeve pulled from Cordelia's grasp as the water thundered around them. Water sluiced across the little girl's face. She coughed and gagged.

Cordelia staggered toward him with her precarious hold on Katie.

"Don't let them die," Frank called, his gaze on his struggling daughter.

When Mackenzie made it to Gideon's side, the water was up to their chests. She grabbed the bookcase, and inch by inch they shoved it just enough to open a narrow gap to the stairwell. While he anchored it in place, Mackenzie swam to Cordelia and escorted her and Katie to the foot of the stairwell.

"Get to the roof," Frank called across the space, then he hurtled away down the rear hallway.

Mackenzie pushed Cordelia and Katie up the submerged steps.

Gideon nodded at her. "Go. Tell Jake we're on our way."

Cordelia held her daughter as high as she could and staggered up the stairs.

Mackenzie looked at the spot where she'd let Frank go.

"Come on," he said over the rush, giving the bookcase a final shove to secure it in place.

Her expression was pure pain as she joined him, and he couldn't bear it, not for a second longer. He took her face in his palms and kissed her cold lips, wishing he could absorb the agony she was experiencing. Her grief appeared as acute as the day she'd told him her brother had been murdered.

His forehead pressed to hers, he said, "You did the right thing, Zee."

Another assault of water shattered the remaining picture window, sending more furniture tumbling with a cascade of glass. Together they squeezed into the stairwell. It was a race against the rising water as they pulled themselves up three agonizing flights, chased the whole way by the reckless flood. The last few steps they had to hold their breath and swim through the stairwell.

They burst out of the final threshold and exited onto the roof, which had become a shallow lake with water up to their shins, rising with every passing second.

Cordelia peered out from the helicopter. Her terror morphed to relief as she saw them. "Hurry! Jake's got to lift off."

He pushed Mackenzie ahead. She was as exhausted as he was, running on a whisper of adrenaline, but rescue was within inches. She'd reached a hand up to propel herself into the chopper when another door opened at the far end of the rooftop. Frank charged through and ran toward the chopper. He wielded a fireplace poker like a club.

Of course he wasn't going to let his family go. Why hadn't Gideon anticipated the attack?

Before Gideon could hoist Mackenzie aboard to safety, Frank slammed the poker into his compromised shoulder. The agony lit Gideon's nerves on fire, and he fell face down in the water.

Sparks of pain burned inside him, and he swallowed a

mouthful of water as he struggled upright, gasping for breath. His vision was blurry, and he fought to keep from collapsing again. As he dashed the water from his eyes, he saw that Mackenzie had desperately clutched Frank around the legs. Furiously, Frank kicked out.

One of his heels caught her in the cheekbone and rocketed her head backward, but she didn't release her grip.

Jake lifted the skids from the roof, rotors spraying foam. Taking off or trying to dislodge Frank?

Gideon threw himself at Frank's torso, pulling on his shoulders, adding his weight to Mackenzie's. Cordelia screamed.

He jerked to see what she was reacting to as a wave the size of a building engulfed the rooftop. The chopper lifted off inches above the liquid frenzy just as a wall of water blasted into them.

He was tumbled over, twisted, and turned until he lost sight of everything. He felt himself picked up like a dried leaf, helpless against the roiling surge.

The raging tumult made it impossible to orient himself, but he felt the scrape of cement as he was dragged along. Something, the edge of the roof perhaps, caught him in the stomach as he was swept over. The breath was expelled from him by the unexpected punch.

His fingers clawed for a way to save himself, to return to Mackenzie. There was nothing to hold on to. The sound of the cacophony changed, and he realized he'd been swept over the roof and deposited into the middle of the maelstrom.

Mackenzie? Frank? Had they been washed over too? He fought for breath, the freezing waves dousing him again and again. Something whipped against his forehead, but he had no idea what it was.

The cold was crushing, the force of the rush irresistible. His strength was all but gone. Another wave picked him up and dumped him deep below the surface.

From underwater, he saw the faint lights of the helicopter as Jake took the bird into the sky, carrying Cordelia and Katie away from the deadly flood. The mother and child had been saved.

But not Mackenzie.

She hadn't made it aboard.

His howl was lost to the waves.

* * *

Mackenzie could no longer feel anything except the bone-crushing cold. Was she in the water or out? She couldn't tell. Possibly she was in the process of dying—or maybe dead already.

She prayed for her parents, that God would eventually soothe the anguish they would feel at losing their remaining child. How thoughtless she'd been of their feelings, ignoring their needs in favor of her own. She prayed that Jake would get Cordelia and Katie to safety. They'd already lost so much at the hands of her father. Why should their futures be denied them like Aaron's had?

She prayed for Gideon.

There were so many things she wanted to tell him, regrets that she'd not spoken of.

All around was darkness and noise and the intermittent glimmer of blurry objects jetting across her field of vision.

Everywhere was an inconceivably vast void. Bottomless water, excruciating cold. No help. No hope.

No Gideon.

The only emotion that penetrated her deadened senses was grief. He was lost out here somewhere, if he was even still alive, because of her. He'd suffered and died, because of her.

Survive, evade, resist, and escape. He'd sacrificed everything for her to do all four. If the chopper had managed to lift off, he'd made it possible for Jake, Cordelia, and Katie to survive. Because of her choices, she was alone out here and dying by inches, separated from him. She hoped it would at least be fast for both of them.

She caught a tiny glimmer of starlight between the clouds. Was it worth it? Her life for vengeance? No, but the price was hers to pay.

Not his.

Not Gideon's.

She thought of his easy smile, the way one eyebrow lifted when she was confounding him, how his family would feel when he didn't return, his parents, his brothers and cousin.

"I'm so sorry," she whispered to him and to God. Her vision blurred as she twirled helplessly.

The sky, or what she thought was the sky, was a black sprawl of nothing, and she looked in vain for the chopper. Another wave slapped against her face and she held on to the one positive thought she could muster. Cordelia had hopefully gotten her child away from her murderous grandfather. Aaron's daughter would have a future. It was some solace, though it didn't penetrate the agony at what she'd done to Gideon. Would Cordelia tell Mackenzie's parents what had transpired? That at the last moment she'd turned away from her vendetta as they'd begged her to?

Her chin sagged. She had no energy left to fight. She abandoned herself to the tug of the water. When the next wave pulled her under, she didn't have the strength to battle back to the surface again. What a way to die, to be slowly inundated and overwhelmed. Would it stop being so cold as her heart ceased to beat?

Something caught her, yanked her head free from the watery grip.

She gagged, trying to expel the water from her lungs and suck in oxygen at the same time. The night was impenetrable, smothering, and she saw nothing but darkness.

Her name . . . Someone was saying her name over and over.

Her mind slowly broke free from its stupor.

Someone was beside her.

Gideon. He was treading water, holding on to her and something else. Or was she dreaming? Her eyes wouldn't focus.

"Zee." He pulled her close. His body was shuddering convulsively like hers. "Thank God."

"Gideon?" She clung to him, crying and laughing. "It's you. You're not . . . I mean . . . you're here."

"Yes, ma'am. We gotta stop meeting like this, huh?"

She squeezed him around the neck, then pressed her head to his chest to reassure herself she wasn't dreaming. "What . . . Where are we?"

"We're in the top of a tree, near as I can figure." He

squeezed her close. “But the chopper made it out, Zee, and Jake saw what happened to us. If he can stand up and be a man, he’ll come back and get us or radio for help.”

Help? Escape? It was hard to fathom when she’d been absolutely without hope a minute before. “A big if. Bullseye threatened his wife.”

“He better come through. There’s nowhere to swim from here.” He paused.

“What . . . happened to Bullseye?”

“I don’t think he made it to the helicopter.”

She silently agreed. He’d gotten washed over with the two of them. He was somewhere out here, maybe clinging to his own branch, which was a temporary reprieve. How did she feel about it? Prison was the destiny she’d have chosen for him, not drowning.

The water stretched around them in a vast, nebulous sprawl.

They were both too cold to get anywhere on their own, even if there was any place nearby above flood level. She saw nothing. Not even the roof of Frank Soliel’s expensive home was visible. It was as if it had never existed.

She felt the branches now, swaying and crackling around her legs, a submerged nest. Unbelievably strange that she and Gideon were stranded in a tree like two half-drowned birds. But he was alive, and all other thoughts ebbed away under that beautiful realization. They were still surviving. Together.

He stroked the wet hair from her forehead. “I’m proud of you, Zee.”

She leaned against him and felt like sobbing. “Proud,

huh? Of the woman who got you stuck in a tree in the middle of a flood?"

"I got myself stuck, and don't dis the tree because it's keeping us from drowning." He kissed her forehead, his mouth only a fraction warmer than the freezing water. "You made a choice back there with Frank. The right choice."

She still didn't know what to think about what she'd done. It was getting more difficult to form thoughts as the water stole away her remaining warmth.

"I couldn't have imagined all that's happened if I tried. To find out that Aaron had a child . . ." The wonder of it stunned her afresh.

He squeezed her, his own teeth chattering. "Who would have thought? You're Auntie Zee now."

Auntie Zee . . . "I hope my parents can meet their granddaughter someday. Maybe . . ." Maybe it would take the sting out of losing both of their children. Because the longer they struggled to stay afloat, the more she understood that they weren't going to escape. There was no sign of the chopper's return. They would gradually become hypothermic until they drifted apart in the floodwaters. She gripped his hand tighter, resolved to keep them together for as many precious moments as she could. That was all she had left.

Survive, evade, resist, escape.

All for what? Now that Frank was likely dead, she had no hope that he'd ever pay for his crimes, not in the way she'd wanted. Her scheduled podcast would go live when the post date came and went, but it would be for nothing.

"My next vacation I'm going someplace warm, like the Sahara," Gideon said.

She laughed, but it was weak. "Sounds like a dream."

He pulled her closer, and she began to cry, quiet sobs, barely audible.

He rubbed her shoulders. "It's okay, Zee. I got you."

She clung to him, the agony of cold beginning to wear off as hypothermia set in. He chafed her arms, but she couldn't feel it any longer. He kissed her, but she didn't feel that either. What had she done to them both? "I'm sorry."

"I know. Me too."

Wind-borne water peppered their faces. A low throb echoed over the surface. She didn't understand what it was.

"Chopper," Gideon said suddenly.

Chopper? She thought she'd imagined him speaking until a light shone down, roving the darkness, blinding them. Gideon waved his arms and she did the same, as much as she could.

"It's Jake all right," Gideon said, his tone ecstatic. "He's dropping a line."

A line. Survival. Escape. A dream? A last-minute reprieve?

It took several passes before Gideon grasped a nylon rope from the helicopter and six tries before he got it tied around them.

"Ready for a wild ride, Zee?"

It could not possibly be wilder than what they'd experienced since the moment she crashed his wilderness class.

"Why not?" she whispered, her strength almost gone.

She clung to him as they were hauled upward and flown out over the raging waters.

EPILOGUE

ON A BLAZING AUGUST AFTERNOON, Mackenzie walked out of the judge's chambers with Gideon beside her. The sunshine was glorious, but she buttoned her suit jacket anyway. Warmth was a commodity she could never seem to get enough of.

Six months after their ordeal in Oakleaf, and she was almost healed from the bumps and lacerations and pneumonia she'd contracted after they were airlifted out of the flood zone. Gideon had fared better, but he was several pounds lighter and his face still had a slightly hollowed look. Even after another surgical repair, his shoulder pained him, though he wouldn't let it show.

A weight had been lifted off her when the robbery charge was dropped in lieu of community service. The court was lenient since Gideon vouched for her and she was cooperating with the police in all parts of the investigation. Sergeant Rodriquez put in a good word for her too. Her punishment was minimal.

Frank Soliel's body had finally been unearthed from where it was entombed under a massive fallen tree a full month after their rescue. Mackenzie knew his crime ring might not have died with him. Another criminal could have stepped in to take his place. The authorities had asked her not to share any details on social media while they continued their investigation.

She'd acquiesced and paused her podcast with a short broadcast relating the facts about the flood and Bullseye's death but omitting any reference to Cordelia and Katie. Her days as a social media crusader would continue, she'd decided. There were many cold cases left to be solved, but the inquiry into Frank Soliel's drug trafficking activities belonged solely to the police now.

Sergeant Rodriquez had been instrumental in having the charges against her contact Lorraine dropped. Mackenzie had visited her after her release and followed through on her promise to help both Lorraine and her mother relocate to Jamaica, where they'd have a fresh start. Kevin was rebuilding his family home. Mackenzie wondered exactly how he had explained everything to the wife he adored.

Gideon took her hand and kissed it. "You look pretty sharp in that silk suit."

She pulled her hair loose from the neat bun and let it fan out around her face. "I can't wait to exchange this outfit for jeans and waders. You promised me a fishing trip after things were settled, and my calendar is now officially clear."

"I'm ready when you are. We can go right now, if you want." He waved a thermos. "This contains Hearty Chicken Gumbo. It's the second recipe in chapter five from the *Three Hundred Sixty-Five Soup Recipes* book."

She rolled her eyes. "I'm beginning to wish you hadn't located another copy of that thing."

"Well, mine was lost in the wilderness, as you know, so it was purely due to my cyber diligence that I found another. This baby is out of print so it's a collector's item coveted by soup lovers everywhere."

"Just how much soup can a person be expected to consume in one lifetime?"

"There's no limit." He arched a brow. "You've loved all the soups I've made so far."

"Not exactly. The gazpacho wasn't a winner."

"Humph. You're a robber, so what do you know about fine dining?" He assumed a wry expression. "And I'd like to register a complaint. The justice system has become entirely too soft. A couple days of community service was a puny punishment for a woman who knocked me down and demanded my wallet."

She laughed. "I'm reformed, I promise. And I'm going to work with the cops on solving their cold case backlog until I figure out what to do with the rest of my life."

"That sounds safer, though I've no doubt you'll find a way to get into trouble."

She pushed her hair behind her ears. "Will you be there to get me out?" She shot him a quick side-glance, gratified when he tugged at their joined hands.

"You know I will, Zee."

It was her turn to smile. And blush. They strolled out into the sunny parking lot. "What's the latest word from Cordelia?"

"Katie's adjusting well in their apartment." They'd rented a unit not ten miles from Mackenzie's parents' home. To be cautious in case any of her father's crime syndicate might still be active, she was using an assumed name and probably always would. The local police were apprised of the situation, which further eased Mackenzie's mind.

"Cordelia's planning to come next weekend to introduce Katie to my parents while she looks for a new location for her stable." The thought of it, their grandchild, her niece, the best part of Aaron and Cordelia, made a lump form in her throat. She'd already been picking out a few toys and activities she could share with Katie when they arrived. She intended to be the best auntie ever to hold the title. "My parents want you to come for dinner tonight, by the way," she said, suddenly feeling butterflies in her stomach.

He gave her a wondering look. "Really? All these months and you haven't exactly wanted me around the old homestead."

Her cheeks warmed. "I wasn't sure about . . . things."

"I am." The shifting light turned his frank gaze from brown to honey. "You know how I feel, Zee, don't you?"

She did. He'd told her he loved her, wanted a future with her, but he wasn't going to push. The notion of being loved by and loving Gideon Landry thrilled her.

But she'd needed time.

To be sure her head was on straight.

To accept that Bullseye was officially dead.

To be certain the feelings pulsing in her heart were not a knee-jerk reaction to a harrowing escape. She was finally certain. Completely.

She took a breath and turned toward him, wrapping her arms around his neck. “I’m sure now.”

He tilted his head and looked at her with such intensity her stomach flipped. Before speaking, he quirked a brow. “Would you like to expound on that?”

“I love you, Gideon. I think maybe part of me always has.”

His grin was as bright as the summer morning as he rocked her in his arms. “It’s ’cause I’m a stud, right? You want to hitch your wagon to a rising star? Gonna be a civilian and run a mega-successful wilderness survival company? And I’m also super handsome? And I know the nutritional value of a praying mantis? And I make the best cup of coffee in the civilized world? Right? Those are only a few of the many reasons you love me?”

“No,” she said quietly and put her finger to his chest. “It’s because of what you’ve got in here.”

His expression softened to an inexpressible tenderness before he kissed her. “I never thought God would give me a chance with you.”

“Maybe he figured if we survived, we belonged together.”

“We do. For now and for always. I love you, Zee.”

She knew she could never hear those words enough even if he said them a million times. “I love you too, Gid.” His kiss was long and lingering.

“This is the best day of my life,” he said.

“Only one thing would make it better. Are you ready to go fishing?” she said, breathless.

He swung her around and kissed her again. “As long as

you promise to keep us out of the water. I've had enough of that."

"Okay," she said, reveling in the joy of her new beginning. "But if you fall in, I promise I'll rescue you."

"Counting on it."

Thermos in hand, he tucked her into the circle of his arm and led the way.

Dear Reader,

We're a drought-ridden state here in California, but ironically, even in our location we have experienced mild flooding. It caught us by surprise. Too MUCH water? We are way more familiar with rationing than filling sandbags. It was good to see the community come together to help those affected by the floods. Have you ever experienced such an outpouring of love? My husband worked for the fire service his whole career, and he always maintained that disasters bring out the best and worst in people. In my story it does just that, but Gideon and Mackenzie survive with grit, faith, and the help of a few characters willing to take a risk. Wouldn't it be grand if we were all able to step up for our neighbors as God intended? Sometimes it requires the help of a faithful friend to stand against the floodwaters. I know I've experienced such support from people who have been the hands and feet of Jesus in my hour of need.

I pray this story has entertained and inspired you, dear readers. Until we meet again in the pages of another book, God bless.

Dana Mentink

ACKNOWLEDGMENTS

When the waters start to rise, I depend on my troop to help keep my head above water: three sisters; one husband and soulmate; two kiddos; a spectacular agent, Jessica Alvarez; and an amazing editor, Kelsey Bowen. You all have a part in keeping this story and this author afloat. Thank you from the bottom of my heart.

Dana Mentink is a *USA Today* and *Publishers Weekly* bestselling author. She's written more than fifty mystery and suspense novels for Love Inspired Suspense, Harvest House, and Poisoned Pen Press. Winner of two ACFW Carol Awards, a Holt Medallion Award, and a *Romantic Times* Reviewer's Choice Award, Dana lives in Northern California with her husband. Learn more at DanaMentink.com.

Sign Up for Dana's Newsletter

Keep up to date with Dana's latest news on book releases and events by signing up for her email list at the website below.

DanaMentink.com

FOLLOW DANA ON SOCIAL MEDIA

Dana Mentink

@Dana_Mentink

@DanaMentink

A Note from the Publisher

Dear Reader,

Thank you for selecting a Revell novel! We're so happy to be part of your reading life through this work. Our mission here at Revell is to publish stories that reach the heart. Through friendship, romance, suspense, or a travel back in time, we bring stories that will entertain, inspire, and encourage you. We believe in the power of stories to change our lives and are grateful for the privilege of sharing these stories with you.

We believe in building lasting relationships with readers, and we'd love to get to know you better. If you have any feedback, questions, or just want to chat about your experience reading this book, please email us directly at publisher@revellbooks.com. Your insights are incredibly important to us, and it would be our pleasure to hear how we can better serve you.

We look forward to hearing from you and having the chance to enhance your experience with Revell Books.

The Publishing Team at Revell Books
A Division of Baker Publishing Group
publisher@revellbooks.com